LOVE AT FIRST SIGHT?

Jackson shifted his heavy briefcase to his left hand and pressed the doorbell. A woman in a uniform answered the door. "You're the accountant?" she asked.

He nodded and extended his hand. "I'm Jackson James, thank you."

"Miss Granger will be right down."

He followed the housekeeper into a room lined with oil paintings and mirrors.

"Tilly, I have your favorite drink," said a musical voice just before the body attached to it entered the room. "Whiskey, a double—" Big blue eyes met his in consternation. "You're not Tilly."

Whoa! He caught a scent that reminded him of the sweetest tease. So this was Lori Jean Granger in the flesh. She looked and smelled good enough to eat. Her skin looked like cream, her lips a deep pink rosebud currently set in a moue of unhappiness, her blonde hair hung just past her shoulders like a silk curtain. Her white cotton dress with tiny red dots skimmed over breasts, which reminded him of ripe peaches, and down over the feminine curves of her waist and hips to just above her knees. She wore red high heels, the kind of heels that could give a man wicked fantasies. They were the kind of shoes a man wanted to see a woman wear when she wore nothing else . . .

*Please turn this page for
reviews for Leanne Banks.*

"A wonderful story filled with romance and humor. *When She's Bad* had me laughing out loud at some parts and sighing at others. Grab a copy and settle down for a great read."
—BookLoons.com

Some Girls Do

"Every girl from eighteen to eighty will love *Some Girls Do*!"
—Janet Evanovich

"A witty feel-good read with charming characters and a page-turning plot."
—*Booklist*

"4½ Stars! From Philadelphia's Society Hill to honky-tonk Texas and back again, everything feels right in this story of three misfits who help each other's dreams come true. This story, full of love and pain and quiet humor, is told by an author at the top of her game."
—*Romantic Times BOOKreviews Magazine*

"Banks's prose sparkles with energy and heart . . . the story strikes a true vein of gold."
—*Publishers Weekly*

"*Some Girls Do* is irresistible! A stay-up-at-night read that keeps you laughing under the covers. Charming, witty, fun—I urge you to read *Some Girls Do*."
—Joan Johnston, *New York Times* bestselling author

more . . .

Trouble in High Heels

ALSO BY LEANNE BANKS

Some Girls Do

When She's Bad

Trouble in High Heels

LEANNE BANKS

FOREVER

NEW YORK   BOSTON

Copyright © 2009 by Leanne Banks
All rights reserved. Except as permitted under the U.S. Copyright Act of 1976, no part of this publication may be reproduced, distributed, or transmitted in any form or by any means, or stored in a database or retrieval system, without the prior written permission of the publisher.

Cover art and design by Shasti O'Leary

Forever
Hachette Book Group
237 Park Avenue
New York, NY 10017
Visit our Web site at www.HachetteBookGroup.com

Forever is an imprint of Grand Central Publishing. The Forever name and logo is a trademark of Hachette Book Group, Inc.

Printed in the United States of America

First Printing: March 2009

10 9 8 7 6 5 4 3 2 1

This book is dedicated to wicked,
wise, and wonderful Sunny Collins and
all the readers who wanted more of her.

Acknowledgments

Special thanks to the incredible people who encouraged me and helped to make this book happen: Cindy Gerard, Rhonda Pollero, Binnie Syril Braunstein, and Tami Peckham.

Thank you also to my fabulous editors Frances Jalet-Miller and Karen Kosztolnyik.

"High heels weaken men's knees."
—SUNNY COLLINS

Chapter One

"Congratulations, Jackson. Because of your hard work and dedication, we've decided to offer you a junior partnership with the firm."

Jackson stared at his boss in surprise. Exhilaration pumped through him. Twelve years ago, he'd been a high school dropout doing manual labor at a ranch in southwestern Texas. He'd moved to Dallas and done everything from waiting tables, to working as a part-time rodeo clown, to being a janitor in the evenings to earn his way through college and get his CPA.

Despite his father's insistence that Jackson would never amount to anything, he had. This moment proved his father wrong. Jackson was a success.

It took a moment for him to find his breath. "Thank you, Mr. Hollingsworth. I don't know what to say."

Mr. Hollingsworth, a fifty-eight-year-old balding man with a shrewd, creative, but always law-abiding mind, nodded. He removed a rumpled handkerchief from his pocket and mopped his shiny head. "You've earned it. Your salary will increase by twenty-five percent, you'll receive an annual bonus, and you can hire an assistant. You'll also be offered Mr. Till's office. He's retiring," he explained.

Jackson immediately calculated the difference in his salary, and three investment possibilities came to mind. He'd shared an assistant with the other CPAs until now, and Mr. Till, who appeared to be approximately three hundred years old, had a *corner office.*

This was the stuff of fantasies for a dirt-poor kid from southwestern Texas. This was like winning the lottery. This was the pot of gold at the end of the rainbow.

He watched Mr. Hollingsworth's head turn shiny with perspiration and felt an itchy sensation. That same itchy sensation had kept him alive in dark alleys and rowdy bars. That same itchy sensation had kept him away from troublesome females. That same itchy sensation had kept him from being gored by a bull.

It was the same itchy sensation that warned him: if it looked too good to be true, then it probably was.

Mr. Hollingsworth smiled at him nervously.

Jackson's stomach sank. *Oh, shit.* Whenever Hollingsworth smiled, there was trouble. Big trouble. He remembered the audit he had managed for one of their larger clients, who had neglected to disclose all their financial activities for a tax return. It had taken months of work to keep the guy out of prison.

Mr. Hollingsworth cleared his throat. "You know we think a lot of you. You've earned the respect of all of the partners and all the clients you've worked with."

Cut to the chase, Jackson wanted to say. He would

have to assess the risk. Life was all about risk. If he could do whatever dirty work the firm wanted him to do, then he could claim his prize.

"Of course, with additional reward comes additional responsibility. We, the partners and I, have carefully evaluated our client list, and we believe you are the man to handle the Granger account."

"The Granger account," he echoed in disbelief. The Granger account was one of the firm's top five accounts. Compared to the Granger account, everything Jackson had done had been chicken shit. He knew a few things about the account, but not much, because old Mr. Till had kept Harlan Granger's financial matters close to the vest.

"As you know, Harlan Granger died six months ago, and most of his estate is being held in trust for his daughter, Lori Jean," Hollingsworth said.

Jackson hadn't ever met Lori Jean personally. He'd just seen photographs of her in the paper at charity functions or at her home while she posed with a prissy white dog that was probably fed filet mignon every night. Blonde, with a melt-in-your-mouth body, the woman was a looker, but she didn't appear to have much upstairs.

Hollingsworth cleared his throat. "Since Mr. Till has retired, you'll be in charge of managing the estate." He cleared his throat again and fingered his tie as if it were choking him. "Some changes in the conditions concerning the dispersal of the trust have recently come to light." The senior partner of the firm rubbed his nose and shrugged. "All in the files. You should go ahead and get started on them so you can meet with Miss Granger as soon as possible."

The itchy sensation climbed up the back of Jackson's

neck again. Something about this just wasn't right. "What about my other clients?"

"Don't worry. They'll be temporarily reassigned. I'm sure you know the Granger account is one of our largest accounts."

So, why were they giving it to him instead of one of the more senior partners? Jackson shoved his hands into his pockets and decided to test Hollingsworth's desperation. He'd learned a long time ago that people would spend a lot of money to protect whatever they held dear. Jackson knew Hollingsworth held the Granger account very near and dear.

"It sounds as if this could be more demanding of my time and energy than what I've been doing here at the firm," Jackson said.

Hollingsworth slowly nodded. "You could say that."

"Do you think it might be more appropriate to give me a raise of thirty percent?"

Hollingsworth paused, then mopped his head and cleared his throat. "I think it could be arranged."

Jackson didn't know whether to shout in victory or brace himself for the depths of hell. If Hollingsworth was willing to fork over the bucks, things must be in a helluva mess.

Three days later, Jackson stood on the grand porch of the mansion where Harlan Granger had spent most of his days since he'd hit the big time as an oil baron. He was one of the few who'd managed to survive and thrive during the rough times, and he'd done it by diversifying. By the time he passed away, Harlan owned a bit of everything.

Taking in the elegant architecture of the whiter-than-white building, large columns, polished brass fixtures, and well-kept porch, Jackson couldn't help remembering the shabby house where he'd lived as a child. The tin roof had leaked, the floors were warped, and it was a wonder the faulty wiring hadn't caused a fire. The hot water system was busted more often than it was working, so cold showers were the norm. He fought a twinge of feeling out of place. For a sliver of a moment, he was thirteen again, without a degree in accounting, wearing hand-me-down torn jeans from the local Goodwill store instead of the Brooks Brothers suit he'd bought on sale.

He didn't belong here.

Jackson thought of Lori Jean Granger. She probably didn't know what a cold shower was, and he was certain her home had always been warm when it was cold outside and cool when the summertime heat hit.

She also, however, hadn't learned to manage her pocketbook, and by the looks of her accounts, he was going to have to teach her. It had taken some persistence, but he'd finally cracked Hollingsworth. Now he knew why no one else wanted this account. And he was still shaking his head over it. He'd imagined every possibility but the one Hollingsworth finally coughed up. As he'd begun to suspect, the woman scared them. Not, however, because she was a raging bitch, but because she was this sweet, helpless woman that men just couldn't say no to—like she had some mystical power over them or something. Jackson rolled his eyes. A Lorelei of accountants, with the ability to sink their careers into the bottom of the ocean. By the looks of her accounts, Till had rarely said no. Jackson snorted. Well, Till had been a fool. Jackson wasn't . . . and he would have no problem saying NO to Lori Jean Granger.

He shifted his heavy briefcase to his left hand and pressed the doorbell. Within a moment, a woman in a uniform answered the door. "You're the accountant?" she asked.

He nodded and extended his hand, a memory of his mother flashing through his mind. She had been a maid, and she'd told him everyone, including the garbage man, deserved courtesy. The lesson had stuck. "I'm Jackson James, thank you. And you're?"

She blinked in surprise. "I'm Mabel, thank you very much." She accepted his hand and shot him a considering glance that gave him the odd sense that she could see everywhere he'd been since he was born. "You're new, aren't you?"

"New to Miss Granger," he said.

"I thought so. Please come into the parlor. Miss Granger will be right down."

Hearing the echo of his shoes on the gleaming marble entryway, he shot a quick glance at the chandelier hanging from the ceiling and the double stairway leading to the second floor. He followed the housekeeper into a room furnished in cherry and walls lined with oil paintings and mirrors.

"Tilly, I have your favorite drink," a young woman said in a musical voice just before the body attached to the voice entered the room. "Whiskey, a double—" Big blue eyes met his in consternation as the woman carried her prissy dog tucked under her right arm and in her left hand Tilly's drink. "You're not Tilly."

Whoa! He inhaled and caught a draft of a scent that

reminded him of the sweetest tease. So this was Lori Jean Granger in the flesh. She looked and smelled good enough to eat. He could see why those doddering old fools would be falling all over themselves. But he wasn't a doddering old fool. Her skin looked like cream, her lips a deep pink rosebud currently set in a moue of unhappiness. Her blonde hair hung just past her shoulders like a silk curtain. Her white cotton dress with tiny red dots skimmed over breasts that reminded him of ripe peaches and down over the feminine curves of her waist and hips to just above her knees. She wore red high heels, the kind of heels that could give a man wicked fantasies. They were the kind of shoes a man wanted to see a woman wear when she wore nothing else.

Jackson pulled his brain out of its death spiral headed straight for his crotch and hardened his heart before another part of him turned hard. He met her gaze and extended his hand. "I'm Jackson James. I've been assigned to handle your account. Mr. Till has retired."

She frowned. "I didn't realize."

Jackson nodded. "It was a surprise to a lot of people." But not to the partners, since Mr. Till had royally screwed up.

She shot him a troubled glance. "Oh, well, would you like some whiskey?"

She looked as if she could use it. He shook his head. "I don't drink on the job."

"Oh, that makes sense." She glanced around and set the drink down on a table and turned back to him. "Mr. James, then." She shifted the dog to the other arm and shook his hand. "I'm Lori Jean. It was kind of you to make a house call. I do need to arrange for some additional funds."

"We should discuss the status of your trust. You've talked to your attorney?" he asked.

She gestured toward a chair. "Please have a seat. Yes, I talked with Clarence. He said something about the possibility of a more recent will."

"That's right," Jackson said, wondering if she was truly in the dark or if she was acting. It didn't matter, he thought as he opened his briefcase and pulled out three fat files. He was ready to turn on the light. "A more recent will has been found, and your father stipulated that half of the trust will be given to you when you're thirty and the other half when you reach fifty-five. Until then, you'll be given a sizable annual allowance. Unfortunately, you're twenty-four years old and you have spent your allowance through your twenty-eighth birthday. Some adjustments will have to be made in your spending."

She blinked at him. "Are you sure? I probably spend too much on clothes, but most of my money goes to charitable foundations." She lifted her shoulders and smiled. "I'm a philanthropist. Tilly always found a way to squeeze some money out of the trust for me."

That was why Tilly had retired. Tilly had skated a fine line of getting the firm in trouble over how much he had allowed the Granger babe to get her well-manicured fingers on.

"Mr. Till didn't have the information regarding the final will."

"So are you saying that my father left me all this money, but I can't touch it even for a good cause?"

"Exactly. You may live in the house and you will be

taken care of, but there is a limit to the amount you are allowed to spend."

Her eyebrows furrowed and she absently stroked her dog. "But what if it's for charity?"

"There is still a limit."

She gave a sigh of impatience. "But this is what I do. I'm a philanthropist. I fund worthy causes."

"Not when you don't have the funds."

"What am I supposed to do until I turn thirty?" she demanded.

"You still have two years' worth of allowance. If you budget your money—"

"Budget!" she echoed. "My father had so much money he couldn't spend it fast enough. I can't spend it fast enough."

"You've made an impressive start," Jackson muttered.

"Budget," she said again. "I can't believe this."

"I can help you. That's why I'm here." It hadn't taken long for Jackson to figure out exactly what his job was and why he had been chosen. His job was to say *no* to Lori Jean Granger because no one else could. His job was to teach the woman some real-world restraint, and the reason he had been chosen was because his bosses knew that when it came to heiresses who spent money with the same ease most people sent water down the drain, Jackson had no heart at all.

Lori didn't like this accountant. She frowned as she watched his face, all stern lines and no-nonsense scowls. She wanted a different one. She wanted sweet old Tilly back. Tilly had chastised her about her donations, but after a double shot of whiskey, he'd always found a way to loosen the purse strings.

The attorney, Clarence, had left her several messages, but Lori had been away visiting one of her sisters and her brother in Philadelphia. Ever since Harlan died, she'd been trying to fill up the empty space inside her, but so far, nothing had worked. Being with her sister Katie and her family had helped a little, but Lori felt useless unless she was helping to fund her charities.

She had felt useless since her horrible horseback riding accident in college several years ago. She'd nearly died, and it had taken three surgeries and months of rehabilitation to put her back together again. Riding had been the passion of her life, and she hadn't ridden a horse since. First, her father had forbidden it. Now, without him, she was too frightened. Scaredy-cat is what her sister Delilah would have called her, and Delilah would have been right.

Lori bit her lip and felt the beginning of an unwelcome but familiar edgy sensation. She was one of four offspring, and she'd gotten lucky with the sperm donor. She'd won the lottery when it came to fathers. Her father had not only loved and adored her, he'd also been loaded. The only thing he'd requested in trade for his devotion and riches was that she leave her mother, half sisters, and half brother behind. She'd been willing to hide her contact with her half sisters and brother until the accident. After that, she just couldn't hide her desire to connect with them anymore, and she feared that was what had broken Harlan's heart.

She'd felt guilty most of her life. Guilty for having a

wealthy father. Guilty for having siblings he didn't approve of.

The nasty, edgy feeling built inside her so that she couldn't sit still. "There must be some way," she ventured. "Some creative accounting way—"

"Creative accountants and their clients often end up in prison."

Lori glanced at him again. She was surprised they'd sent someone so young. He didn't seem the least bit affected by her appearance. She wondered if he was gay. He didn't look gay. Except for his suit, he didn't look like an accountant, either. He was tall, with broad shoulders. His nose looked as if it had been broken, but he wasn't ugly. He wasn't handsome, either. Strong jaw, she noticed. She had the un-fun sense that he would be stubborn.

"There's got to be a way around this," she said.

He placed a file of papers on the coffee table. "I'm leaving you with a copy of the will and the amount of the allowance you're due for the next six years. We can meet again tomorrow," he said, then paused. "Provided you don't start any new charitable foundations or go on any shopping sprees."

She frowned at his dry tone. "I don't like your attitude, Mr. James. I'm not sure I want to work with you. Perhaps I should call Mr. Hollingsworth about working with someone else."

"Good luck," Mr. James said in a confident tone that grated on her.

"Why good luck?" she demanded.

"Because everyone else said no to the job. I'm the only sap they could talk into taking you on. They're all afraid you'll turn them into mush and send their careers down the toilet."

"I'm not that difficult to work with! I'm not rude or arrogant or—"

"No. You just come across as so sweet and helpless that you make men feel like they have to take care of you. They want to give you everything you ask for, everything you wish for."

She didn't like the image he was painting of her. She didn't like it at all. "I'm not helpless."

He cracked a half smile that didn't reach his piercing eyes. "Here's your chance to prove it."

> *"For most of us, there always seem to be enough bills to cover whatever money we make."*
> —SUNNY COLLINS

Chapter Two

The following morning, Jackson James arrived just as Lori was eating the last bite of her breakfast of fresh fruit and granola. She made a face when Mabel told her he was waiting for her. After looking over the paperwork he'd left her last night, she'd barely been able to sleep. She truly hadn't realized how much money she'd spent since Harlan had died. It was embarrassing. Most of the money had gone to good causes, but seeing the numbers in black and white was disconcerting, to say the least.

Now she had to pay the piper, face the music, suffer the consequences. Lori suspected that working with Jackson James would give new meaning to the word *suffering*.

There was another way, another choice. Unspoken and unspeakable, but available nonetheless. Lori considered the option for a half second and wrinkled her nose. She wasn't that desperate.

Taking a sip of coffee, she braced herself for another

meeting with this Scrooge with linebacker shoulders. She slipped her feet into her shoes and walked down the gleaming wood floor of the hallway to the parlor. "Good morning, Mr. James," she said and waved him to a seating area. Choosing the ivory leather chair, she sat down. She noticed the navy suit jacket he wore today didn't fit any better than the one he wore yesterday.

"Did you have a chance to look over the folders I gave you?" he asked, sitting across from her with a bulging briefcase.

"Yes, I did," she said. "Things have been such a blur since my father died, I didn't realize how many donations I had made."

He gave a neutral nod, but disapproval emanated from his dark eyes. "That's why we need to set up a budget for you, so you don't get caught short in another year. It's my job to identify possible areas where you can—" He paused as if searching for the right word. "Economize," he said, his voice full of irony. "For example, I notice you spend a significant amount of money on clothing, particularly evening wear. Here's an area that could be trimmed."

"I wear the dresses once, then donate them to the women's shelter," Lori said and shrugged. "A Granger doesn't repeat wearing a dress to a social event during the same season, and by the next season, they're out of style."

"I don't think the women staying at the women's shelter are going to have too many places to wear couture evening dresses," Jackson James said.

"The evening dresses are sold, and the proceeds go to the women's shelter," Lori told him.

"Admirable, but not economical," he said without missing a beat. "If you want to keep donating all your dresses, then you need to hit some sales."

The housekeeper entered the room carrying a brown package and several envelopes. "Morning mail, Miss Granger."

"Thank you, Mabel."

Jackson gave Mabel a nod of welcome, then continued. "Now we need to pare down this list of charities you contribute to on a regular basis. Cat and dog groomers for rescued animals? I wasn't aware cats allowed anyone to groom them."

The way he said it made it sound silly. "For some rescued animals, mostly dogs, grooming can be a health issue," Lori said, determined to keep a defensive tone from her voice.

"At a hundred dollars a pop?" he asked with a raised eyebrow. "I don't spend that much on a haircut for myself."

Lori glanced at his hair and resisted the urge to point out that her stylist wouldn't cut the top quite so short. "I can direct my resources toward one of my other charities for the time being."

"And about this grooming for your dog? I think we can find something more reasonable than what you're doing now."

"Kenny gets nervous around water. He requires a special touch."

"You can buy a bottle of dog shampoo and save five hundred dollars a month. Hell, I'll give him a bath for five bucks a pop."

She wouldn't let him anywhere near her dog. He would probably drown Kenny.

"I'll make other arrangements," she said, picking up the stack of mail.

"Here's a charity for cultural arts appreciation for preschoolers? Why would anyone want to take a two-year-old to the opera?"

"One of my sorority friends founded that charity. It sounded like a nice idea at the time," she said, feeling more idiotic with each passing moment. The trouble was that everything sounded worthy and good at the time. She flipped through the mail.

"And what is this purchase of collectible teddy bears?" he asked.

Lori Jean winced. She'd gotten a little carried away with that one. "It's a worthy cause. The fire department and rescue squads like to give children teddy bears when they have to be treated or taken to an unfamiliar place."

Jackson James met her gaze. "Do the bears need to cost two hundred dollars each?"

Resisting the urge to squirm, she lifted her chin. "Of course not, but I sponsored an advertisement for that charity, and they needed some bears for the photo shoot."

"For this price, you could have gotten real bears," he muttered.

He was going to pick her to death, she thought as he continued. Mentally muting him, she caught sight of a return address on an envelope that snagged her attention. Virginia Dawson. *Miracles in Motion Ranch.* Lori tore open the envelope and read the letter. She felt a stab of grief at the news that Virginia's husband, Skip, had suffered a long illness and died. As she read on, a knot of distress formed in her chest. Virginia was going to have to shut down the ranch. She didn't have the financial backing to continue. Miracles in Motion was a combination working/therapeutic ranch. Children with disabilities came to the facility to ride the horses.

Guilt twisted through her. She bit her lip. She hadn't been in touch with Virginia or the ranch since her accident. Before her accident, she had spent two summers at the ranch to gain the practicum credit her degree required. She had loved working at the ranch, loved the people, the horses, the children. It had been one of the few places where she'd been valued and accepted for herself, not for her father's wealth.

Another sharp pain stabbed at her. Another loss, she thought. She hated the idea of the ranch closing down. She'd witnessed the improvements children had made during their visits there. What a rotten time to get the news. Any other time and she could write a check without blinking.

Miserable and hating the overwhelming feeling of helplessness, she sighed.

"Miss Granger, this is important. Are you listening to me?" Jackson James demanded.

Blinking, she met his hard gaze and moved her head in a circle. "Yes," she said with a shrug. "And no." She fought a flurry of nerves in her belly at the dark expression on his face. "I just received some bad news. An old friend has passed away."

His eyes gentled a fraction. "I'm sorry."

"Me, too. And now Virginia is going to have to sell the ranch. I have to do something."

"What do you mean you have to do something?"

"I mean I can't let this happen." She waved the piece

of paper. "I can't let Virginia lose the ranch because Skip died. I have to do something."

Jackson James set down his pen and looked at her as if she were a couple cookies short of a dozen. It wasn't the first time he'd looked at her that way. "Who are Virginia and Skip? And why do you have to do anything with this ranch?"

Restless, Lori stood. "Virginia and Skip run—well, they ran," she corrected herself and frowned. "They ran a combination working/therapeutic ranch where handicapped children came and rode horses. It was a wonderful place, the employees, the horses, the children. It would be a crime to let it fail. I can't do it."

"What do you have to do with this ranch?"

"I worked there for two summers during college break. I need you to help me find a way to help them."

Jackson shook his head before she finished her request. "No can do. Between the teddy bears, the preschool visits to the opera, and everything else, you have to help yourself now." His mouth settled into a firm, unyielding line. "I have to help you help yourself."

Lori began to pace. "You really don't understand. You can take away my shopping trips. I'll wash Kenny myself, although someone else will have to trim his nails, because I refuse to hurt him. I can't let this fail. It would be wrong."

Jackson looked at her for a long moment and sighed. "This must be like an addiction or something to you. You find some needy cause and you have to shell out the bucks to—"

"This is not an addiction!" she shouted, rounding on him. Her heart raced with anger, fury pounded in her head. She felt her left eye begin to twitch. She glanced at the Waterford crystal vase of flowers and itched to throw it at him. She couldn't remember when she had felt so strongly about something. Not since her father died. Maybe not even since her accident.

She could look at Jackson James and see that he didn't respect her. She couldn't really blame him. She wasn't sure she even respected herself. But this was different. She really didn't want to let Miracles in Motion go under.

She took a deep breath. "This is different. This was a very special place. They liked me and valued me, not just because of who my father was."

"If they're asking you for money now, how can you be sure of that?" he asked, reeking cynicism and disbelief.

At that moment, Lori really hated the man, and she couldn't remember ever hating anyone. "It must be sad to be you, to never be able to see the good in people, or just the possibility of good in people."

A sliver of surprise came and went in his eyes, and his jaw hardened. "This isn't about my personal abilities. This is about your financial situation."

"You're right. You're exactly right. Thank you for reminding me. And your job is to help me accomplish what I believe is important. And this is important."

"Are you willing to fire your assistant and other members of your staff to accomplish it?"

Lori blinked. She hadn't even considered that. "I—don't see how. Merilee has a son in college, and Dena's husband hurt his back, so he can't work. She's the sole support of their family."

"Then where do you propose to get the money?" he asked.

Lori drew a blank. The truth hurt, but the truth was she knew much more about spending money than making it. "That's part of your job, isn't it?"

He raked his hand through his hair. "I'm gonna have to think on this. The general rule is you don't expand expenditures when you're short of cash."

"There's got to be a way. Maybe a loan."

He shook his head. "Yeah, you need that like you need a root canal. There's always the alternative condition your father left . . ."

Lori felt bitter disgust back up in her throat. "You mean that archaic, chauvinistic, insulting clause that if I get married and remain married until I'm thirty, then my husband and I can have more access to my inheritance, but my husband will have to approve major purchases." She gritted her teeth. "I still think Daddy must have been mentally half-gone when he put in that provision."

Not only was it insulting, it was also embarrassing. The ultimate no-confidence vote. Her father had loved her with all his heart, but he obviously hadn't believed she was capable of looking after herself. The terrible question whispered in her brain like a hissing poisonous snake.

What if she wasn't?

Before Lori Jean Granger drove him completely out of his mind, Jackson decided to drive his Chevy Blazer to a barren area past the outskirts of Dallas. This was where he came when he felt the corporate demands sliding around his neck to choke the life out of him. With his jacket already ditched, he tugged his tie loose and undid the top button of his shirt. It was still hot as hell outside, and even though he'd been wearing suits since he graduated from college, he'd never grown accustomed to it. No matter what brand he wore, he always felt as if he was wearing a straitjacket and a silk noose.

He got out of his truck and watched the sun ease down the horizon. Two hundred acres of scrubby land. The only good thing about the acreage was the accessibility to the highway. Anyone else looking at the expanse of barren land would see an ugly, useless plot of real estate.

But not Jackson. Jackson saw well-manicured lawns with houses that oozed comfort. He saw paved driveways and neighborhood streets with lights. He saw a playground for children and a community clubhouse and swimming pool. He saw everything he had wanted as a child and didn't have.

An image of the shack he'd grown up in flashed through his mind. He heard his father's anger and his mother's tears. He smelled the alcohol on his father's breath and felt his rough slap across his cheek as if it were yesterday. He saw the bruises on his mother's face and felt the horrible helplessness.

Something inside him hardened like granite.

He would never be helpless again. He would make his own way.

The rest of the firm would fall out of their chairs if they knew that Jackson James had every intention of becoming the next real-estate tycoon of Texas. The partners and everyone else thought he was a heartless sonovabitch determined to make his living through accounting, but Jackson had always known accounting was just a means to an end. The kind of success he wanted required a vision and heart his peers thought he didn't possess. It also, however, required financial backing, and that would take some time. He sucked in a draft of hot summer air and narrowed his eyes. It may look like a piece of crap now, but this was going to be one building block of his fortune. Jackson owned a couple of houses in town that he rented and added the monthly payments to the special account for Jackson Place.

"Jackson Place," he echoed, and his lips twitched with self-derision. It was egotistical as hell to name a real-estate development after himself, but he didn't want anyone mistaking who founded this successful venture.

Jackson Place would be the first of many successful ventures. He knew it in his bones. Nothing would stop him, especially not the whiny, nerve-racking Princess Granger, who had somehow managed to pussy whip even the toughest accountant. The Granger account was just one more little battle to conquer, and both heaven and hell knew he'd fought tougher opponents than Lori Granger.

"You will always be my little sunbeam."
—SUNNY COLLINS

Chapter Three

Lori sat on her bed with Kenny by her side as she looked at the contents of the package she'd received earlier that afternoon. She couldn't remember being this angry in her life.

She snatched another Oreo from the plateful on her bedside table, then lifted the nearly empty bottle of Cristal champagne and guzzled it straight from the bottle. She'd smashed her crystal champagne flute against her closet a couple of minutes ago.

Her personal line rang, and she was so disgusted she almost didn't answer. Glowering, she snatched up the receiver. "Hello," she said in a voice that sounded both slurred and cross to her own ears.

"Lori Jean? Is that you?"

Lori immediately recognized her sister Delilah's voice, and something inside her eased. "It's me. I am so angry at my father I could scream."

"What's wrong? You don't sound like yourself at all."

"Probably because myself is so furious I can't stand it."

"I know Harlan had almost as much money as the devil himself, but what could he do from the grave that would piss you off this much?"

"It's not what he did from the grave. It's what he did before," she said, scooping up a pile of letters from her long-deceased mother. "Did you know Momma sent me at least three letters a week until she died? He kept them from me. Even after she died, he didn't let me see them."

"I'm sorry, sweetie. If it helps any, my father wouldn't let me read them, either. He was actually worse, though. He burned them right in front of me."

Lori knew Delilah's father had been downright harsh. He'd even been known to beat Delilah. It was a miracle Delilah had turned out as loving and successful as she had. No one would have predicted she would marry one of the Houston Huntingtons and start having babies right away, but Delilah had always been one for the unexpected.

"Your father was a toad. He was worse than a toad," Lori said.

"Lori, sweetie, you sound very strange. What are you drinking?"

"Cristal, but I'm balancing it with Oreos since you're not supposed to drink on an empty stomach." She glanced around her room. The decor hadn't changed much since she'd first moved here as a frightened young girl so many years ago. Once Harlan had learned that his quick affair with her mother, Sunny Collins, had yielded a daughter, he'd smeared Sunny's reputation in court and won custody so fast it made heads spin. He had been a doting but controlling father, determined that Lori not go the way of her slutty mother.

Delilah snickered. "I approve the champagne, but you're gonna feel horrible in the morning."

"I've felt horrible for the last few days, so it won't be anything new. I knew my father was controlling, but this, this just takes the cake. Between the will and the letters, he was—"

"What about the will?" Delilah asked.

Lori winced. She hadn't wanted Delilah to know about the will and the trust. "It's nothing, really. He was just being his regular controlling self, wanting to control my entire life. I swear if he could have put strings on me to make me dance like a puppet, he would have done that." She picked up another letter addressed to her in her mother's flowery script and felt a dull pain behind her ribs. "I don't know if I'm going to be able to forgive him for this." She felt so betrayed, so horribly betrayed. She had longed to contact her mother, but Harlan had prevented every effort. All because he was terrified that she would end up a floozy like her mother.

"Lori? Lori Jean, are you still there?"

"Yes, I'm still here," she muttered, picking up the bottle of Cristal and swallowing the last drops.

"As much as I can sympathize with your anger and your desire to tie one on when you found out about the letters, you're gonna pay for this big-time in the morning. Trust me. I want you to promise me that you won't drink any more champagne tonight."

That was easy. The bottle was empty. "I promise," she said, smothering a burp. "No more champagne tonight."

"You promise?" Delilah repeated skeptically, as if she knew she'd extracted the agreement too easily.

"I promise. I not only promise. I promise to keep that promise."

"You're really loaded, aren't you?"

"Don't worry. I'm not driving."

Delilah chuckled. "I may have one of my Dallas managers check in on you tomorrow," she said.

Delilah had expanded her spa business so that she now had an additional location in Dallas. Lori could feel the haze of alcohol closing over her brain, but she didn't want Delilah worrying about her. "I'm fine. I'll be fine. Remember, I'm surrounded by people eager to do my bidding."

She slumped down against her pillow and yawned, closing her eyes.

"If you're sure," Delilah said.

"I'm sure. I'm really sure," Lori said, absently stroking Kenny.

"Well, I doubt you'll remember this, but the reason I called is to tell you that I'm pregnant."

Lori's eyes popped open. "*Again?* That's three times in three years!"

Delilah gave a low chuckle. "What can I say? Benjamin inspires me."

Lori felt the slightest stab of envy but pushed it aside. She knew Delilah had suffered before she'd found her dream man. "Is Ben excited?"

"Of course, and he's so sweet about morning sickness. He brings me crackers, caffeine-free soda, and a prenatal vitamin every morning before he leaves for the office."

"Must be nice to have a man so crazy for you."

"The feeling's mutual, but I don't want to gush too much. Something tells me you might be dealing with a queasy stomach in the morning for a totally different reason."

"Well, I won't need any prenatal vitamins, that's for sure." She closed her eyes again. "Congratulations on the new baby, sis."

"Thanks, Lori. I'll call you tomorrow afternoon. Don't forget to wash off your makeup and take an Advil before you fall asleep."

"Absolutely," she said, wishing her voice didn't sound so slurred. " 'Night, Dee."

As she began to fall asleep, she muttered to herself. "I'm going to fix my father. I don't know how, but I am really going to fix my father good."

The next morning, Lori awakened to the sound of Kenny barking and a pain in her head that felt as if she were being hit with one of her father's ten irons. She opened her eyes with effort, recalling that she hadn't washed her face. Her makeup felt as if it were cracking on her skin.

Lori made a face and lifted her head. Her stomach turned and her head pounded. "Oh, I should have taken that Advil. Why didn't I take the Advil?"

Kenny continued to bark, no doubt wanting to relieve his little bladder. The sound abraded her senses. Her fingers holding either side of her head, she gingerly made her way to her bedroom door. "Hang on, Kenny. It'll be just a minute. Just a minute." She turned the doorknob and he rushed down the stairs.

The only way Lori could imagine getting downstairs was either crawling or throwing herself over the railing. She fumbled for the button for the intercom. "Mabel?" She paused and waited, hearing Kenny's staccato yips jab at her brain like knives. "Mabel?" she repeated, hearing the desperation in her own voice.

No answer. She walked down the hallway and covered her eyes to shield herself from the bright, offensive sunlight streaming through the half-circle window above the front door.

Peeking down at the ominous grand stairway, she adjusted her peach sundress, bit her lip, and sat down. Her head throbbing with each movement, she scooted her feet forward and followed with her bottom, step by step, until she reached the foyer, where Kenny danced on the tile floor.

The doorbell rang. "*Where* is Mabel?"

Glancing through the peephole, she caught sight of Jackson James. Lori scowled. *This early?* She looked at the grandfather clock and was shocked to see the time was 11:00 a.m.

Looking down at her mussed self, she shook her head. He couldn't see her like this. He already had a superior attitude toward her. This would only make it worse. "Oh," she groaned as the pain shot through her skull. "Kenny, you're just going to have to pee in the backyard. C'mon," she said, lightly clapping. "Back door."

But Kenny continued to bark and dance in the foyer, even though she gestured for him to follow her. "Kenny, c'mon."

The doorbell rang again. Kenny raised his leg. "Oh, no. No, no, no."

She opened the door and set the dog outside, where he proceeded to take a leak on Jackson James's black shoes.

"Oops." Lori cringed, noticing that Jackson moved quickly for a man his size. "I'm really sorry. Kenny rarely has accidents, but I couldn't get Mabel and I didn't realize how late it was and—" She broke off when she noticed him staring at her face. Oh, God, she hadn't even glanced in the mirror, but she could well imagine what she looked like, mascara under her eyes and her hair a rat's nest. Lori shuddered.

"Please take off your shoes and I'll get you some new ones in no time. When I find Mabel, I'll ask her to take the shoes out to the garbage. I apologize for running late for our appointment, but I have a few things I need to do."

"I don't need to throw away these shoes just because your dog sprinkled a little on them. I just need to clean them off. It won't take me but a minute, and we can go ahead and get to work."

Except I'm not ready. "Fine. Let me find Mabel," she said, heading down the hallway. "Mabel? Mabel?"

"Yes, ma'am. I was just emptying the trash in the backyard."

Lori pulled her housekeeper aside. "Kenny had a little accident on Mr. James's shoes, so I was wondering if you could get someone to clean them. I also need to shower, so I need you to occupy Mr. James with something," she said, searching her foggy brain for possibilities. "Food. Just give him food, please, and I'll be down as soon as I can."

Her head still pounding, she dragged herself up the back staircase, so she wouldn't run into Jackson again. She ate a couple of leftover cookies and downed the Advil she should have taken the night before, then stripped and got into the shower. Although she would have loved to linger, she knew the clock was ticking. Quickly lathering herself from head to toe, she rinsed and got out of the shower. She rubbed herself dry, put some gel in her hair, slapped moisturizer on her face, and applied lipstick, concealer, and mascara. After brushing her teeth twice, she pulled on a red cotton sheath and stepped into red heels. Red made her look more confident, even if she didn't feel it.

Sometime in the middle of her Cristal-enhanced sleep, Lori had dreamed the solution to her problem. She would beat her father at his own game of control, and Jackson James was going to help her. Despite her headache and queasiness, she felt completely resolute, and all she had to do to turn her conviction to concrete was to look at the box of letters Harlan had kept from her.

She walked down the front stairway with a clearer head and entered the parlor, where Jackson James was reviewing some papers. A tray of food that Mabel had left him appeared untouched. The man must have the self-discipline of a priest. No one could resist Mabel's cinnamon rolls.

He glanced up at her, his gaze sliding over her in quick neutral assessment. "Nice of you to come," he drawled, standing.

She nodded. "I already apologized."

"Too much partying last night?" he asked.

"I'm not sure I would call it a party," she said. "Please sit."

He shrugged and sat down. "How does your head feel?"

"Like hell," she said with a smile. "But you already knew that. I need to discuss something else with you. I made a decision last night, and it will impact your duties."

He raised an eyebrow. "What decision is that?"

"I've decided I want to get married, and I want you to help me find a husband."

"Dogs are generally more devoted than men are."
—SUNNY COLLINS

Chapter Four

Jackson stared at the insane woman in disbelief, but he didn't need to ask Lori to repeat herself. Her words would ring in his ears at the top of his list of unforgettable requests. He stood and shook his head. "No, ma'am."

With perfectly manicured, unsteady hands, she poured herself a cup of coffee. She rattled the china so much he took the cup and saucer from her, for fear she would drop them. Jackson poured the coffee and nodded toward a chair. "You need to sit down," he said. "You drank way too much last night if you think I'm going to find a husband for you."

Lori sat down and immediately slipped off her shoes. She tucked one leg behind the other, beauty-queen style, and gingerly sipped from the coffee, wrinkling her nose. She closed her eyes for two seconds, then fixed her baby blues on him. "This is the perfect solution to my financial situation. Find a man who agrees to be my husband until

I turn thirty, pay him for his services, then divorce him so I can do what I want."

"Have you even considered that a budget could be a better solution? You need to learn how to responsibly manage your inheritance."

Lori rolled her eyes. "You and I both know that even at the rate I spend, I would have to throw away a lot more money on a daily basis in order to go through my father's fortune during my lifetime. My father wrote his will to control me. He always tried to control me, and a lot of the time, he succeeded." Her eyes turned dark. "Now it's time for me to take control. That's why I'm getting married on my terms." She took another sip and grimaced. "That's where you come in."

"That's where you're wrong. I manage your finances, not your love life."

She shook her head, then pressed her fingers to her temple. "This has nothing to do with my love life and everything to do with my finances."

His stomach twisted at the determined expression on her face. She looked angry, resolved, and a little nuts. "Marriage is serious business, Lori."

"Exactly," she said, meeting his gaze. "Business. That's why you'll be the perfect matchmaker for me. You can vet prospects, arrange for background checks, and coordinate a prenuptial agreement with an attorney. Plus, you've got that whole emotionally detached accounting thing going for you."

She was serious. This kooky rich girl was serious. He swallowed an oath. "You've got the wrong man. There's no way I'm going to be your matchmaker. No way."

As he bolted from the Granger mansion, Jackson felt

steam rising from his head, and it wasn't because of the August heat. It was all internal. Lori had fried his brain circuits with her idiotic proposal.

Driving to the office, he strode directly to Hollingsworth's office and tapped on the door. His boss's assistant looked up at Jackson and frowned as if she weren't going to let him inside, so he went ahead and opened the door.

"Jackson?" Mr. Hollingsworth mouthed, cradling a telephone receiver to his ear.

"Excuse me, sir—"

Hollingsworth held up a finger. "I look forward to meeting with you. Friday at 10:00 p.m. We'll have your favorite cigars." Hollingsworth laughed. "Sure, see you then."

Jackson felt movement behind him.

"I'm sorry, Mr. Hollingsworth," the assistant said, frowning at Jackson in disapproval. "Mr. James got past me before I had a chance to stop him."

"That's okay," Hollingsworth said, studying Jackson for a few seconds. "This time," he added. "Come on in, Jackson. You can close the door behind you. Hold my calls."

Jackson closed the door and walked to his boss's desk. He cleared his throat. "Mr. Hollingsworth, I'll put my accounting background against anyone's in the firm, but I can't fulfill Lori Granger's latest request," he said with a bitter taste filling his mouth.

"Have a seat," Hollingsworth said, motioning to the leather chair in front of his desk.

Jackson reluctantly sat. He was still stifling the urge to scream.

"Did she ask you to commit a crime?"

Jackson blinked and shook his head. "No, no," he said.

Hollingsworth stood and walked to the side of his desk. He lifted the lid of his humidor. "You see what's in this humidor?"

Jackson looked inside. "It's empty."

"Right. I hate cigars. They're nasty, and the odor clings to everything. But Friday this humidor will be filled with the finest Jamaicans money can buy, because a client with a multimillion-dollar account will be walking through that door. He'll light a cigar, and so will I—even though I hate them. Dealing with top clients means you're willing to work with their eccentricities. If these people weren't rich, they'd be called freaking weirdos instead of eccentrics. Now, I'm not going to ask what Lori Granger wants you to do. I'm just going to tell you that this is part of playing with a big fish." He leaned forward and clapped Jackson on the shoulder. "We believe you can handle this account." With a smile reminiscent of Jack Nicholson's I-couldn't-care-less grin, he waved the hand toward the door. "Now have a nice day."

Nodding, Jackson rose and strode from the office to his vehicle. He got inside and felt himself boil with frustration. At least he understood the rules. He could expect zero backup from the partners, and he was expected to fulfill Lori Granger's most insane wish as if he had a magic wand. Hey, he'd dodged a roaring, snorting bull, mad with the urge to kill, before. He should be able to manage a female mad with the urge to marry.

Swearing under his breath, he started the vehicle and shifted it into gear. Who was he kidding? This job was going to be a bitch if ever there was one.

Needing silence and sense, he drove to his house and walked inside. His black Lab, Sadie, greeted him by rising and walking toward him. "How ya doing, girl?" he asked, petting her silky coat. He really hadn't had room in his life for a pet, but when he'd found Sadie abandoned and emaciated from lack of food, he hadn't been able to leave her. After they'd come to an agreement on her chewing habits, she'd become an easygoing buddy for him.

Hanging his suit coat on the back of a chair, Jackson lifted his phone and checked his voice mail. One message from his mother, another from his brother, another from a tenant. The tenant needed a faucet. No problem. Jackson could take care of that tonight. His mother and brother needed money, he suspected. Whenever both of them called, they didn't come out and ask for money, but they needed it. Since his father came and went as he pleased, Jackson sent money to fill in the gaps, with the understanding that his mother use it strictly for herself or his teenage brother, Adam.

Grabbing a beer from the refrigerator, he unbuttoned his shirt and pulled off his tie. He sat down in a wooden kitchen chair, put his feet on the chair across from him, and looked out the window. The view wasn't anything to scream about, just a couple of trees and brown grass singed from the unrelenting hot sun, along with the back of a neighbor's house. It soothed him because it was normal. He could use a lot of normal after the last few days.

He took another long drink from the can and let the silence and sanity seep inside him. He took a deep breath and felt his muscles loosen. Grabbing a notepad, he began to scribble notes, questions. Within twenty minutes, he formulated a plan for how to help Lori Jean Granger find a suitable husband, all the while trying to drown out the sound of the theme song from *Mission: Impossible* in his mind.

The following morning, Lori made sure she was ready early for Jackson, since he'd called her assistant and told her to expect him at 10:00 a.m. sharp. She was still stinging from the fact that he'd caught her in such an embarrassing position the morning before. She had no doubt that Jackson was mentally tough and she would have to stay on her toes at all times to keep up with him. He'd already let her know he was no pushover.

Grimacing at the prospect of meeting with him again, she checked her watch: 9:55 a.m. The doorbell rang. What an anal man, she thought, at the same time conceding that most good accountants probably were detail-oriented. It was a necessary trait for the job. She wrinkled her nose. The fact didn't make working with him any easier.

She opened the door and caught a look of surprise on his face. "What?" she asked, immediately feeling defensive. "You expected me to have another hangover? I'm not a drunk."

He shook his head. "I didn't say you were a drunk. I was surprised Mabel didn't answer the door," he said and entered the foyer.

"Oh." She felt as if someone had pricked her balloon. She met his level gaze and felt unsettled. "I'm assuming you've decided to work with me on my husband hunt."

He cleared his throat and narrowed his eyes in irritation. "Against my better judgment." He jerked his head impatiently. "If you're dead set on it, let's get on with it."

"I'm definitely dead set," she said, sensing his supreme

disapproval of her and trying not to feel on edge because of it. Walking with him toward the study, she told herself she didn't care what Jackson thought of her as long as he helped her accomplish her goal.

He held the door open for her, then waited for her to sit before he took his seat across from her. Pulling out a pad of paper and a pen, he sighed and scratched his head. "I have some questions I need you to answer. Do you have an age preference for your husband?"

She blinked. "I hadn't really thought about it. If he were going to be a real husband, I don't think I would want to marry someone too old. Older than me, though." She shrugged. "But since I'm only going to be married to him for a few years, it doesn't really matter, does it?"

"Unless he dies," Jackson muttered.

"Which would make me a very young widow—" Lori broke off. "I wonder what the requirements are if I'm widowed. If I married someone really old, maybe—"

Jackson groaned. "If you married someone really old, you'd have to contend with his heirs."

Lori made a face. "Oh, well, scratch that idea."

"Age preference," Jackson repeated.

"Twenty-eight to forty," she said.

He scratched her answer on his pad of paper. "What about education?"

"What about it?"

"Do you care if this guy has a college degree or not?"

Lori sighed. The truth was that she didn't want to overthink this. She just wanted to do it so she could get it over with and have it interrupt her life as little as possible. "I suppose so."

Jackson nodded and made another note on his paper.

"Do you have a preference about his physical appearance? Height, weight, body type, hair color, that kind of thing."

Lori gnawed her lip. "I'm not sure you're getting this. I don't really want to have to be married. I don't want to spend much time with this man. Any time," she added. "I want this to be a strictly business arrangement."

"And you don't care what the press will say about it?" Jackson asked, his gaze level.

Lori opened her mouth to answer *no*.

"You don't care what your friends will say behind your back. You don't care what kind of impact this may have on a future real marriage."

Lori felt her stomach twist. "I may not want to get married."

"What if you do? What if you have children?"

She bit her lip hard. He didn't know what he was talking about. He obviously didn't know that she probably couldn't ever have children because of the terrible horseback riding accident. "I don't think I'm cut out for motherhood," she managed in an airy voice, ignoring the stabbing sensation inside her.

He gave her a long, considering glance, as if he were weighing his opinion of her. His gaze swept to the pad of paper, and Lori experienced that old, familiar feeling of not measuring up.

She felt naked and vulnerable, but not for long. Self-righteous anger burned to the surface. She clenched her fingers into a fist to keep from throwing something at him.

"No children," he said. "Does that mean no sex?"

The question took her off guard. The whole discussion unnerved her, but Jackson's tone was deep and rich, edged with a tinge of huskiness that teased something inside her. She met his dark gaze and felt an odd tugging sensation in her belly. She wondered what kind of lover he would be. Passionate, she decided. Whether a little rough or a little tender, he would be passionate when he made love to a woman. She wondered how he chose his lovers.

Lori caught herself. What was she thinking?

He was so anal he probably had some sort of numerical rating system and checklist.

"I already told you this is supposed to be a business arrangement," she said.

"So is it okay if this guy gets taken care of on an extracurricular basis, or does the poor sap have to sign a chastity agreement?" He paused. "For that matter, what about you?"

"No, he doesn't have to sign a chastity agreement," she said, feeling more huffy by the moment. "He just needs to be discreet."

"Discreet as in down the street, out of town, or out of the country?"

Lori frowned. "I'm sure we can work out the details later."

Jackson shook his head. "You can get in a lot of trouble not taking care of details."

"Spoken just like an accountant," she muttered under her breath.

"I heard you," he said. "Just remember, you asked an *accountant* to find your husband for you."

Lori bit her tongue to keep from sticking it out at him. "Okay. Discreet means in a different city and not in view of the press."

"For you, too."

She looked at him in confusion. "What do you mean, me, too?"

"You'll be discreet, too, by going to a different city when you have your affairs."

Lori wrinkled her nose. "You make it sound slimy."

He lifted an eyebrow but said nothing. Aloud, anyway. His expression said he thought the whole thing was slimy. Lori couldn't stand his censure another moment. "I'm not slimy."

"I didn't say you were."

"You might as well have." She pointed at his face. "Your eyebrow said it."

His lips twitched in amusement. "I didn't know eyebrows could talk."

"Well, yours can," she said, her hands on her hips.

"I don't think you're slimy. I think you're desperate. Desperate people do stupid things."

Her anger kicked up another notch. "I'm not stupid, either."

"I didn't say—"

"Close enough," she said, cutting him off. "You know, you don't understand because you're a guy and you don't know what it's like to be female when your father was a wonderful man but he was also sexist, chauvinistic, and controlling." She sighed. "This is my way of taking control of my life."

He shrugged. "As long as you're sure living on a budget wouldn't be easier than getting a husband."

"I have people counting on me. You obviously don't understand. You must be free as a bird with no responsibilities, don't have to answer to anyone . . ."

She blinked, and he was looming over her. Her heart slammed in her chest at the dark expression on his face.

"You make a lot of assumptions about me," he said in a quiet, too-controlled voice.

She refused to be intimidated. Even if her legs felt a little shaky. "You haven't presented yourself as particularly compassionate."

He was silent for a long moment. Lori felt some kind of weird energy zinging between them. If the humidity and outdoor temperature hadn't been ninety percent and ninety degrees, then she would have thought it was static electricity.

"It's not my job to be compassionate. It's my job to help you learn to live within your means."

"Tilly was nicer than you are."

"No," Jackson said, shaking his head. "Mr. Till was a pushover."

"And you're not," she said. "Darn shame."

"You need—"

"Don't you dare say I need a firm hand," she interjected.

"You need someone who will tell you the truth. I think you know that I'll do that. That's the reason you want me in charge of your harebrained scheme to get a husband. Because you know I'll tell you the truth."

Lori tried not to squirm, but his words felt razor sharp. Even though Jackson lacked charm, she did feel she could trust him.

"Stop making assumptions," he said.

"Okay," she said, still feeling dissatisfied. "As long as you stop making assumptions about me. Yes, I've been overprotected. Yes, I've lived a privileged life. But I'm not selfish. I'm not stupid. And another thing," she added. "People sometimes make assumptions based on lack of information. If you want to change my impression of you, give me different information."

"Deal," he said and glanced down at his pad of paper. "I have one other question regarding your prospective husband. What did you have in mind for his annual salary?"

Lori resisted the urge to wrinkle her nose. Despite the fact that she'd decided this was a business arrangement, the idea of paying a man to be her husband was one more thing that made the whole plan feel icky. "I haven't thought of a figure. Have you?"

He lifted his eyebrows and shook his head. "I think it's going to have to be seven figures."

Stunned and a little insulted, Lori gaped at him. "I can't believe it's going to be that much of a horrible job." She lifted her shoulders. "What is this guy going to have to do? Pretend to like me, marry me, then go away with a settlement."

"You're a beautiful, generous woman, but this kind of thing would drive a lot of men crazy. Think about it. No sex and putting your future on hold for *years*."

"I didn't say no sex," she insisted.

"Just no sex with you or with anyone in the same town as you. Most heterosexual men can't handle that kind of you-can-look-but-you-can't-touch policy for a night, let alone years."

Something about the way he said *sex* got under her skin.

"You're just not going to be great wife material."

"If animals don't like your boyfriend, it's not a good sign."
—SUNNY COLLINS

Chapter Five

"You're headstrong and you won't compromise," Jackson continued, infuriating her even further.

"What you mean to say is I won't cave to instructions just because they're given to me by a man. I'm trying to remember the last time someone working for me said something so rude to me."

His eyes darkened. "Don't pull rank, Lori. You've turned this into a circus, and I'm just trying to keep it within three rings. Part of the success of my assignment will be based on your expectations. If you don't know what your expectations are, then you need to figure them out and tell me."

But that was the problem, she thought, balling one of her fists and swallowing the urge to shriek. She'd already figured out she didn't want to overthink this. She just wanted to do it. "I want a polite, discreet, and clean man who will sign an agreement to be married to me for six years, who will accept a settlement of divorce and then get out of my life." She refused to talk about it anymore. The intense discussion was upsetting her stomach, or maybe it was the expression in Jackson's eyes. "And stop judging me. You've never walked in my shoes."

He glanced down her legs at her high heels and his lips twitched. "I can't disagree with that."

"Hallelujah, have we actually found something we agree on?" she said more to herself than him. He unnerved her. She'd been in his presence only a little longer than ten minutes, and she was already feeling restless. "Okay, I think you have enough to get started. Let me know when you have some prospects for me." She bit back the urge to say *Now shoo*. Jackson didn't strike her as the kind of man to accept *shoo-ing*.

"Thank you for coming," she said, reluctantly extending her hand but figuring it was the most polite way to dismiss him.

His large hand swallowed hers the same way his whole persona seemed to dwarf hers. The strength in his clasp was appealing, and while his confidence in himself made her all too aware of her lack of it, she couldn't fight a grudging admiration. What she wouldn't give to have that kind of confidence. She wondered how he had gotten it and suspected it hadn't been the easiest path. Rock solid, so sure. The qualities were so attractive to her. But she knew he was a man who would only marry a submissive, agreeable woman—someone he could control. Not her, she told herself, and she gave his hand a firm shake.

Just as she had for the last few nights, Lori nixed social outings in favor of reading letters from her mother. There were so many it was going to take a while to read all of them. Her mother's letters were full of warmth and her distinctive wisdom. The early letters, filled with news about Katie and the pets Lori had left behind, made her stomach clutch with emotion.

She glanced around her room, now redecorated in soft tones of mauve and blue, and remembered how when she'd first arrived here she'd been afraid the big bed would swallow her up in the dark.

The doorbell interrupted her reverie and she frowned, glancing at the clock. Nine o'clock. Curious, she rose from her bed with the letter still in one hand and her glass of champagne in the other. She was limiting herself to one glass so she wouldn't make a fool of herself in front of Jackson again. She walked down the hall and had partway descended the steps when she stopped at the sound of a male voice.

"Speak of the devil," she murmured to herself, when Mabel allowed Jackson inside the door.

He was dressed in jeans and a dark T-shirt that accented his biceps and the exaggerated V shape of his body. His hair was the same, his face was the same. He was even holding a folder in one of those large hands of his. Without a suit, he seemed even more masculine to her.

As if he felt her studying him, he glanced up at her, and she felt his quick but thorough survey. She wore shorts and a summery tank top. His gaze lingered on the bare sliver of belly the shirt revealed, and she fought the urge to cover herself. Silly, she told herself. She wasn't naked. She just felt as if she was.

"I have a few prospects for you to look over," he said.

Surprise rushed through her. "Already?"

"You gave the impression you didn't want to drag your

feet," he said. "And based on your spending, we need to get moving."

"Okay," she said, feeling anything but okay. Nodding, she walked down the rest of the stairs.

He lifted a brow at the sight of her champagne glass and the letter she held. "What did I interrupt?"

"I wasn't getting drunk," she assured him. "Just reading some old letters."

He nodded, studying her face. "From your father?"

She shook her head. "No. My mother. My father—" She stopped, feeling a sharp jab of hurt and anger all over again. "My father kept them from me until he passed away."

Jackson's mouth rounded in a low-voiced "Oh." He was silent for a long moment that felt thick and full of emotion for Lori. "I could see where that might piss you off."

She gave a rough laugh. "That would be an understatement."

"Just how old are those letters?"

"This one's about eighteen years old."

He gave a whistle. "And your mom is—"

"Dead," she finished for him. "He didn't tell me about that until she had been gone, either. Nor did he tell me about my half brother." She felt her anger building. When she'd first found out about her mother's death and her half brother, she'd been angry, but her concern over her father's heart condition had kept her from letting him have it. Now that he was gone and she was left to deal with his controlling ways, she was having a tougher time forgiving him so easily.

"Well, that puts a different spin on things," Jackson finally said in a thoughtful voice.

For once, he wasn't looking at her in disapproval. The knowledge made something inside her loosen and sigh. Confused, she swallowed a sip of champagne. "It's all pretty complicated."

He nodded and glanced at the folder in his hand, then the letter in her hand. "What'd your momma say?"

She smiled. "She told me how my kitty cat was doing and how much she and Priss and Delilah missed me."

"Priss and Delilah?"

"Half sisters. We all had different fathers," she added. "My mother was always looking for the knight in shining armor to rescue her. She was gorgeous, and men were crazy for her. At least temporarily." She grimaced, recalling some of the stories her sisters had told her. "Unfortunately, she was a little blinded by her hope in eternal love."

"And you're not," he said.

She shook her head. She couldn't help feeling a pinch of longing when she looked at her sisters' happy marriages, but Lori had the strong sense that since she'd had the good life during her childhood, it would be too much to hope for that she would experience eternal love as an adult.

Sure, she'd been obsessed with those singers from the short-lived rock group Extreme, and she'd fantasized about Luke Perry from *Beverly Hills, 90210,* but she'd never lost her heart to a man. Of course, the fact that her father had threatened every guy she ever dated with his life hadn't helped matters.

"It's not that I don't think it's possible," she said. "For other people," she added. "I just get the impression I might have better odds on a slot machine in Vegas."

"Lucky with the slots?" he asked, his dark eyes amused. Something about his easy manner quieted her, made her feel less frantic.

She shook her head. "Not at all."

"Ever thought you might just need some time to figure out what you want for yourself, let alone in a man?" he asked.

Lori didn't want to go there. She didn't even want to consider the possibility. "Due to my dearly departed father, I don't have the luxury of time right now." She sighed. "I know I want to make this money work for good, and I don't want to wait."

He nodded and handed her the folder. "We're back to square one. Here are your first two prospects. I'll have more by the end of the week."

"Thanks."

He paused a moment. "Don't drink too much champagne."

She smiled. She supposed she'd earned his cautionary comment, since he'd witnessed the worst hangover of her life. "I won't. One glass, two Oreos, and as many letters as I can read."

"Aren't those letters depressing?"

Lori laughed. "Depressing letters from Sunny Collins?" She shook her head. "My momma was a firecracker."

He narrowed his eyes in speculation.

She couldn't resist prodding him. "What? What are you thinking?"

"Maybe that firecracker gene is hereditary, and maybe your daddy was scared to death of it."

"Maybe," she said, remembering her father's overly protective ways. She'd spent so much of her life not wanting to hurt him that she'd resisted any urge to rebel, with the exception of visiting her sisters and brother once they'd reunited several years ago.

He glanced at the folder. "Those guys have no idea what they're in for. Be gentle with them."

Impatience hissed through her. "There's nothing to worry about. I was raised well. I've always been described as well-mannered and polite."

"That was when Harlan was watching every step you took. Now that you have the opportunity, you may want to—" He paused as if he was searching for the right word and dropped his hand to rest on his hip. "Experiment."

Distracted by his large hand on his lean hip, she felt herself grow warmer. She dragged her gaze up from his hips, taking in his muscular chest. She'd bet he looked great without a shirt on. She bit her lip in surprise at herself. Her sex switch had been turned to the permanently off position so long, she'd begun to wonder if she was abnormal. And now she was getting turned on by her accountant? How wack was that?

She muffled a sound of strangled frustration. "You're talking about sex again, aren't you? I'm starting to wonder if I had you all wrong and if you aren't obsessed with it. I don't foresee that I'm going to suddenly go wild, but if I do, don't worry, I'll use protection." She desperately searched for a way to diffuse her strange attraction to Jackson. "Auntie," she added impulsively.

His eyebrows shot upward. "Auntie?" he echoed.

"Yes. You remind me of a nanny I had for several years. Auntie Pauline." This was a stretch. "She left just before I started driving, and the last three years, all she did was warn me about boys and sex."

Scrubbing his forehead with one of his big hands as if her logic was too much for him, he shook his head. "Whatever. You've been warned. You're of age, even if you don't always act like it. That'll have to be good enough for me. Let me know what you think of the contenders. I'll talk to you tomorrow," he said and opened the door.

"Thanks," she said.

"Just doing my job," he said, then shot her a dry sideways glance. "Such as it is."

The following day, Jackson arrived with information on three more contenders. He noticed Lori fidgeted as she reviewed the file contents. She tapped her bare foot on the floor. Her dog, seeming to sense her unrest, trotted restlessly around her feet.

"What do you think?" Jackson asked.

"I don't know," she said with a frown. "There's something missing."

"What's missing? You have photographs, family history, health history, education, and financial status."

She sighed and shrugged. "It just seems like a bunch of facts and numbers. What about their personalities? Their interests?"

The woman was a moving target, and Jackson hated moving targets. "I thought you said since this was going to be a business relationship, their personalities and interests wouldn't matter."

"Technically, I guess they don't. But I would just feel better if I knew a little more about their interests before I see them. Can you do that?"

"Yes. Are you interested in seeing any of them?"

"Not until I have a little more information about their personalities."

"Anything that you know is a dealbreaker up front?" he asked.

"He needs to be kind. Now that I think about it, even though I'm not going to be emotionally involved with this man, I don't want to live with someone who isn't kind."

"Define *kind*," he said.

She gave him a blank look. "Oh, I can see why you would need a definition. *Kind* means somewhat compassionate, not nasty or sarcastic in a mean way. Kind means polite. Kind means not making a joke at someone else's expense or being happy at someone else's failures. Oh, and he needs to be nice to animals. If he's not nice to animals, then he's got to be a total loser." She picked up her Pomeranian and nuzzled his neck. "Right, Kenny?"

Jackson squeezed the bridge of his nose and resisted the urge to run screaming out the door. "I'll do my best, but some people are experts at covering up a lot of nastiness."

"True," she murmured. "Maybe you could get a character reference or two, and if I get serious about one of them, you could do a deeper personal review."

"Okay, I'll take care of it this afternoon, give you the results, and maybe we can get a face-to-face tomorrow."

"Tomorrow?" she said, her voice filled with uncertainty.

Jackson was ready to toss his notebook on the ground and say to hell with it. "You need to make up your mind. Are you ready to do this or not? If you're serious about pursuing marriage, you need to get on with it. Don't get me wrong. I still think it's a crazy idea and you would be much better off just living by a budget—it would be a maturing experience for you."

"So will marriage," she said and took a deep breath. "I'll be ready to begin tomorrow."

Two days later, Jackson introduced prospect number one, Allan Sunday, to Lori. He stayed long enough to encourage pleasantries, although pleasantries were difficult because Lori's dog, Kenny, barked throughout the exchange. As soon as Lori led Allan to the living room, Jackson excused himself.

He stepped into his car, loosened his tie, and shook his head. So, this was what his life had come to? Finding a temporary husband for a kooky heiress. Swearing under his breath, he turned up the volume on the radio, allowing Eminem to express his rage for him.

He hoped Allan would work out. He seemed like a nice enough guy, although a bit on the geeky side. He'd graduated from college several years ago and wanted to start his own business. He had no history of drug abuse, he wasn't a Romeo, and his record was so clean it squeaked.

Jackson pulled into his new parking space at work and felt a surge of optimism as he opened the glass doors and strode toward his office. Allan met all of Lori's qualifications. There was no reason prospect number one shouldn't become Lori's groom.

"Mr. James, Miss Granger is waiting on line one," the receptionist told him.

Jackson's stomach fell. A call from Lori this soon wasn't a good sign. "I'll take it in my office."

He pulled the door closed behind him and picked up the phone. "Jackson James."

"Hi, Jackson, this is Lori."

"I know. Is Allan still there? Did you already reach an agreement?"

She gave a nervous-sounding laugh. "I guess you could say that."

Jackson felt an itchy irritation climb the back of his neck. "What kind of agreement?"

"Well, Allan had a little problem, and we're just not going to be able to live together."

"What could be wrong with him? The guy is perfect. No record, no bad habits."

"He's allergic to dogs."

Jackson groaned.

"It's a problem. It doesn't seem like it should be that big a deal, but I keep Kenny with me all the time, and Allan is very allergic. I couldn't put him through six years of asthmatic reactions. That would be too cruel."

"Have you considered confining Kenny to part of the house so Allan could have a dog-free zone?"

Silence followed. "Kenny is going to be around a lot longer than any husband."

"When you're a teenage girl, think of dating as a visit to the candy store. Remember you can visit more than once, and make sure to try everything that looks interesting."
—SUNNY COLLINS

Chapter Six

Bachelor number two was Ian Thompson. He seemed nice and sufficiently bland. Although a college dropout, Ian was brilliant. He wanted money to fund his inventions. During the dinner she shared with Ian, Lori had difficulty following Ian's thought patterns, but that wasn't the major problem, and Lori dreaded telling Jackson why Ian wouldn't work.

"He smells funny?" Jackson echoed, staring at her in disbelief the morning after the date. He set his cup of coffee and bagel aside. Darn, the food wasn't going to be a good enough distraction. "You won't marry him because he smells funny?"

Lori folded her hands in her lap and sat up straighter in the parlor chair. It might sound nuts to Jackson, but it was more important than he thought. "It's an issue. Think about it. I'll be smelling this man for six years."

"He could change his soap," Jackson said.

"It wasn't soap or cologne. It was just him."

"How did you get that close to notice?" he asked, lifting his dark eyebrow. Lori would swear Jackson's eyebrows could scold her and he wouldn't even need to say a word.

"We sat next to each other in the same vehicle," she explained. "It was easy to smell him."

Jackson looked at her as if he would rather chew nails than the lovely spread her housekeeper had prepared.

"You shouldn't underestimate the importance of smell. My sister Delilah chose her husband partly because she loved the way he smelled."

"But you don't want to love this man. You just want to marry him."

"Yes, but I don't like the way he smells, so I'm not marrying him." He made it sound ridiculous. Lori frowned. He made nearly everything she said sound ridiculous.

He rubbed his hand over his face in exasperation. "How am I supposed to screen a guy for smell?"

"You can't," she said. "You're probably not very sensitive to smell, anyway. You don't know what works for me and what doesn't, so I'll do the scent test."

"If you keep finding reasons not to marry the candidates I bring to you, I'm going to start thinking that you really don't want to get married, after all," he said, his gaze entirely too sharp.

"It would have been nice if one of your first two candidates had worked out, but I don't think it's unreasonable for me to need to see more than two men before I feel comfortable getting married."

"It's going to be impossible for me to help you find a

husband if you keep adding requirements to your list that can't be quantified, such as smell," he said as if it were the most ridiculous thing in the world. As if *she* were the most ridiculous person in the world. "You're creating a moving target and . . ."

Distracted by noises coming from the foyer, Lori didn't catch the rest of Jackson's lecture. Hearing a voice that sounded familiar, she tilted her head and listened to a woman's laughter. Shock and pleasure raced through her.

"Delilah," she whispered, rising to her feet.

"What?" Jackson said, also rising.

Lori heard more voices. "She brought the kids!" Two seconds later, her sister Katie, also known as Priss, and Delilah burst into the room with their children.

"Sorry for the lack of notice," Priss said, opening one of her arms for an embrace. With her other arm, she held a toddler on her hip. Lori immediately gave her oldest sister a hug and kissed the baby.

"Speak for yourself," Delilah said. "The surprise was my idea. You've been holed up in your fortress too long," she scolded, pulling Lori into her arms while her small children tugged at her legs.

Lori's heart swelled and her eyes filled with tears. "Oh, you two have no idea how great it is to see you."

"Hold that thought," Delilah said, eyeing the table of food. "Do you mind sharing your picnic with my little monsters?"

Lori smiled. Amazing how Delilah could infuse so much affection into the word *monsters*. Delilah, with the reputation of man-eater and flirt, had become supermom, and from the glow in her eyes, her sister was loving every minute of it.

Delilah tore off pieces of pastry and motioned for her small children to sit on the floor. She gave them plates with bits of pastry and fruit.

"And who is this?" Delilah asked in her best man-eater voice.

Lori whipped around to look at Jackson as he offered a grape to Katie's daughter. Her gaze locked with his, and she felt a kick of panic and something else she couldn't name. How could she explain Jackson? She refused to tell her sisters about her marriage plan. They would try to talk her out of it. Delilah and Katie were too sharp not to ask questions if she told them he was her accountant.

"I'm sorry. I should have introduced you, Jackson. These are my sisters and their children. Delilah," she said, pointing to her middle sister. "And Priss—" She corrected herself. "Katie. This is Jackson James. He's my, uh, my—new assistant," she invented.

Glowering at her, Jackson didn't appear to like her invention. He gave a curt nod of his head. "Hi," he said simply.

Delilah gave a throaty laugh. "Is he your personal assistant? What kind of duties does he perform?"

Biting her lip at Delilah's suggestive tone and Jackson's growing scowl, Lori stepped toward the door. "He's the most efficient assistant I've had. He keeps me from double booking and double spending all the time," she said. "Speaking of booking, Jackson, there was something I wanted to tell you before you left. Excuse us just for a moment," she said to her sisters and urged Jackson out the door with her.

Reaching out, she grabbed his arm and led him down

the hallway into the butler's pantry and closed the door behind them.

"Assistant?" he echoed.

"I didn't know what else to call you," she said. "I don't want my sisters to know about the marriage thing. They won't understand."

"Good to know someone in the family is rational," he said in a dry tone. "Assistant," he repeated, lifting the dark eyebrow again.

Lori resisted the urge to force the eyebrow back down. "I don't want them to know about my finances, either," she whispered. "They'll feel like they have to rescue me, and I absolutely don't want that. I want to handle this myself."

"By pretending you're not planning to marry for money and telling them your accountant is your assistant."

Lori frowned at him. "It's just for a couple of days. We'll visit a children's fun palace, eat out, then they'll go home. You don't even need to come over very often for the next couple of days. Just maybe once or twice. I'll tell them you're taking care of some errands or I let you have some time off."

"You don't have time to procrastinate, Lori," he reminded her, making her stomach knot.

"I know, I know. You can use this time to set up several dates for me with different men. Maybe five," she said, watching his eyes widen in surprise. Yep, that was the solution—she needed to keep Jackson busy during the next two days. "You're a goal-oriented type. Five men. There's got to be someone I can stand for several years out of five men."

"As long as they smell okay and Kenny likes them," he muttered.

"Yoo-hoo," Delilah's voice called from the hallway. "Lori-girl, my youngest needs a diaper change. Where would you like me to—"

Lori pushed open the door. "Would you like the blue suite on the second floor? There's a connecting room with another bed, and we could put a crib in it if you like. Mabel keeps a few of the guest rooms ready all the time."

"Your Mabel is a goddess," Delilah said, craning to look beyond Lori's shoulder. "Did I hear you talking? Did I interrupt something?"

"Not a thing." She felt Jackson step behind her and bit back a groan at Delilah's curious stare. "I was telling my assistant that I need him to take Kenny for his grooming appointment." She turned and smiled at Jackson, avoiding the look of murder in his eyes. "I just need to give him the address."

"Hasn't he ever taken Kenny before?" Delilah asked.

"Did I mention that I'd just hired Jackson? He's been busy putting my social and charity information on the computer."

"Good for you. Jackson, do you have a college degree?"

He gave her nosey but charming sister a quick nod. "Business."

"Business," Delilah echoed. "Aren't you overqualified for this kind of—"

Lori stifled a sigh. "Delilah, quit harassing my employees. This is a temporary job for Jackson. Since the hours are flexible, he can pursue other opportunities at the same time."

"Such as?" Delilah asked.

"Delilah, stop—"

"Real-estate development," Jackson said.

"Really?" Delilah said.

"Really?" Lori echoed, then cleared her throat at the skeptical expression on her sister's face. "Of course. But it's none of your business. So leave him alone. Jackson, could you wait just a sec while I take Dee upstairs to her suite?"

"No problem," he said, but his eyes said there would be hell to pay.

Lori led Delilah to the guest room, thankful her sister's little daughter was demanding her mom's attention. At least she had a temporary reprieve from the inquisition. She walked back down the stairs and found Jackson waiting for her in the foyer with Kenny in one of his large hands. Her pet appeared totally content and safe. He flashed a business card at her. "I got this from Mabel. I'll do the spa run this time, but don't ask again."

"I won't," she said. Besides, she rarely sent Kenny for grooming more frequently than every two weeks. Her sisters would be here only two days. "Thanks."

He shook his head. "You're digging one hell of a hole for yourself, Lori."

She bit her lip. No, she wasn't. She would make it all work out. She was determined. "Just set up those dates. I'll surprise you."

"You've already done that," he said, but it didn't sound like a compliment.

She smiled. "Save your flattery for a more susceptible woman."

His lips twitched and his gaze skimmed over her, making her skin feel sunburned. "As if you need any flattery," he said.

"You're right. I don't. But I don't know anyone who doesn't appreciate a sincere compliment or even just a positive comment every now and then instead of unrelenting criticism."

He held her gaze for a long moment. "Okay, you are the most generous woman I've ever met. In fact, you're too—"

"Nuh-uh," she said, covering his mouth with her hand. "Stop there. That sincere compliment was about to become a criticism. Let me savor the moment," she said in a half-mocking voice, but underneath it all, his words were a soothing balm over the cactus prickles he usually presented her.

Catching her hand with his, he flicked his thumb over the inside of her wrist where her pulse picked up. "You're a tough one to figure, Lori. One minute, you're asking your accountant to find a husband for you. The next, you're sending cashier's checks to three women in Tennessee, Virginia, and Oregon."

Shock raced through her. She thought she'd been so careful to keep those payments concealed. "How did you know about those? I used cashier's checks."

"It's my job to know."

Her throat closed in panic. "I'm serious, Jackson," she whispered. "Those women aren't just counting on my support. They're counting on me to keep their whereabouts a secret. How did you know?"

"Your trash," he said.

Lori opened her mouth to scream, but her vocal cords were frozen. She'd thought she'd been shocked before, but she'd never expected this. "My trash," she finally managed in a voice that sounded weak to her own ears. "My trash," she repeated. "What were you doing in my trash?"

"Hey, you were going to be the biggest assignment I've ever been given. After a few of our discussions in the beginning, I needed to know what I was dealing with. Everyone's trash tells a story."

Lori felt violated. She felt so furious, so powerless that she wanted to slap him. "You're a disgusting person. You call me manipulative and helpless, but you enjoy intimidating me, violating my privacy, and making me feel like crap. You're disgusting."

He shrugged. "Fine, call me disgusting. I call it survival. You forced Tilly into an early retirement. You're not taking me down, too."

Lori balled her fists. Oh, how she wanted to slap him. *Just once*, she thought. Her fingers itched. She lifted her hand slightly and eyed his jaw.

He must have read her intent when his gaze caught sight of her hand and the blood that was in her eyes, because his eyes widened like golf balls. "You really think you're going to slap me?"

"I want to," she said. "I want to, but that's one of the differences between one who's been raised to behave in a civilized, gentle manner and one who has not."

"Is there a problem with the dog?" Delilah called from the top of the stairs. "You two look a little intense."

Lori took a deep breath. "No problem. I was just repeating the instructions to Jackson. I'll be right with you." She glanced at Kenny, then at Jackson. "Hurt my dog and you'll pay in ways you've never imagined."

Jackson ignored her, dipping his head toward Delilah. "Nice meeting you," he said.

"The pleasure's mine," Delilah returned in the same flirty voice she'd used to lay men at her feet for years.

Lori opened the front door and resisted the urge to slam the hard frame into Jackson's own buns of steel. Closing it carefully, she counted to ten and prayed that her color would return to normal. She could still feel her pulse pounding in her head.

"I like your taste in employees," Delilah said, descending the stairs with her toddler on her hip. "He's got a great body."

"I hadn't noticed," Lori muttered.

"Is that so?" Delilah asked, stepping in front of Lori. "Then why do you look like a ripe tomato? I saw him take your hand earlier."

"It's not what you think it is, Delilah," Lori said. "Jackson and I don't have a romantic relationship. He's temporary."

Delilah moved closer and touched Lori's cheek with sisterly concern. "You could use a temporary diversion."

Lori shook her head. "Not him. He's a bit too sexist, controlling, and just—" She couldn't find the right word.

"Hmm," Delilah said. "But is he any good in bed?"

Lori groaned. "I remember when you kept hounding Katie to take a lover. Sex doesn't solve all problems."

"No, but good sex can sure make problems seem easier," she said, stroking her daughter Maggie's hair. "And in my case, I sometimes get a bonus."

Lori smiled at her little niece. "I can't disagree with that." She extended her arms. "Your mom gets you all the time. Come to Auntie Lori for a hug."

Her niece pitched forward, and Lori caught her small body. Maggie wrapped her arms around Lori's neck and squeezed. Lori felt her heart swell with affection. "You are the sweetest girl in the world," she said to her niece. "How many are you going to have?" Lori asked Delilah. "Two out and one on the way. Are you going for an even dozen? If so, may I put in an order for one?"

Delilah shook her head. "I'll pause at three and stop at four." She studied Lori. "You should get married so you can start making some of your own."

Lori fought a quick twist of pain at Delilah's suggestion. Neither of her sisters knew the true extent of damage Lori had sustained from her accident years ago. Delilah didn't know Lori may not be able to have children.

Lori flashed a teasing smile at her sister.

"I can't believe my unconventional sister is telling me to get married."

"Well, on second thought, Harlan left you so much money, you could raise twelve of your own. You could probably afford to just get pregnant through artificial insemination, but where's the fun in that?"

*"The true test of a man's ardor is if he will go
shoe shopping with you on Black Friday."*
—SUNNY COLLINS

Chapter Seven

Geoffrey Taylor heard the chord in his head. It would lead into the bridge of his current musical creation. He heard the sound of a cat screaming in the background, beyond the closed wooden door of his music room, and he tried to shut it out, narrowing his concentration on the beautiful sounds inside his head.

He stretched his fingers into a chord on the century-old grand piano and played. He frowned. Not quite right. It didn't quite match—

The wooden door burst open. A plump woman with wet orange hair and a wet red face shrieked at him. "Geoffrey, the loo is broken again! We need to get it fixed! Permanently," his stepsister, Danielle, added.

Geoffrey frowned. He wanted that note, that chord. If he could just get that one chord, it would be enough for now. Holding up his hand and mentally shutting off his stepsister's shrieks, he continued on the keyboard. Almost there, almost—

"Geoffrey!" His stepmother's voice interrupted his concentration.

Geoffrey gave up. His stepmother's voice was the ultimate mood killer. He looked up at the face that had made his late father tumble like the proverbial Jack from Jack and Jill. Although her youthful glow was dimming and lines were beginning to appear around her eyes and mouth, her skin still looked like a porcelain doll's, her lips were lush and pink, and her eyes were blue like the summer sky.

Geoffrey knew the truth, however. Behind those innocent-looking blue eyes lurked the instincts of a killer shark with a voracious, unquenchable appetite for designer clothing, jewels, antiques, holidays in Monte Carlo, and generally living beyond her means.

"Geoffrey, look at your sister. This has gone entirely too far. The manor is in total disrepair. Your father never would have permitted the home of generations of Taylors to deteriorate into this kind of condition."

His father wouldn't have been permitted to permit it. Charlene would have nagged him twenty-four hours a day, and then his father would have gone into debt to keep his yellow rose from Texas happy. "I'm sorry, Charlene, but as you know, my father may have left his title behind, but he didn't leave the kind of money you've grown accustomed to spending."

Geoffrey couldn't recall how many times he'd repeated the same words to Charlene during the last three years.

"Yes, but Gilmore is your responsibility now. You are

the heir. Your father trusted you to care for Danielle and me."

Unlike his father, Geoffrey wasn't the least bit chauvinistic. As far as Geoffrey was concerned, it was high time Charlene got a job to help support her spending habits. "I'll remind you that my father was deeply indebted and we almost lost Gilmore because of it. I managed to cover his debts and provide us with a modest income."

"Selling collectibles on eBay," Danielle said with a snort. "Why can't you get a real job instead of spending all your time in here playing your weird music?"

Geoffrey ground his teeth. He was a classically trained musician with special abilities in composing music. He knew that one day he would be paid well for his work. Until then, he needed to continue the discipline of putting down on paper the music that soared through his mind. He also needed to be frugal.

"Danielle needs to go to college," Charlene told him. "NYU in Manhattan."

Geoffrey tensed, feeling a sickening sense of foreboding. "But she hasn't been accepted, has she?"

"Of course she has," Charlene said. "I met the wife of the president at one of the parties I attended in New York several years ago. We stayed in touch."

"Does she have a scholarship?"

"No, but Danielle has worked hard on her studies the past two years. She took her father's death very hard. Despite that, she's done well, and her efforts should be rewarded."

Geoffrey bit the inside of his cheek. "That's going to be dreadfully expensive. Are you sure there isn't another—" He cleared his throat. "—more reasonable option?"

Charlene narrowed her eyes to slits. "You have a lot of nerve considering you've spent years in the finest schools earning a doctorate that will qualify you to ask the question 'Would you like fries with that?' "

"I was offered scholarships," he retorted.

Charlene's cheeks turned scarlet, almost purple. The color of her rage, he thought. He'd seen it many times before.

She pursed her lips. "Danielle, I need to speak to Geoffrey alone. Run along and clean up."

"But Mother—"

"Now," Charlene said.

Danielle gave a huff and left the room, slamming the door behind her.

Charlene closed her eyes for a moment and inhaled deeply.

"Are you feeling faint?" Geoffrey asked hopefully.

"No. I'm aligning myself with my inner core."

Her inner core? He hadn't known she had an inner core. In fact, Geoffrey had always suspected Charlene's backbone was formed from some slimy form of rubber. Her morals depended on the day, the situation, whom she needed to impress, and, most important, what she wanted.

She opened her eyes. "A week ago, I did something which I believe will ease the burden you have felt in providing for Danielle and myself since your father passed away."

Geoffrey's stomach dropped. "You didn't sell the piano," he said. The piano had been in his family for generations. It was his prize possession.

It was his prize possession even though it technically

belonged to his stepmother. In a fit of passion-driven insanity, Geofrey's father had altered his will immediately after his marriage to Charlene and left some of the contents of the house to his new bride. Those contents included the piano. He would live in a box in order to keep that piano.

"No, although I've considered it once or twice. Since you're quite obsessed with continuing to pursue a career in music despite the fact that you haven't profited from it in any shape or form, I decided it was time to take extraordinary measures."

A terrible dread grabbed at his throat. "What extraordinary measures?"

She cleared her throat and lowered her voice as if she were taking him in her confidence with a juicy piece of gossip. "A friend of mine in Texas told me that a very, very wealthy heiress wants to get married and her business manager is screening prospects. I faxed in your information, and I'm happy to say they're willing to give you a chance to meet her."

Horrified beyond words, Geoffrey stood. "You're joking."

"Not at all," she said and swept her blonde hair behind one ear. "It's the perfect solution. If you marry this woman, you can fulfill your father's request that you take care of Danielle and me and at the same time continue your endless pursuit of your musical career with no pressure."

"You've gone mad. I'm not going to be bartered off like some—some prize cow so you can shop yourself into oblivion." He raked his hand through his hair. "It's barbaric."

Charlene planted her perfectly manicured hands on her

hips and rolled her eyes. "Oh, don't be a pussy. Women have been doing this kind of thing for years. It's the perfect solution. It's not as if you even have a love life." She paused a half beat. "You haven't gone to the other side, have you?"

Geoffrey stifled a groan. *The other side* was Charlene's way of referring to homosexuality. Since Charlene preferred generalizations and Geoffrey had been musical his entire life, he knew the possibility of his being gay lurked in her devious small mind. Being gay right now would come in bloody handy. He was almost tempted . . . But no, knowing Charlene, she would find another way to torture him.

"Just because I'm heterosexual doesn't mean I'm a candidate to stud this woman from Texas," he told her. "If marriage is such a great solution, why don't you do it again?"

Her eyes widened, and she lifted her hand to her throat in a perfectly choreographed gasp. "I can't believe you'd suggest that to your father's wife. You have no heart, no honor."

Geoffrey looked heavenward for help. *Oh, no. Now he would get the martyred-widow speech.*

"I was married to your father for twenty years. I took you as my son."

To his eternal regret.

"I bore him a daughter."

Charlene had moaned and groaned through the entire nine months.

"We loved each other dearly."

She'd loved his *title* dearly.

"I'm not going to marry some woman I've never met

and live in Texas. You may as well be sending me to hell," he said. "Besides, she probably wouldn't find me her type."

"I've already thought of that," she said with unflattering speed. "I've made an appointment with my hairstylist for you. I've also arranged a facial for you. Those circles under your eyes are dreadful. We can't do much about your body on short notice, but we can probably make you look a little more firm with a few hours at the gym and some new clothes. Then all you have to do is try to be charming, which I realize will be a stretch, darling, but I have some reading material for you to peruse between now and Tuesday."

Geoffrey didn't think she could have horrified him more, but he'd underestimated her. "You've lost your mind. I don't know who this woman is. I don't even know her name, what she looks like. She could be a descendant of Attila the Hun for all we know."

"You'll find out who she is when you arrive in Dallas. The important things that you need to know are that she wants to get married and she's loaded. Your job is to be charming."

Geoffrey put his foot down. "I'm not doing this, Charlene. And don't try shoving any more guilt trips down my throat, because it won't work. This would be the same as prostitution. I will not do it. There's nothing you can say to make me change my mind."

She met his gaze and sighed. "All right, I'll give you a choice. Find a way to get Danielle's tuition by Tuesday, or you're getting on the plane to Dallas. Otherwise . . ."

Her voice drifted off and she gave his piano a longing, sinister glance. She slid her fingers along the wood lightly.

His gut clenched. "You wouldn't," he said.

"It would never be my first choice," she said. "But oh, yes, Geoffrey, I would." She met his gaze again. "Much luck on eBay."

Jackson was going insane.

Lori's sisters had stayed longer than two days. It was up to four, and he'd culled five prospects from a long list. He'd put a shrink at the top of the list. If ever a woman could use one, he'd say Lori Jean Granger could. Late at night, she preyed on his mind. He was starting to wonder if she was a witch. Or a fairy.

"No fairy," he said, shaking his head and splitting a piece of grass in half as he sat on his back porch with a beer. She just *thought* she was a fairy. She thought she was the Miss Fix-It Fairy with unlimited dough, and he was the heartbreaker who had to inform her of the sad truth that she was mortal like the rest of us.

He remembered how her face had paled when he'd told her he knew about the payments she was sending to the three women hiding from their abusive husbands. Jackson thought of his own mother and how she continued to hang in there with his father, despite his father's verbal abuse. No matter how many times his father left, his mother took him back. He remembered begging her to change the locks, move away, but she would do neither.

He felt a slice of envy that Lori had been able to help women who were strangers when he hadn't been able to get through to his own mother. He wondered how she'd done it—what kind of magic she possessed to help a beat-up person find the courage to follow through and make a new life.

Of course, nearly unlimited money didn't hurt, he thought cynically and crushed his beer can against his chair.

Jackson was still torn about Lori. The rate at which she disposed of her fortune gave him hives. At the same time, he was starting to see how serious she was about trying to make a difference. Finding out about those women touched a sore point inside him. Her determination to keep it secret grabbed at him. In elementary school, he remembered that a history teacher had said that what a person did in secret said a lot more about what they were made of than what they did in public.

In public, Lori wore designer clothes and donated her money to crazy charities. In private, she clung fiercely to her independence at the same time she looked to her dog for acceptance while she tried to take care of the world.

Jackson felt oddly protective of her. He still wanted to talk her out of the marriage deal, but he was starting to understand her point of view, her impatience with her father's manipulation.

He picked up the file of prospects again. One of these men was going to go through six years of heaven and hell. Heaven to be close to her. Hell not to have her.

Lori had a case of cold feet. After being around her sisters for the last several days and overhearing their lovey-dovey phone conversations with their husbands, she couldn't help rethinking her decision to marry for access to her money. If only it wasn't necessary, she thought, frustration zooming through her as her chauffeur negotiated the heavy traffic.

But it was, and Jackson had left a message that he wanted to meet with her tonight to show her the dossiers on five prospective husbands.

She felt another chill run through her—all the way to her feet.

It was temporary, she told herself as a doorman allowed her into the exclusive nightclub charity party. A band played in a back room while servers floated through the space with trays of champagne and food. A barrage of children's paintings and baskets loaded with giveaways were arranged on tables for a silent auction. Lori's friend Chloe was chairing a fund drive for children's art programs. Lori had promised to attend, and she always tried to keep her promises.

In the back of her mind, she imagined Jackson James frowning in disapproval at her. He didn't want her to spend a dime until she was married.

Lori made a face and wrote a bid for one of the children's paintings. "It's for a good cause," she murmured.

Someone jostled her from behind, and her pen went flying.

"Bloody hell, do watch where you're going," a male voice said in a British accent. "Excuse me, Miss."

The sound was so different from the Texas twang she was accustomed to hearing that it immediately caught her attention. She glanced around to find a tall man with floppy brown hair accepting a napkin and an apology from a server. He mopped at his damp jacket.

"Good start," he muttered. "Spend the rest of the night

smelling like a wino." He glanced up at her. "Did he get any on you?"

She patted her hands over her black dress and shook her head. "No. I think you got the worst of it. Sorry," she said, feeling pity for him. He looked so frazzled. Cute in a lost-puppy-dog sort of way.

"Par for the day. I should have gone to bed after that flight from London, but I promised a relative I would attend this function for her."

"Would you like some champagne to *drink*? Would that help a little?" she asked, waving at a waiter.

"A bottle of scotch would be better," he muttered. "But thank you. Champagne will be fine. What is this party for, anyway? My stepmother told me, but I forgot."

"Development of the arts for children."

He narrowed his eyes at the painting she'd just bid on. "Good cause. Definitely needs development," he said and tossed back the champagne in two gulps.

Lori frowned. "That's not very nice. A child painted it. You shouldn't expect perfection. Unless you're a snob," she added.

Chagrin crossed his face. "Forgive me. I shouldn't have come tonight. I've been sent to do something I don't want to do. It's put me in a bad mood." He glanced at the painting again. "You like it?" he asked doubtfully.

"I like the colors. They're bright and cheerful."

"Where the devil would you hang it?"

Lori couldn't help smiling at the question. "My decorator would hang it in the closet," she admitted. "I would put it somewhere prominent. The foyer," she fantasized.

Mr. England smiled at her, his eyes glinting. "Ah, you're a rebel underneath it all. Kindred spirit. So am I."

He dipped his hand. "Geoffrey Taylor. Pleased to make your acquaintance."

What lovely manners, she thought and shook his hand. "My pleasure. I'm Lori Jean—"

"Lori Jean!" a feminine voice shrieked, interrupting her. Looking over her shoulder, Lori saw a blur of her friend Chloe, dressed in a garish combination of chartreuse and orange, just before Chloe enveloped her in a huge embrace. "I'm so glad you came. What do you think? Is it fabulous? Do you think I'll raise any money?"

Lori smiled at Chloe's enthusiasm. Chloe was one of the few people with whom Lori felt totally comfortable. She wore her motives and her heart on her sleeve and didn't fit in with the die-hard society types. Everyone except Lori had been surprised when a leading heart surgeon had swept her off her feet.

"You've done a beautiful job, and I know you're going to raise money, because I already see three pictures I'm bidding on."

"Oh, perfect! Let me get you some more champagne so you'll pay exorbitant prices and drive the demand through the roof."

Lori laughed. Out of the corner of her eye, she saw Geoffrey watching her curiously. "Oh, excuse me. I should have introduced you. Chloe Braunstein is the hostess of this lovely party. This is Geoffrey—I'm sorry, I didn't catch your last name."

"Taylor, Geoffrey Taylor. I'm pleased to meet you, Mrs. Braunstein. My stepmother, Charlene, asked me to attend on her behalf."

Chloe's eyes widened. "You're the duke! Or the duke's son," she said, waving her hand. "I'm not sure how all that works. Love the accent. My stepmother is friends with Charlene. When she told us you would attend, we were all excited. Please have some more champagne. Bid astronomical amounts on a drawing or two." She waved her hand toward a waiter. "More champagne here. Do you mind if I steal him away for a few minutes?" she asked Lori. "Alison Crandall will have a cow when she learns I have a *duke* at my event. She's such a snob." She turned back to Geoffrey. "You don't mind if I briefly exploit your title, do you?"

He looked momentarily speechless, then shot Lori an uncertain look.

"You did say you were a rebel at heart," Lori reminded him.

"So I did."

"And it's for a good cause," Chloe said.

He gave a short nod. "In that case, I'm at your service."

Lori snickered as Chloe ushered Geoffrey away. Poor thing, she thought. He would become the prize steer of the evening. Taking another sip of her champagne, she meandered around the room, enjoying the children's art. She placed bids on three pieces that grabbed her and was writing a bid for another when a large male hand closed over hers.

Lori's heart stopped. *Oh, no, not him.* She cringed, closing her eyes, wishing she were anywhere but here. Wishing Jackson hadn't found her.

"I thought we agreed you were going to rein in your spending until you take care of your inheritance."

Lori took a deep breath, inhaling his masculine scent, and wiggled her fingers as a broad hint for him to let go of her. "My spending is relatively reined," she said. "I haven't bid on every piece of art I've seen."

"Four," he said. "And you offered six figures for one of them. You should change your bid."

Horrified, Lori turned, noting that he wore yet another dark jacket that didn't fit him properly. "Absolutely not. That would be like welshing. I couldn't do that to Chloe. Besides, it's for a good cause."

"Welshing?" he echoed, lifting that dark fussy eyebrow at her again. "What about your agreement to meet with me tonight to review your candidates? What do you call your failure to show up for that?"

Lori barely resisted the urge to squirm beneath his penetrating gaze. "I forgot about a previous engagement," she said, trying to effect an air of importance and suspecting she wasn't succeeding.

"Spending money you don't have yet," he said.

Her discomfort rising a mile a minute, she lowered her voice and stepped closer. "People are starting to stare. Could we conduct this conversation somewhere else?"

He ground his teeth. "Fine," he said and grabbed her arm. "I'll find a place."

Lori raced to keep up with his long stride as he led her out of the main room and down a hallway. He opened a door and pulled her inside a utility closet. Flicking on a switch, he closed the door. "Is this private enough for you?"

"Lust is not a bad thing. It just means you're alive."
—SUNNY COLLINS

Chapter Eight

Lori's heart hammered in her chest. She stepped backward and her foot ran into a bucket. Jackson immediately put his hands on her shoulders and steadied her. She took another deep breath and felt oddly dizzy. "This isn't exactly what I had in mind," she said.

"Me, neither," he muttered. "I didn't think I would have to be chasing you down in some nightclub and tying your hands to keep you from writing checks for money you don't have."

"You weren't very nice about it."

He shot her an incredulous look. "How do you think I felt when your housekeeper told me you'd gone to a charity event instead of meeting with me? I've been waiting for days for your sisters to leave. If you're really going to carry out your insane plan, then we need to get moving. At the rate you're spending, you're going to end up in a tent by the end of summer. And you don't strike me as the type that loves camping."

"Oh, you're exaggerating."

"Not by much," he said grimly.

"You and I would get along much better if you would be a little more flexible," she told him.

"Somebody has to hold the line," he said with a growl in his voice. "I'm the unlucky guy."

She could tell he didn't enjoy his position any more than she was happy with hers. Lori sighed. "Are you nicer to your other clients? Can't you be just a little nicer to me?"

"My other clients haven't made any complaints, but I haven't had to be as firm with any of them. The problem with being nice to you, Lori, is you are the proverbial example for give-her-an-inch-and-she'll-take-you-for-a-hundred-miles."

"Another exaggeration," she said.

"Six figures for a finger painting," he reminded her. "Six figures."

"All right, all right," she said. "I guess you should tell me about the prospects for the job as my husband."

"Do you want to hear about it now or at your home?"

"Go ahead," she said with a shrug. "I need to get my head turned back around to this idea. I may as well start now."

He paused, studying her. "Second thoughts?"

She didn't want to admit it, but he was clearly the kind of man who could smell any weakness a mile away. "Yes, and there will be more, but it doesn't change my situation and it doesn't change my decision," she added quickly before he could interject anything. "I'm going to do this."

"You have other options," he said.

"This is the best plan. It's just being around Delilah

and Katie and hearing them talk about how much they love their husbands. And my little nieces and nephew, they're so sweet, and—" A lump of emotion crowded her throat and she bit her lip. "And I need to stop thinking about it, because I'm on a different track. There."

"Lori, are you sure?"

She met his gaze and felt his strength bolster her. Strange, she thought, that a person who annoyed her and frustrated her could make her feel more certain. "I'm sure," she said and smiled. "Tell me about my future husband."

He paused, and she saw a sliver of something almost like respect deepen his eyes. It was gone so quickly she wondered if she had imagined it.

"Bachelor number three," he began.

"Let's start with a fresh page. The first ones didn't count."

"These do," he said firmly. "Bachelor number one is Dr. Frank Liebowitz. He's a little older, but he has an excellent reputation and excellent communication skills. He would like to have money for research."

It was weird, but Jackson approved of this guy just a little too much. "Why isn't he married?"

"His wife passed away. He's a widower," he said.

"Oh," she said, feeling sorry for the doctor she'd never met. "What kind of doctor is he?"

"A—" Jackson cleared his throat. "A psychiatrist."

A shrink, Lori thought, noticing the way Jackson's eye twitched. "Not very subtle."

"This isn't a bad idea. Maybe he could do double duty. Help you with some of your—issues," Jackson said and cleared his throat.

"As if I want someone around twenty-four seven putting me under a microscope, examining my every move, word, and thought. Wouldn't you just love that, too?"

"This isn't about me. He's a respectable man. Worth your consideration," Jackson said in a rock-hard voice.

"Tell me about the rest," she said, inwardly fuming. He wasn't joking when he said he thought she was nuts. He really believed it. Even though she knew her plan was unusual, she wanted to feel as if she and Jackson were a team. Knowing he really thought she was insane bothered her so much she barely heard him list the other prospects.

"And the last one is an English duke, if you're into titles at all. He's a financial loser, and I think he could be the most expensive of all of them. That's why I put him last. He's got these old mansions that need a bunch of repairs. From the list of repairs, it looks to me like they should ditch the current buildings and start over. Plus he's got a stepmother who needs to be sent off for a twelve-step program for her shopping habits. Geoffrey Taylor can be a last resort."

Lori brightened. "Geoffrey Taylor. Did you say Geoffrey Taylor? I met him! And I liked him. Somewhat," she added, remembering he'd been a grouch at first.

"You did?" Jackson asked, surprise crossing his face.

Lori nodded. "I did. He was appealing in a lost, out-of-his-element way. He needed a haircut, but . . ."

Jackson was looking at her with a stunned expression. "You actually liked him?"

"I *like* a lot of people," she said, miffed at his implication that she didn't like people.

"So you might be interested in marrying this guy?"

Her stomach clenched. "I don't know. I have to see how Kenny responds to him."

"How'd he smell?"

"I'm not sure. I think a waiter had just spilled champagne on him, but I didn't notice anything that bothered me."

"You didn't find anything objectionable about him?"

She shrugged. "I liked that he had a sense of humor. I think a sense of humor is going to be important for this situation."

Jackson gave a growl-like laugh. "That's an understatement. A great sense of humor or medication," he said. "Maybe both."

His sarcasm poked at her. "Do you have to be so insulting? You act as if I'm the worst person in the world a man could be stuck with for six years. Did you ever think that maybe you have the problem?" she asked, daring to poke his hard chest with her finger. "Maybe you're not a people person. Plenty of people enjoy my company. You may not, but plenty of people actually think I'm charming. Plenty of people actually like me."

He grabbed her finger and held it still. "You don't get it. I feel sorry for the guy who agrees to do this because he's gonna spend every day of his six-year sentence being close enough to smell you and touch you, but he won't be taking you to bed. And if he's a normal heterosexual man, being that close to you and not having you will drive him insane."

Was that heat in his gaze? Lori wondered, feeling her pulse race. She felt an odd warmth flare across her skin, starting at her toes and moving up to her cheeks. She tried to take a deep breath, but her lungs would allow only a puny shallow one.

She cleared her throat. "The way you say that makes me think you almost find me somewhat attractive."

"That would be wrong," he said. "I don't find you somewhat attractive. Despite the fact that you think I have computer wire for veins, I'm like the rest of my gender. I know you're a knockout. I wouldn't be male if I didn't wonder what it would be like to take you to bed. The big difference between me and the other guys is if I got sexually involved with you, I could lose everything. Baby-blue eyes with the too-generous pocketbook, you could blow me away in bed, but I've been protecting my rear for long enough to know I need to protect it more than ever now."

Lori didn't know whether to be flattered or insulted. "I didn't ask you to go to bed with me."

"Not in so many words, but there's something there."

She looked at him in surprise. "Pardon me?"

"I've seen the way you look at me when you think I'm not looking back. You're curious about me."

"I—I—I—" she sputtered, embarrassed beyond words.

"It's no big deal," he said in what she guessed was his effort to reassure her. "We're both curious. We're both attracted. It doesn't matter as long as we don't act on it."

The air in the closet suddenly felt thick and humid. Her mind shifted with rapid-fire speed to a vision of Jackson pulling off the jacket, whose seams strained from the breadth of his shoulders. His tanned skin revealed he spent some of his off-time in the sun. She could easily imagine the sculpted muscles of his chest and a six-pack abdomen. He would accept no less for himself, not out of vanity, but for strength.

She wondered where his tan line started—just below his belly button or lower. His strength and size were overwhelming to her. More than one thing about Jackson suggested he was just this side of civilized.

She wondered what that meant about his lovemaking.

He gave a swift, short oath. "It's not gonna help matters if you keep looking at me like that."

"Like what?" she asked and tried to pull her curiosity away from what kind of man he was out of his clothes.

"Like you're curious about my body and how it would feel. How I would feel naked against your naked skin. How I would take you."

Turned on, embarrassed, and not sure which sensation was more unwelcome, she closed her eyes. "This conversation is crazy."

"Crazy, but necessary," he said. "As long as you and I admit we're both tempted, then we can both avoid temptation."

"I'm not admitting anything," she retorted. "I would have to be a masochist to be attracted to a man who thinks I'm a twerp."

"Keep telling yourself that, baby girl, and we'll be just fine."

The first sign of a serious problem was the jammed-full voice mail on the cell phone Jackson had dedicated to the Lori marriage project. He'd turned the damn thing off late last night to charge, and it was only 6:30 a.m.

Not a good sign, he thought as he finished drying off from his shower. He listened to the first message.

"Greg Staunton here. I'm calling to be considered as a candidate for Lori Granger's husband. I'm an entrepreneur and was very successful until the market caved in on the dotcoms. I'm willing to submit a blood test and—"

An undertow of dread tugged at his gut. How had Greg Staunton heard about Lori's plan to get married? Jackson swore, punching the delete key.

"My name is Rose McKinney, and I'd like to suggest my grandson as the perfect husband for Lori Granger. He'll be eighteen years old next May—"

Starting to sweat, he punched the delete key again.

His home phone rang and he snatched up the receiver. "Jackson James."

"Houston, we have a problem," Lori said.

His stomach twisted. "What do you mean?"

"I mean my phone has been ringing since six a.m. Six men asking for my hand in marriage have already been turned away."

He cringed as her voice rose.

"And ten more are on my front porch. What did you do? Take out an ad in the newspaper? This was supposed to be confidential."

"There's obviously been a leak," he said, his mind clicking into emergency mode. He'd known all along the news would get out sometime. He'd just hoped to get Lori safely engaged and married by then. He would alert Mr. Hollingsworth so that his boss could take care of the source.

"What am I supposed to do with all these men on my front porch?"

"Sit tight," he said, pulling underwear out of a drawer. "Pack a suitcase with just the essentials. I'm taking you away."

"Where?"

The strong note of distrust he heard in her voice irritated him. "Where no one will look for you. Get packed. We need to move fast."

"I need to know where I'm going so I know how to pack."

Jackson rolled his eyes. This woman didn't know what essentials were. "Pack underwear, jeans, and shirts. And any medication you're taking."

"I'm not taking any medication," she said, her voice dripping with ice.

"I keep hoping," he muttered. "Trust me. You won't need your tennis bracelet where we're going."

"This wasn't supposed to happen."

"Maybe it wouldn't have if you had told me your husband needs to pass the sniff test and the Kenny test."

"Oh, no. You're not pinning this on me. I haven't told anyone what I planned to do. Not anyone but you."

Jackson eyed a box of bullets in the back of his closet. This woman could make him chew the whole box. "You want to waste time arguing whose fault this is? That line of men is just going to get longer. Every loser in Dallas is going to be knocking on your door."

"I was so stupid," she said. "You're so committed to being ethical that I was sure I could trust you."

Jackson felt an unwelcome bitter taste in the back of his throat. "Looks like you've got a choice, then. I can bow out, and you can handle this on your own or with some other sap."

Silence followed. "It's an impossible choice, but I'm not letting you off that easily."

Thirty minutes later, after asking his neighbor to take care of Sadie, Jackson wove his way through snarling rush-hour traffic to the back entrance of Lori's home. He dashed out of his vehicle and inside her house, expecting Lori to be ready to go. Instead, she stood gaping out one of the front windows.

"Where's your luggage?" he asked.

She tore her gaze from the window for a second and pointed her finger upward. "Upstairs in my bedroom." She turned her head to look out the window again, shaking her head in a combination of horror and wonder. "I'm shocked that this many men would be interested in marrying me."

"For your money," Jackson emphasized, glancing outside to see a line of men standing on her front lawn.

She threw him a look of irritation. "You say that as if I couldn't find someone to marry me for love. Or at least intense like," she added.

"I didn't say anything about you finding someone to marry you for love. You're the one who decided it should be a business proposition. This is like one of those reality TV shows where people agree to marry for a million bucks, except in your case, the guy gets a lot more than a million bucks." His exasperation at the turn of the situation soared. "C'mon, let's get going."

"I need to take Kenny out to tinkle before we leave."

"Can't your housekeeper do that, since you're leaving him here?"

She looked at him as if he'd sprouted an extra head. "I'm not leaving him anywhere. Kenny goes where I go."

Jackson groaned. "Well, you better hope Kenny can hold it, because we'll be on the road for a long time. And I'm not stopping every fifteen minutes for your dog." As he stomped up the stairs to get her luggage, he heard her mutter.

"Crab."

"I heard that," he tossed over his shoulder.

"Good," she tossed back.

Jackson growled under his breath. This trip was going to be hell. Neither of them was starting out with a great attitude. He pushed the door open to her bedroom to find five suitcases stacked beside each other. Shaking his head in disbelief, he called down to her, "You're not seriously planning to take all this luggage, are you?"

"Serious as a heart attack. I don't know how long we'll be gone; therefore, I don't know what I'll need."

"So she just packed everything," he said to himself and juggled the suitcases downstairs. He loaded them into the car and waited impatiently for Kenny to do his business.

He hustled her and the dog in the car, then got in the driver's seat. Starting the ignition, he glanced at her as she arranged herself and Kenny in the seat. "You need to duck until we're out of your neighborhood."

"Duck?" she echoed in disbelief.

"Hide," he repeated. "Put your head down."

She looked at him for a long moment. "I can't believe that anyone will notice me in—"

"This has gotten out of control. We're not taking any chances," he said. "Either lie down in the back seat, or duck."

In order to keep her head out of Jackson's lap, Lori had to smash her rear end against the door of the vehicle, and Kenny didn't like being on the floor at all. Although she found herself staring at the dash, she was still entirely too aware of Jackson's proximity. He might be cranky, but he'd responded to her crisis with gratifying speed. Despite the fact that someone had leaked her secret, she still felt safe with him.

Because she represented the most important account he'd ever been assigned, she told herself. It had nothing to do with integrity or the kind of man he was, she tried to tell herself, but something inside her disagreed. She would think about that later, she brooded, stroking Kenny to comfort him and herself.

"So the whole world knows I'm willing to buy a husband," she said, her stomach twisting at the thought. It was bad enough that she'd privately concluded that love wasn't in her future. Knowing that everyone else knew she was so desperate she had to pay a man to marry her was mortifying. "How are we going to pull this off now?" she asked. It sure looked futile to her.

"The whole world doesn't know," he said. "Just Dallas," he added, his words offering little comfort. "This will blow over. It's the gossip of the week. The important thing is to take you out of the public eye for a while. We still have four prospects, five if you include the broke duke."

Craning to look at him, she lifted her head. "But how am I going to meet with them if I'm staying out of the public eye? And for that matter, where are you taking me?"

Jackson pushed her head down. "Stay down," he said. "I've put the word out that you've taken a trip to Europe."

Lori Jean brightened. "Paris? Tell me it's Paris."

"It can be wherever you want it to be, because you're

not really going there. I'm taking you to Miracles in Motion. It's perfect. It's in the middle of nowhere, and no one will expect you to be there."

She automatically lifted her head. "But I don't ri—" —*de horses anymore*. Lori barely managed to swallow the entire confession. She felt a sinking sensation in her stomach. She didn't want Jackson to know she didn't ride anymore. The last thing she wanted was to admit any frailty or insecurity to him. It would only give him another reason to think less of her.

Jackson glanced at her. "Damn it. Keep your head—" He glanced back at the road and swore again, jerking the steering wheel to the right.

The sharp swerve sent her over the dash, her head poised above Jackson's crotch.

"Crazy driver, pick a lane and stay in it . . ."

He continued to mutter while Lori tried not to notice the way his worn jeans outlined his powerful thighs and the bulge between his legs.

She closed her eyes, and an image sneaked into her brain of her skimming her hands down his hard belly and him urging her on.

Lori started to sweat. Giving her head a small shake, she told herself she definitely needed to move.

Jackson abruptly stopped muttering and swearing, prompting her to steal a glance up at him.

He met her gaze, then she felt his gaze linger on her mouth, causing her lips to feel burned.

"Now, that's a sight I won't forget for a long time."

> *"Sometimes you have to take a step backward to know which direction you want to go forward."*
> —SUNNY COLLINS

Chapter Nine

"Here we are," Jackson said as he turned onto a dirt road.

Lori looked at the battered sign for the ranch and a wave of nostalgia mixed with apprehension. She remembered arriving at the ranch during her college years and how quickly she'd felt at home here. Her father's name hadn't mattered. Nor had her mother's notorious love life. Her willingness to work and her ability with the horses and children had earned her acceptance by the rest of the staff.

She thought of Skip Dawson and felt a stab of loss at the wise, gentle man with a deadpan sense of humor. She'd often laughed at his puns because they'd been so dreadfully corny. Now he was gone. "Why do the good ones have to die?" she murmured.

"What?" Jackson asked.

She glanced at him and shook her head. "I was thinking of the owner, Skip, and wondering why good people seem to leave too quickly."

Slowing, he pulled to a stop and looked at her for a long moment. "You liked Skip."

She nodded. "He was the best. He was like a second father to me when I was here at the ranch." She paused, feeling another pang of loss. "I haven't been close to that many people." She shook her head, feeling her throat tighten. "I don't like losing the good ones, the important ones."

"Like Skip," he said.

"And Daddy and Momma, and for a long, long time, my sisters."

"What do you mean your sisters?"

"Daddy wouldn't let me contact my sisters or my momma after he took me away from her. He was afraid I would turn out like her or Delilah or Katie Priss."

He shook his head and gave a low whistle. "Did they go to jail? Were they prostitutes or murderers? What was so bad about them? You told me about the letters from your mother, but not about your sisters."

"I lost them for over ten years," she murmured. "He was afraid I would become a floozy like my mother. And he thought Delilah was nothing but trouble."

"What about your older sister?"

"Guilty by association. She was pure as the driven snow. He tried to make up for it, but I couldn't help feeling like a part of me had been amputated." A familiar guilt trickled through her, making her stomach hurt. She'd been the lucky one. Her sisters' childhoods had been much more difficult than hers. She took a deep breath and forced a smile. "I'm being silly. I've lived like a princess. I have no room for whining."

She bit her lip, wishing she hadn't blurted her feelings to Jackson. Of all people, he probably wouldn't understand. It was clear that he thought she was spoiled and unreasonable. She looked away, hoping he would take the hint and finish the drive to the ranch.

His hand on her arm took her by surprise. She automatically turned to look at him. He slid his fingers up to cup her jaw. "You're a screwy little mix, Lori. You pick the strangest things to kick yourself for. When it comes to parents, we all get the luck of the draw. When we grow up, life's what we make it." His eyes gentled. "You feel like an orphan no matter when your parents die. You're left behind to deal with your life on your own. That's all understandable, but it's better to have had someone terrific in your life even if you lose them."

Surprised at his expression of sympathy, she held his gaze and felt a wave of deep understanding flow between them. "Better to have loved and lost than never to have loved at all."

"Something like that," he said and cracked a smile. "In your case, better to have been loved and lost than never to have *been* loved at all."

His sympathy touched her. She leaned toward him and brushed her lips over his cheek. "Thanks."

"For what?" he asked, looking surprised.

"For being nice," she said with a shrug.

His lips twitched, and he turned back to the steering wheel and put the car in gear. "Don't get used to it," he said in a gruff voice.

She wondered what experience had made him adopt his philosophy. She wondered what his family life had been like. "You know, we haven't talked much about your family," she ventured.

"That's right. And there's no need to change that now."

"It's not fair that you know almost everything about me and I know nothing about you."

"You know enough. You know I'm your accountant and you can trust me not to give in to your wiles to get more money and you can trust me to find a temporary husband to meet your specifications. You can trust me to look out for your best interests, because your best interests are my best interests."

She wrinkled her nose. "It's still not fair."

"Fair enough," he said firmly and pulled to a stop in a graveled parking lot close to the main ranch house.

"What's your mother like?"

"She's a hard worker. Always has been. Always had to be." He muttered the last part under his breath.

"And your father?"

His eyes narrowed, and she saw a dozen emotions come and go in his gaze. "Undependable. Sometimes there, but usually not. Sometimes working, but usually not. It would have been easier if he hadn't been around at all. Then my mother and brother wouldn't hope he would come through when he didn't."

"Oh," she said, at a loss.

"Yeah, *oh*," he echoed, meeting her gaze. His facial features were neutral, but the way his hands clenched the steering wheel revealed his anger. "Aren't you glad you asked?"

"Yes and no," she said, knowing she was treading on eggshells. "Yes, because it makes me understand you a little better. No, because the subject is obviously a painful one for you."

"Painful," he mocked. "You have to give a damn in order to feel pain. I don't."

It might have been wiser to let it go at that. There was really no need to disagree with him, but Lori had glimpsed his honesty. She skimmed her fingers down his arm to his still-clenched fingers on the steering wheel. "I think I feel some *damn* right about here," she said gently, rubbing the tense tendons in his right hand.

His eyes darkened with an emotion that made her feel a little nervous. She almost retracted her hand and her statement, but she had the odd sensation of playing truth or dare, and if she didn't take the dare, then he would never respect her. She would Super Glue her lips together before she confessed, but she wanted Jackson's respect in a big way.

His right jaw twitched once, twice, and he narrowed his eyes as if he were trying to sustain the anger but was having a tough time. He cleared his throat and took a deep breath. "I've never heard anyone suggest that my hands had some damn in them," he said.

"Well, they do. Look at them," she said, but his hands were relaxed now. "Okay, well, they *did* have some damn in them."

"Sure you didn't imagine it?"

She dropped her jaw in surprise. "Absolutely not, and you know it. Your hands were—" She broke off when she saw the beginning of a chuckle. He was teasing her. She punched his bicep.

"Ouch!"

"Oh, right," she said. "Like you barely even felt that. You think you're so clever."

He grabbed her hand. "There's more to you than meets the eye. And what meets the eye is enough to cause trouble," he said with a sigh and tugged her closer. "I don't like talking about my father," he said, his mouth a breath from hers.

The atmosphere changed in an instant. Passion took the place of anger. Her heart slammed against her rib cage.

"If anyone else had said what you did, I would have cut them off right away."

"Maybe you can't resist my girlish charm, after all," she managed in a husky whisper, feeling out of her depth but determined to stay in the water with him.

"We're in trouble if I can't," he said and lowered his mouth to hers, barely touching her lips.

Lori strained to press her mouth more fully against his. Her reaction was so fast and instinctive it took her by surprise. Where was this coming from? Why did she want him?

He groaned. "Just this once," he muttered and really kissed her, shoving her questions far from her mind. Sliding his hands behind her back, he pulled her against him and devoured her mouth with his. His strength, physical and sexual, made her dizzy. He slid his tongue past her lips and demanded a response from her. She felt her nipples grow taut and her internal temperature ratchet upward.

Echoing his moves, she slid her tongue into his mouth and he gave another groan that vibrated all the way down to her toes. She'd been kissed nearly to the point of no return before, but no one had ever made her feel so hot she was certain steam would rise from her skin.

Something about him made him seem so much more like a man to her. Something about him made her wish she was more experienced so she could make him half as hot as she was.

She rubbed her achy breasts against his chest and he took control of the kiss again, sliding his tongue over hers. She suckled it, drawing him deep into her mouth, and she felt his thumbs brush the sides of her breasts.

More, more, more. She wriggled against him and lifted her hands to slide her fingers through his hair.

She felt his thumb move closer to her nipple and a wild, carnal need ricocheted through her like a sparkler on the Fourth of July. *Touch it, touch me.*

He moved his thumb away and she couldn't quite swallow the whimper crowding her throat.

"Oh, you like that," he muttered against her mouth. "You want more."

He rubbed his palm over her nipple and she shuddered.

He swore. "I didn't think you would be this hot." He French-kissed her again, still rubbing his palm over her breast. "All it takes is a touch and you kiss me like you'd spread your legs and let me take you right here, right now. I bet you're already wet."

Lori felt her cheeks heat at his words. He was right. She was wet and wanting, but she didn't want him to know. It wasn't fair that he still sounded in control when she was hot and bothered.

Taking a deep breath, she pulled away from him. She cleared her throat. "That was educational. Now that we've done that once, we won't need to do it again."

He gave a nonchalant nod. "If you can control yourself."

His attitude nettled her. "I didn't start it."

"The way you look at me started it. You look at me like you want to rip my clothes off and indulge your darkest, baddest thoughts."

"I do not," she lied. "You have an inflated opinion of

yourself, but that's no surprise. Your arrogance isn't the least bit seductive."

"Well, something about me works for you, because you were begging me to kiss you and touch you. You were begging for more."

"Don't take it so personal," she said, feigning a breezy air although she still felt jittery. "It's been a while for me. I'm going inside to see Virginia."

Frowning, Jackson watched Lori get out of the car and walk across the rough parking lot. Although she wore jeans, she also wore heels, which were impractical as hell. The heels, however, did things to her gait that kept his gaze fastened to her backside.

He remembered how she'd felt and tasted and grew hard again. Swearing, he adjusted his jeans and narrowed his eyes at the woman who, just minutes ago, had acted like a scorching man-eater determined to consume and be consumed.

Kissing her had been a mistake. Knocked sideways by the strange conversation they'd shared about their families, he'd told himself and her it was just that once.

But now he knew how she felt and tasted. Now he knew she was hotter than black pavement in Dallas in August. He had the unsettling feeling that he'd opened Pandora's box by kissing her.

She'd seemed cool as a cucumber when she'd stepped out of the car and left him with a lingering whisper of her French-perfumed scent, but the way she'd responded to him made him doubt her easy dismissal of her reaction to him.

"Actions speak louder than words, princess," he muttered. No matter, he told himself, his arousal finally starting to wane. If she was determined to be Miss Cool, then all the better. As long as she didn't toss him those I-want-you-now looks, then they would be just fine.

Lori climbed the slanting wooden steps of the large farmhouse. The house needed a new coat of paint and a few repairs, she noticed as she felt a board wiggle beneath her foot. As she approached the screen door, however, she smelled the scent of a fresh-baked pie. She inhaled and closed her eyes. Cinnamon, apples . . . Eager to see Virginia, she knocked on the door.

A moment later, a beautiful young Mexican woman, with long dark hair and a scar that slashed across her cheek, stood at the door. "Good afternoon," she said and studied Lori for a long moment, her eyes hinting at disapproval. "You must be Lori Granger. I'm Maria. Come in. I will tell Virginia."

Lori stepped inside the foyer while the woman disappeared to the back of the house. She heard a low voice followed by a peal of delight and immediately smiled at Virginia's response.

"Lori," the older woman said as she rounded the corner, dressed in an apron, with Maria following slowly behind her. "You came! It's been too long, sweetheart."

Virgina's hair contained far more gray than before, and she was thinner. Her eyes held a combination of sadness and weariness, but her wide smile was still full of magic. Lori immediately rushed into her open arms. "Virginia, I'm so glad to see you. And I'm so sorry about Skip."

Virginia sighed and gave her a squeeze. "You've had a tough time, too, sweetie, with your daddy passing." She pulled back and looked at Lori. "We're pleased as punch to have you, but I didn't quite understand what that Jackson man was telling me. Your visit needs to be confidential? You're not running from the law, are you?"

Lori laughed. "No, nothing like that. Jackson's just being protective."

"He's a bodyguard?"

Lori shook her head. "Not exactly. My accountant," she said.

She noticed Virginia looking past her outside the door. "That's your accountant?" she said in a lowered voice, and Lori didn't have to turn around to know that Jackson was climbing the steps of the porch. Lori noticed Maria staring with an assessing expression that made Lori feel, well, weird.

The situation was strange enough, and she didn't want Virginia or anyone else to pick up on the dynamics, whatever they were, between her and Jackson, so she took the high road of civility. "Virginia and Maria, this is Jackson James. He's my accountant and advisor. I'm sorry we didn't give you much notice for our visit, but both of us would like to help while we're here. And if you don't have room, I'll totally understand."

"Nonsense," Virginia said. "Of course we have room. We always have room for you. And right now, I can offer you pie."

Jackson entered the house and Lori introduced him to Virginia and Maria. He greeted each of them. "Thank you for letting us come on such short notice."

"Lori is always welcome here. We loved her from the first summer she spent here at the ranch. She was great with the horses and the kids."

"Really," he said, surprised by the woman's assessment of Lori. It was tough for him to visualize Lori doing such hard physical labor. "I'm hoping we won't need to stay long."

"Don't worry about a thing. Now, as I was saying," Virginia said. "The pie is ready. Would you like a piece?"

Jackson inhaled the mouth-watering scent. "I never turn down just-baked pie," Jackson said as the four of them returned to the kitchen.

Virginia urged Lori and Jackson into kitchen chairs around a small breakfast table. "Do you have any campers?" Lori asked. "Are they out on the horses or resting?"

"We'll have campers in a couple days," Virginia said as she served the pie. "I'm low on staff this summer, so you can be sure we'll be busy. Thank goodness some family members and counselors will come with the campers and serve as helpers."

"I can help," Lori offered.

Jackson nearly choked on his pie in surprise.

Virginia's eyes rounded with excitement. "That would be fantastic. The campers will love you, and we have some new horses that you will love."

Jackson watched Lori bite her lip. "I'm a little rusty with the horses. Maybe I could help in the kitchen or with the housekeeping duties." That made sense, he thought. No heavy lifting for the princess.

Virginia paused, then gave a slow nod. "That will work, too. I just thought you would enjoy working with the horses more."

"Oh, I'm sure your routine is different now. It will be easier for me to jump right in with helping in the kitchen."

"Okeydoke," Virginia said. "Two more hands. Maria, the jackpot arrived at our front door, didn't it?"

Maria gave a neutral smile. "We're always grateful for volunteers."

Maria was no fool, Jackson decided. He suspected the striking Latino woman had already rendered judgment on Lori as useless. Which wasn't completely true. Even though Lori had been a major pain in his ass, he knew she had a good heart.

"If you have any repairs you need done on the house, I can help with those," he said to Virginia.

The older woman lifted her hand to her throat. "Oh, stars, you have no idea what you're offering. I hate to take advantage of you, but I'm desperate enough to do just that. There's a loose board in the front porch."

"I noticed that," he said. "I could probably take care of it this afternoon."

Virginia beamed. "Well, isn't this too good to be true? Jackson, you can work on the house, and Lori, Maria can get you started on some casseroles and cutting and chopping of vegetables. We like to do as much ahead of time as we can, since things get so hectic when the kids are here." She smiled at Jackson. "You want another piece of pie?"

That afternoon, Maria gave Lori the recipe for a chicken-and-stuffing casserole. Lori hit a little snafu when she overlooked the instruction to precook the chicken and chop it into pieces. Not understanding the use of soups, she prepared them according to the instructions on the can. When she pulled the huge casserole out of the oven, it was a mess.

Maria stared at her in chagrin. "You could not read

the recipe?" she asked. "You did not see that you are supposed to cook the chicken first? And the soup?" She shook her head and went off in a spate of Spanish that Lori couldn't interpret word for word. She got the gist, however, that Maria was pissed.

"I'm really sorry," Lori said. "I'll pay for the ingredients. I'll—"

Virginia entered the kitchen, and Maria immediately began talking to the woman in excited Spanish. Virginia looked at the casserole and grimaced, then looked at Lori.

"Carrots," the older woman said. "We need chopped carrots, potatoes, and onions. And after that, you can snap beans. Maria, why don't you take some of the horses for a ride?"

Lori meticulously chopped carrots until dinnertime, when Virginia appeared again. "Oh, my, you didn't get to the potatoes yet, did you?"

Lori felt a sinking sensation at the surprise in the woman's tone. "Was I supposed to chop them first?"

"No," Virginia said. "I just thought we might use some of the vegetables for dinner tonight." Virginia paused. "But you know, it's so hot, I think sandwiches and chips would be a great idea for dinner." She squeezed Lori's shoulder. "Sweetheart, are you sure you wouldn't rather work with the horses tomorrow?"

"Oh, no. I'll get faster," Lori said. "I just haven't done much cooking lately." Or ever, she silently added.

Maria swept into the kitchen and glanced at the bowl of carrots. "Carrots? She has only sliced the carrots?"

Virginia gave a determined smile. "I've decided on sandwiches for dinner. Everything okay with the horses?"

"All good," Maria said. "Holt and I took them for rides."

"Holt?" Lori asked.

"He's a neighbor who helps part-time when he can. Used to ride the rodeo. He's great with the horses," Virginia said. "Maria, let's put some sandwiches together."

"I'll help," Lori offered.

"That's sweet. Would you mind setting the table?"

The following morning, Lori was put on housekeeping detail. She dusted and mopped the floors of the two cabins, and cleaned bathrooms and windows. She even vacuumed the curtains the same way she'd seen her housekeeper do. Exhausted by the end of the day, she returned to the main house.

She smelled something delicious baking in the kitchen and walked inside. Jackson sat in a kitchen chair, chatting easily with Maria and Virginia. She felt a twinge of jealousy at how quickly the women had accepted him. Maria shot him a teasing smile, and Lori felt the twinge turn to a stab that went deeper. Frowning at the feeling, she brushed it aside.

Virginia looked up at her and smiled. "There's our little cleaner. Come on in, sweetheart. The cabins all spick-and-span?"

"Both of them sparkle," she said, proud of herself for doing a good job.

"Both?" Virginia echoed.

"Both?" Maria repeated. "You only did two of them?"

Lori blinked. "There are more? There were only two when I was here before."

Maria sighed. *"Ay caramba . . ."*

"No, hold on just a minute, Maria," Virginia said. "Lori is right. We built the other two cabins the spring after she worked here."

Maria tossed her dish towel aside and met Lori's gaze. "All right. I will finish the other two cabins and eat my dinner later."

Lori felt her pride roar to the surface. It was as if that dish towel was actually a gauntlet. "Oh, no," she said. "I'll do it."

"It will take you all night," Maria said, shaking her head as she moved away from the counter. "The cabins have to be ready for the campers tomorrow."

Lori stepped directly in Maria's path. "I said I would do it, and I will," she said firmly, then glanced at Virginia. "Virginia, would you toss me one of those apples? That should get me through."

"Of course, dear, but you don't have to—"

"Excuse me, but yes, I do," Lori said and surprised herself when she caught the apple. Maria made her feel small and inept. That was bad enough, but the fact that she did it in front of Jackson made Lori understand the concept of catfight. Which was crazy. She shouldn't and didn't care that Jackson viewed her as vapid and useless. If she kept telling herself that, she would believe it.

> *"If you must do a nasty chore, listening to rock and roll will help the time pass more quickly."*
> —SUNNY COLLINS

Chapter Ten

Jackson walked into the barn to check on a loose stall door and heard the scrape of a shovel from the other side of the barn. The horses were out for an afternoon ride with the campers, so he figured it was a good time to take care of cleaning stalls. He checked three of the doors and found the third one was the culprit. Pulling out his tools, he replaced the stripped screws.

Just as he finished the job, he heard a feminine voice humming. He didn't recognize the song until the voice put words to the Justin Timberlake number about bringing sexy back. His lips twitched. If he didn't know better, he would swear that was Lori's voice, but she couldn't possibly be mucking out horse manure.

He couldn't resist a peek at the songstress, and his jaw nearly dropped to the floor at the sight of Lori wearing a hat, gloves, boots, and borrowed jeans that didn't fit. Swinging a fork and her butt, she moved in time to an MP3 player in her pocket. She was so intent on her job and the music, she didn't notice him.

Unable to tear himself from the unlikely sight, he stared for several moments.

Lori turned around, saw him, and screamed.

Jackson grimaced and moved toward her with his hands lifted. "For Pete's sake, it's just me."

She pulled earphones from her ears. "I didn't know anyone was there." She narrowed her eyes at him. "How long have you been watching me?"

"Not long," he said. "Just long enough to know you're not a contender for *American Idol*."

She scowled at him. "Thank you very much. You can leave now."

He crossed his arms over his chest. "With this kind of show? No way." He glanced at the stall. "You've done a damn good job."

"Of course I have," she said, grabbing the wheelbarrow and pushing it out of the stall.

He walked along beside her. "I didn't know mucking out stalls was on your usual list of activities."

"It isn't now, but I did it all the time in college and during my summers here." She dumped the contents of the wheelbarrow into a predetermined pile. "I've actually spent much more time taking care of horses than cooking or cleaning."

"That's right. Your major was equestrian studies. So why aren't you helping with the campers?"

"Cleaning stalls is one of those things that comes right back to you. But I haven't ridden in a while. I'm rusty."

"Why not?"

"I took a few spills, broke a bone or two. Daddy refused to let me get back on a horse."

"Daddy's gone now," Jackson said.

"True," she said and shrugged. "But if I want to be helpful, I need to stick with an area where I'm sure I'm competent."

"I'm stunned. I never would have pictured you, Lori Jean Granger, heiress to millions, doing something like this."

She met his gaze. "I guess that means you either underestimated me or overestimated me. I wonder which," she said and moved on to another stall.

"You know you may need to stay here at the ranch for at least a couple of weeks before everything dies down in Dallas?"

She glanced over her shoulder at him. "I'm fine with that. I've always liked it here. The only part about waiting is that I need to get married so I can help out Virginia financially." She shrugged. "But I guess that's more your problem than mine."

"Mine?"

"Yes, you have to bring in the prospects. It might be tougher getting the right man for the job to come all the way down here."

Jackson swore. She was right about that one.

"It wouldn't hurt you to show a little patience," Virginia said as she pulled hot biscuits from the oven.

Maria rolled her eyes as she packed the dinner baskets assigned to each cabin. "It would be easier if she weren't so useless. All that food she wasted, and then she took forever to clean the cabins. I bet she doesn't even know how to make a bed."

"She does," Virginia said. "It's just been a while. If you understood how overprotective Lori Jean's daddy was, then maybe you wouldn't be so hard on her."

"Overprotectiveness was never an issue with my father," Maria said, unable to keep the bitterness from her voice. Her father had been so abusive she'd repeatedly run away from home, but every time she'd left, he'd found her and beat her. She rubbed the scar on her cheek. The last time Maria had run away, she was eighteen and Virginia and Skip had intervened.

"I know, sweetheart," Virginia said and gave Maria a quick hug. "I wish Skip and I could have done something for you sooner, but we didn't even know you existed until we found you sleeping in the barn."

"Lucky for me," Maria said. "But how long do we have to let Lori stay here?"

"As long as I told you that you could stay here," Virginia told her in a firm voice.

Virginia had assured Maria that she could stay on the ranch as long as she wanted. "But I was helpful," Maria said. "I didn't ruin entire meals."

"Give Lori some time. She'll be helpful, too. You may not see it, but she has a heart of gold."

"If she has this heart of gold, then why doesn't she just give you the money for the ranch?" Maria demanded.

"I don't know the answer to that," Virginia said. "I just know that if she needs a place to stay, I'm going to give it to her."

*   *   *

Two nights later, after everyone appeared to have gone to bed and Lori read more letters from her mother, she went to the barn. As soon as she stepped inside, she smelled the scent of horseflesh. Fear immediately wrapped around her throat like a vise. She closed her eyes and forced herself not to run away.

It wasn't as if she was going for a ride. She was just going to look.

Biting her lip, she moved farther into the barn with quiet steps. She didn't want to disturb the horses. She heard a soft whinny and a stomp. Someone was awake.

In a darkness where only moonlight offered relief, she stepped in front of one of the stalls and stared at the mare inside. She glanced at the name above the door. Christy.

Lori smiled. Lady was still there, too—she had been a filly when she'd spent her second summer at the ranch. And Lilly stood in resting position, her back legs locked. No matter how many times she observed it, a horse's ability to sleep while standing amazed her.

The sound of another whinny and stomp interrupted her, and she wandered deeper into the barn. All the way at the end, a black horse with a white marking on its nose poked its head out of his stall. She glanced over the door and read the name. Rowdy.

Watching him stomp his foot and snort, she agreed with the name. "Everyone else is asleep. You should be, too," she said in a low voice.

Rowdy snorted again.

In another life, she would have mounted him and taken him for a ride to help him get rid of his excess energy. Remembering the metal plate that caused a hassle every time she went through airport security, she shook her head. Not now.

"Making friends?" a male voice said from behind her, surprising her.

She jumped and turned toward Jackson. "How long have you been here? I didn't hear you."

He rested his hands on his hips. "Just long enough to see you tell this guy he needs to chill." He stepped toward the stall and rubbed Rowdy's nose. "There you go. Counting sheep just doesn't do the trick when you want to run, does it?"

As if he understood, Rowdy nodded and stomped. Lori smiled. "Looks like you two understand each other."

"Sure we do," Jackson said, rubbing Rowdy's nose again. He glanced at Lori. "Why don't you take him for a ride?"

She shook her head. "It's been a long time. He's too young for me. I bet they don't use him with the children yet."

"Probably not," Jackson said, then moved to the next stall. "What about this one?" He glanced at the name above the door. "Peace. He's sleeping."

Lori peeked inside the stall at the palomino gelding. "They may have named him Peace out of wishful thinking."

Jackson grinned and shook his head. "You sound skeptical. That's not like you."

"It depends on the situation. I think I'll head back to—"

He stopped at Lady's stall. "What's not to love here? She looks as gentle as rain."

"I don't know," she said, crossing her arms over her chest.

"What? Would you prefer a wooden rocking horse?"

She met his gaze defiantly. "That would work."

His eyebrows furrowed. "What aren't you telling me?"

"Nothing you really need to know," she said, turning away.

"Wait," he said, and she felt his hand on her shoulder. "Why don't you ride?"

She took a deep breath. "I told you I got thrown several years ago."

"If you ride long enough, everyone gets thrown."

"Hopefully not like I did."

"What do you mean?" he asked as he turned her around to face him.

His closeness did things to her. His strength almost seemed to invite her to lean against him and let him wrap his arms around her. The feeling, she knew, would be delicious. She sighed. "You don't want to know."

"Yes, I do."

His intent, searching gaze made her heart skip. She swallowed. "Like I told you, I was thrown. I didn't land well. I broke both legs, one of my shoulders, and my pelvis. I had to have emergency surgery to remove my spleen, then two more surgeries on my ankle. Rehab was a nightmare. It took months to walk again. And I have inner jewelry now," she said and shot him a sexy smile that clearly took effort. "A metal plate."

He stared at her in shock and swore. "How come I didn't know anything about this? Your folder practically details every mole you have."

"It's top secret," she said. "My father didn't want any-one to know. He said he didn't want anyone thinking I was damaged goods."

"Damaged goods," he repeated, feeling as if he were in a boxing match with his hands tied behind his back. "Where the hell did he get that idea?"

"Well, you know, Daddy could get a little dramatic at times. And stubborn. Very stubborn. But I suppose I in-herited some of that stubbornness, because the doctors said I wouldn't walk without a pronounced limp. And to forget high heels."

He looked into her big baby blues with a new feeling growing inside him. Some kind of feeling that included respect and maybe even admiration. "I still don't get the damaged goods remark."

"Think about it. Combine the accident with my wild mother. His goal was to keep me and, perhaps more im-portantly, my reputation from anything negative."

"But working your way through rehab, that showed you had guts and determination. It showed that you weren't a sissy."

"I can see this is a shock to your system. You were so sure everything had come easily to me, weren't you?" She gave a slow smile and her hand rested on his arm. "I ac-cept your kind apology for making negative assumptions about my character."

He slid his hand over hers before she could take it away. He liked the way her hand felt on his arm. He suspected he would like the way her soft hand would feel all over his body. "I can't apologize for what I didn't know."

Her gaze strayed to his hand on hers, giving him the

impression that the connection distracted her. "But you still jumped to negative and erroneous conclusions."

"True, but now I know your top secret."

She met his gaze. "That was my father's top secret. Mine could be different." She glanced at their entwined hands again. "I should go. It's late."

Jackson reluctantly released her. Damn it, the more he learned about her, the more he wanted to know. The woman acted as if she were a simple blonde bombshell, but he'd seen glimpses of the layers. He couldn't help wondering what other secrets she hid.

Geoffrey Taylor used his most persuasive voice with his rental car as it stalled for the third time in an hour. "Just a little farther," he coaxed, turning the key in the ignition and pushing the pedal to the floor. He glanced outside the window at the dry, barren landscape and grimaced. "I realize this is some of the most godforsaken territory you've ever seen, but you just need to make it a little farther. According to the GPS, we're almost there."

There being the Miracles in Motion horse ranch. At first when he'd heard Lori was staying at a ranch, he'd gotten excited. It would be like those old western movies where all men, including him, would be cowboys.

The spare, dusty terrain, however, was causing his asthma to act up, and the employees at the last gas station where he'd stopped had been wearing gangsta clothes, eating donuts, and watching some sort of reality dancing competition on television.

His romantic image was shattered as he reached for his inhaler again. The engine sputtered to life and he immediately put it in gear and floored it. It was near sunset, and he didn't want to get stuck in the dark in the middle of nowhere.

Fifteen minutes later, the car died again. Geoffrey gave his usual pep talk and turned the key in the ignition six times. The engine refused even to turn over.

"Bloody hell," he muttered. What was he supposed to do now? He sincerely hoped his family appreciated the sacrifices he was making on their behalf. When word had gotten out that Lori Jean Granger was in the market for a husband, he'd known he would need to cut himself out of the pack in order to win her. He already had a foot in the door. He'd known she was at least amused by him. Everyone knew women preferred men who could make them laugh.

He climbed out of the car and put his GPS, his cell phone that stubbornly proclaimed no service, his inhaler, and the bottle of ale he'd picked up at the last stop into the leather pouch he carried for traveling. He pulled the GPS out and saw that the ranch was fifteen miles away.

He was young and healthy. He had beer and his inhaler. Fifteen miles should be a snap.

After ten miles on what he was certain was the road to hell, Geoffrey decided to cut through some fields. After all, the shortest distance between two points was a straight line.

He didn't count on sudden holes or bug bites that itched like the devil, and he'd forgotten about the possibility of bloody poisonous snakes. Damn it, he was probably going to die, and if that happened, the future of his family would definitely be ruined. He glumly swallowed his last sip of beer but continued walking.

In the middle of his misery, he heard the distant sound of pounding hooves. His heart lifted. He felt a surge of hope. "Help!" he called. "Help!" He yelled again and again until a black horse came into sight.

His breath caught in his throat at the sight of the woman rider. Long black hair flowed over her shoulders. As she came closer, he saw the lush curves of her body. Her breasts bobbed with the movement of the horse.

For a moment, he feared she was an apparition. She moved closer and looked down at him. "You're trespassing. Who are you, and what are you doing here?"

"I'm Geoffrey Taylor. My car broke down. I'm trying to get to the Miracles in Motion Ranch."

"Why?"

"I'm supposed to see Mr. Jackson James and Miss Lori Granger."

"You have an accent. Where are you from?"

"England."

She rolled her eyes and then let out a spate of Spanish. It seemed to be of a derogatory nature. At the end of her rant, she gave a big sigh. "Okay, I'll give you a ride back to the main building. They can decide what to do with you there. Hop on," she said, moving the horse closer to him.

Geoffrey eagerly put his foot in the stirrup she offered for his use and hoisted himself upward. But unfortunately not far enough. He fell backward into a bush.

"Bloody hell," he said, scrambling to his feet, his manhood wounded. For some reason, he didn't want this hot little senorita thinking he was a complete dork.

This time she extended her hand. He took it, noting the fact that it was small but calloused. He swung over the back and clung to her waist.

"Hold on, pretty boy," she said. "Rowdy's still a little green."

Holding on necessitated that the entire front of his body be meshed with the entire backside of her body. Senorita had an amazing ass. By the end of the ride, he had an amazing hard-on.

"Virginia," Maria called as she pushed open the screen door and held it three seconds for Geoffrey Taylor to get his English body inside. He reminded her of a young Hugh Grant. Cute, but useless. "We have another mouth to feed. No apparent skills."

Virginia stepped into the foyer. "What are you talking about?"

"Him," Maria said, pointing to the man behind her. "He was stranded on the far end of our property."

Lori came down the steps from the second floor. "What?" She met Maria's gaze, then her eyes widened as she looked past her. "Geoffrey?" she said in surprise.

"In the flesh. I was determined to meet you again, but my car broke down," he said with a strained smile on his face. "Miss—" He broke off. "Excuse me, but I'm at a disadvantage. I never learned your name."

"Maria Espoza," she said, realizing he'd been chasing Lori. She should have known.

"Thank you very much for rescuing me, Miss Espoza. I'm in your debt."

"Join the club," Maria said. "Do we have any tequila?" she asked Virginia.

Virginia shot Maria a quelling glance. "It sounds as if you've had a rough trip, Mr. Taylor. Can I get you something to eat?"

"Oh, no. I don't want to be a bother."

"Too late for that," Maria muttered.

"I can fix a sandwich for you," Lori offered.

"And we have some pie left over from dinner," Virginia said.

"That was my piece of pie," Maria said.

"You must have it," Geoffrey quickly said in a gallant tone. "You deserve more than a piece of pie for rescuing me."

"Isn't his accent wonderful," Virginia said with a girlish smile that stunned Maria. "I'll bake an entire pie for you if you'll just keep talking."

Geoffrey gave a half smile. "I should imagine that won't last long," he said. "I fear I'll bore you out of your mind."

"Oh, I don't know," Maria said. "Any man who gets stranded on a ranch while he's carrying a pocketbook could provide some entertainment."

Geoffrey shot her an indignant glance. "It's not a pocketbook. It's a pouch."

"Whatever," she said and turned to leave the room.

Geoffrey bent his head toward her as she passed and spoke in a low voice. "Just because you're beautiful, sexy, and accomplished doesn't mean you have to be nasty," he said.

Maria stared at him, speechless. And flattered.

"It's not fun, sunbeam, but if you're afraid of something, you're eventually going to have to face it down, or it will own you for the rest of your life."
—SUNNY COLLINS

Chapter Eleven

Lori glanced at her diamond-encrusted Rolex as she left the cabin in sparkling-clean condition behind her. If anyone had told her that she would spend her days trying to set a new record for cleaning toilets, she would have laughed them into next week. Glancing up, she nearly ran into Geoffrey.

"There you are," he said. "I was hoping you could show me around today. Last night we didn't have an opportunity to share much time together," he said, dressed in khaki slacks and a white shirt.

He really was cute, Lori thought. Floppy light brown hair, crooked self-deprecating grin, tons of polite British charm. She wondered if she could get along with him for six years. "Sounds lovely, but I need to clean two more cabins, and the clock is ticking. Maria will hiss at me if I don't get them done."

He lifted his eyebrows. "Maria? Why would she hiss at you? You're doing her a favor by cleaning."

"Not fast enough," Lori said, then decided to give the duke a little test. "Would you mind helping me?"

He blinked for a solid moment, then seemed to force himself to shake his head. "Clean," he repeated as if it were a foreign word. "Of course not." He gave a slightly forced smile. "I'm happy to help. Lead onward."

Lori bit her lips to keep them from twitching. "Thank you so much. The other cabins are this way."

As soon as they stepped inside the first cabin, she gave him a feather duster and a mop. "I'll do the bathrooms. They take the most work." After a few moments of scrubbing, she called out to him. "Everything okay?"

"It's fine," he said and sneezed. "Everything's fine."

Lori shined the mirrors. "I'm surprised you were able to find me at Miracles in Motion."

"Your housekeeper took pity on me. I begged her. And gave her a one-hundred-dollar bill."

Lori glanced outside the bathroom door. "A hundred dollars?"

He nodded and flicked the duster over a dresser. "I started low, but she wouldn't budge."

"I'm flattered that you were so determined, but I'm kind of surprised. We only met that once."

"I thought we connected well. That and I wanted to cut myself out of the pack of wild dogs barking at your back door," he said.

She laughed. "They all want the money. What they don't understand is that they'll have to sign an iron-clad prenup."

His dusting abruptly stopped. "Is that so?"

She nodded. "Of course. But whoever I marry will be generously compensated."

"Really?"

"Until I'm thirty."

The duster dropped to the floor. "Pardon me. Did I hear you correctly? Did you say until you reach thirty?"

She glanced outside the door at him. "Yes. The real reason I'll get married is just to get access to my own money, which is unfortunately held in trust."

"And what do you want to do with your money?"

"Give it away," she said and gave the tub another swipe.

She heard a crashing sound and glanced outside the door. "Problem?"

"No, I just—" He picked up his broom and looked at her in confusion. "Why would you want to give away your money?"

"Because I have tons of money and I'm a philanthropist. Prime example is this ranch. Virginia really needs some money, but I can't give it to her until I can access it." She rinsed out the tub.

"Lori Jean," Geoffrey said from directly behind her, startling her.

She whirled around to find him kneeling on one knee. "I didn't know you were right behind me."

"My apologies," he said, mop and duster in his hands. "But would you do me the honor of becoming my wife? I think we could help solve each other's problems. I've been told I'm not a bad man to have around. Amusing, clever, agreeable, not too demanding. I'm not a playboy, but I've also been told I'm not bad in the sack—"

Lori held up her hand. "That's the thing. I'm not sure I want to have sex."

"Oh," he said, pausing for a long moment. Then she would swear he was mentally calculating how many years of abstinence would be required. He cleared his throat. "It might be difficult, but I suppose—"

"It might be okay with me if my husband—" She hesitated, searching for the right words. "If he took care of his needs with someone else, as long as he was discreet."

"Ah, well, as you know we British are the epitome of discretion."

She felt an odd lump in her throat. Marriage. Did she really want to go through with this? With him? "Would you mind if I think this over?"

He shook his head. "Of course not. It's a big decision. For six years. You probably have some questions for me."

"Right," she said.

They stood staring at each other, awkwardly silent for a long moment.

The doorway swung open and Maria appeared. She lifted her eyebrow. "You haven't finished yet?" she asked.

Lori hated the suggestion that she wasn't good enough. "Three down. One to go. Getting faster."

Maria tossed her hair. "So you are. With help from your English boy."

"He's not a boy. He's a man," Lori cooed, just to see if she could poke even a tiny hole in Maria's thick hide. "But I guess since you don't get many gentlemen around here, you wouldn't know how to treat them."

Maria blinked and gave Geoffrey a second assessing look. She opened her mouth and worked her jaw, but nothing came out. "Just finish the other cabin," she finally blurted and stomped away.

"Moody," Lori said.

"Fiery," Geoffrey said, staring after Maria.

"She has zero patience," Lori countered.

"She's stacked better than the Oxford Library," Geoffrey added.

Lori met his gaze, unable to keep her lips from twitching in humor. "Can't argue with that."

Geoffrey suddenly seemed to realize that he'd practically drooled over another woman in front of the woman to whom he'd just proposed. He grimaced. "Bloody hell. Well, you're very well stacked, also," he said. "Very well stacked. Better than Oxford. You have some kind of enormous library here in the States. What is it?"

"Library of Congress," Lori said.

"Exactly," he said with a firm nod. "You're stacked better than the Library of Congress."

"Thank you," she said. "We still need to clean the last cabin."

"Right-o. Lead on."

That evening, Lori read another letter from her mother as usual before she went to bed, but her mind kept wandering to the prospect of marrying Geoffrey. After thirty minutes, she gave up, got dressed, and headed for the barn.

Did she really want to do this? Could she really go through with a business marriage? She thought of her sisters and their happy and passionate marriages. Maybe this was a weird twist-of-fate payoff. Since they'd had the tough upbringings, they were due love happily-ever-after. If the flip side were true, since she'd had the cushy childhood, she wouldn't get the love connection.

It was terribly naive to think all her secret wishes would come true. And when she thought about it, if she got everything she wanted, she'd probably be exactly what Jackson had thought she was—a spoiled brat.

She wandered inside the darkened wooden building and inhaled deeply, wanting to recapture the way she had felt before the accident. Back then, there had been something peaceful about the barn at night. The horses rested easily. It was almost like watching a baby sleep, she thought as she looked into Lady's stall.

She heard footsteps behind her and felt her heart kick a little as Jackson came into view. He was such a man. A man's man. Strong, no-nonsense, sexy. The last description stopped her. Sexy? He was just different, she told herself, because he wasn't falling all over himself to be with her. If she was attracted to him, it was just some sort of sick thing about wanting something she couldn't have. But something had changed between them since they'd kissed. She couldn't look at him without being aware of him as a man.

"Is this becoming a habit?"

She shrugged, leaning against the stall door. "There are worse habits."

"I thought you'd be spending the evening with the English lord," he said, standing beside her.

"Duke," she corrected. "I spent a good part of the day with him," she said.

"He must be very interested if he was willing to drive down here to see you."

"I'm sure he is. I'm loaded and can solve most of his financial problems," she said.

She felt his gaze on her. "You want to expound on that?"

"Not really," she said with a breezy smile and moved toward the next stall. "I came here for the peace and serenity of the barn at night. Don't feel you need to stay."

He gave a rough laugh. "Dismissing me already?" he asked, joining her. "Are you sure you want to do that? I have some sugar in my pocket," he said in a seductive voice.

She whipped her head around to meet his gaze, and then she was unable to stop herself from looking at his *pocket*. "I don't think I've ever heard it called that before."

He laughed again, this time more loudly. "Sugar cubes," he said. "Get your mind out of the gutter, sweetheart."

She scowled, but he ignored her, moving farther into the barn. "Let's see who is awake," he said.

"Probably Rowdy," she said, curious.

"Peace is peaceful as usual," he said. He walked a few steps farther and there was a sound of a hoof on the floor. Seconds later, Rowdy poked his head out of his stall door. "Looks like you were right. You want to give him a sugar cube?"

Lori immediately felt herself stiffen with fear. The dark feeling circled around and inside her, sucking away her breath and nerve. She took a careful breath and tried to appear nonchalant. "That's okay. You brought the treat. You can give it."

She moved closer, though, and watched as Jackson stretched his hand out flat for the horse. Rowdy politely took the sugar cube with his mouth instead of his teeth.

Jackson glanced at her. "You sure you don't want to give him one? I have more."

She considered the offer and felt her palms immediately go damp. It wasn't riding, she reminded herself. It was just a damn sugar cube. She took a deep breath. "Okay."

"Come here," he said and put the cube into her open palm. He slid his arm around her back, and Lori felt a sliver of tension leave her body. Willing herself to remain calm, she tentatively lifted her hand toward Rowdy.

When he nodded his head and whinnied, she stiffened but kept her hand steady. She watched as the horse moved his super-soft lips over her hand and took the sugar cube.

She looked at Jackson and couldn't help smiling. "I'd forgotten that their mouths feel like velvet."

"Yeah, velvet," he said, but he was looking at her mouth.

She felt as if she were going up the down elevator. She met his gaze and another crackle of electricity snapped between them. Was it just her? Was it some kind of masochistic tendency inside her that drove her toward him? Because he clearly didn't think much of her.

Lowering her gaze to grab her equilibrium, she bit her lip. "Thanks for sharing your sugar," she said, hoping she bothered him at least a fraction as much as he bothered her.

Geoffrey was bored out of his mind. He joined Lori to help clean the cabins and tried to engage in conversation, but she seemed distracted. After lunch, Lori announced her plans to muck stalls, and he bailed. She hadn't accepted his proposal, and he was getting dishpan hands from his cleaning chores.

Wandering outside the barn, he walked toward the corral, where Maria and several others were helping a group of five disabled children ride horses, one at a time.

The children appeared to suffer a range of disabilities, some physical, some mental, and some both. He stared at Maria as she comforted a young boy. She hugged and cuddled him against her full breast as she murmured in his ear.

Lucky kid, Geoffrey thought. Bloody hell, he was sick. Jealous of a little kid. Shaking his head at himself, he continued to watch. As the lesson drew to a close, however, he went to the barn and got a soda for himself from the small refrigerator. On impulse, he pulled out an extra and met Maria as she walked toward the barn.

"Care for a refreshing beverage?" he asked her, offering her the can. "I thought you might be hot."

She studied him for a moment as if she hadn't quite made up her mind about him. *"Gracias,"* she said. "Very nice of you. Was there something you wanted?"

"Not particularly," he said. "I don't suppose this place has any musical instruments hidden anywhere?"

She frowned thoughtfully. "I may have seen a piano in one of the rooms upstairs in the house. I don't know if it's playable."

"Would you mind showing me where it is?"

"You play?" she asked in surprise.

He nodded. "It's a passion. Much more so than my day job, but family duty calls and all that rubbish."

She smiled. "Sounds like you don't want to answer the call of family duty?"

"You're very perceptive. Now, the piano?"

"This way," she said and guided him back to the house and upstairs. "I'm surprised you're not spending the afternoon with Miss Granger."

"I helped her clean the cabins this morning," he said.

She murmured something in Spanish. "She *needs* help. She is so slow."

"Better slow than not at all, yes?" he said.

She shrugged as she led him to the end of the hall and opened the door.

"Pardon me, but I must ask, how did you end up on this ranch, of all places? You're so beautiful you could have been a model," he said.

She stopped and stared at him.

He cleared his throat, feeling like a fool. "Well, I'm sure I'm not the first man to tell you that you're beautiful."

A trace of vulnerability deepened her eyes for an instant. She took a deep breath, which drew his attention to her prominent breasts. "Of course not," she said. "But *gracias*." She cleared her throat and pointed inside the room. "The piano."

Geoffrey strode inside and swept the cover off an old spinet. It would probably sound like hell, he thought, but he ran his fingers over the keys anyway. "Needs to be tuned," he said, continuing up the keyboard. He found a broken key that wouldn't play. "Do you think Mrs. Dawson would mind terribly if I called a professional tuner? I would bear the cost."

"I could ask her for you."

"Thank you," he said, taking her hand and lifting it to his lips. "You are truly a goddess."

She met his gaze for a long moment as if she couldn't

decide how to take him. "I can't tell if you are *loco* or just strange."

He smiled. "Why can't I be both?"

Her mouth stretched into a smile that showed her white teeth against that gorgeous tanned skin, and then she gave a husky laugh that somehow managed to grab him by the heart and balls at the same time. *God, what a woman.*

That night around ten o'clock, Lori debated walking down to the barn again. She didn't want Jackson to think she was going down there just to see him. And truthfully, she wasn't. Even though the thought of riding a horse nearly made her break out in hives, the quiet of the barn calmed her.

Walking to the window of her small bedroom, she looked out at the clear night sky. Without city-light glare, the stars shone like diamonds on a blanket of indigo. The moon was a few days away from full but lit up the landscape below almost like a floodlight.

Sighing, she wrapped her arms around her waist, giving herself a hug. Soon she would need to give Geoffrey an answer to his proposal. That answer should be yes, and then she and he would begin their six-year sentence.

"Sanity is overrated."
—SUNNY COLLINS

Chapter Twelve

The thought of her impending marital sentence made her want to vault out of her second-story window. Lori shook her head. The comfy room suddenly felt too small, her skin too tight. Was she doing the right thing by getting married? By the time she turned thirty, what kind of woman would she be? Would an empty marriage change her? Would she become cynical?

Desperate to escape her thoughts, she gave in to her urge to go to the barn. She would take an apple this time to give one of the horses, to prove that she wasn't expecting Jackson to be there.

The apples looked so juicy and inviting in the bowl that she grabbed two and nibbled one along the way. The dry grass crunched under her feet. Lori inhaled deeply. She loved it here. No need for a new dress for every event. She wasn't cooped up in her house trying not to think about her father or mother too much. Glancing down at her manicure, or lack thereof, she laughed. Her polish was chipped, her nails breaking, and her hands looked three hundred years old from being in water so much the last couple of days.

She took another bite of her apple and smiled. Who cared? Slowing down as she approached the barn, she walked inside and found it dark and quiet. Jackson didn't appear to be here. Brushing off a twinge of disappointment, she took a few more steps and the tight feeling in her shoulders eased.

"I wondered if you were going to come," Jackson said from behind her.

Startled, Lori stifled a shriek and whirled around, breathless. "Did you have to scare me half to death?" she whispered. "Is it too much to ask you to give me a little warning if you're going to come up behind me in the dark?"

"Sorry," he said, but his tone said he was much more amused than apologetic.

She took a deep breath, then another, then turned away from him. "Yeah, whatever."

"Looks like you dropped your apple," he said.

"Good thing I brought another one," she said, glancing inside each stall at the resting horses. She already knew who would be awake.

"Is that for me?"

"Absolutely not," she said. "It's for Rowdy." She stopped for a moment and listened. Sure enough, she heard the horse's steps at the other end of the barn. Smiling, she walked toward his stall.

"You're getting more brave all the time," he said. "Soon enough, you'll be ready to ride."

A shiver of fear immediately rushed through her. "Ha, ha. Feeding is one thing. Riding is another."

"When do you think you'll be ready?"

"I don't know. No time soon," she said and turned to face him. "What's it to you?"

He shrugged. "I guess I think that if you got so much pleasure from riding before, it would be good if you could do it again."

"Except I don't get pleasure from it anymore."

"You don't know that, do you?" he asked.

She opened her mouth, then shut it. "I know I break into a cold sweat just thinking about getting back on a horse again. For now, my riding days are over."

"Unless you decide differently," he said.

"What do you mean decide something differently? You think I'm overreacting. You think I'm a wuss, don't you? You try breaking your pelvis and legs and doing a year of therapy and we'll talk, okay?" She turned away, resenting Jackson because he was destroying her Zen experience in the barn.

His hand on her shoulder stopped her. "I didn't say that. I don't think you're a wuss. I think you're brave to come within a few feet of horses. This may sound crazy, but I'd like to help you."

A sensation of warmth slid through her, and she met his gaze. "Why?"

"Glutton for punishment, I guess," he said with a crooked grin.

She rolled her eyes. "Okay, well, thanks, but I'm just offering Rowdy an apple tonight." She walked to his stall and the gelding came over to gawk at her. He nodded and dipped his head as if to greet her.

"He's flirting with you," Jackson said from behind her.

"How do you know that? Are you a horse whisperer?"

"It's a guy thing," he said. "We just know. There's a pretty woman around and one guy is going to try to hog her attention. That's what Rowdy is trying to do."

"He's so gorgeous," she said, admiring his silky coat.

"And he's succeeding," Jackson continued in a dry tone.

"He just smells my apple and wants it," she said.

"I could say something about your apple—"

"But you won't," she said and put the apple on her flat hand and gingerly lifted it toward Rowdy. He scarfed it into his mouth in a flash. She felt a crazy little rush of triumph. She'd done it on her own, and she was sweating only a little bit.

"I did it again," she said to Jackson. "It wasn't a fluke."

"Yeah, you did," he said, meeting her gaze. "You sure you don't want to pet him?"

"I don't know," she said. "One step at a time." She looked at Rowdy for a moment, but Jackson's gaze on her made her feel strange. Avoiding his gaze, she backed away. "I guess I should go. G—"

She felt his hand close over hers and gently tug her toward him. For some reason, she allowed it. She would have to think about just why later. Some part of her craved the sensation of his touch. She would love to feel the strength of his chest against her back. She would love to feel more.

"You're different here," he said in a low voice as he

rubbed his thumb on the underside of her wrist. "On the ranch."

She closed her eyes and took a deep breath, catching just a hint of his scent. "It's easier. I don't feel pulled in so many different directions. I still want to fix things, but a lot of it is so basic. Clean cabins, muck out stalls." She gave a breathless laugh. "Even I can do that."

He turned her around to face him, and she forced herself to meet his gaze. She didn't want him to see how much he affected her. Smiling, she lifted one of her hands and wiggled her fingers. "Are you saying you like my new barn manicure? Didn't you know it's the latest trend?"

Jackson looked down at her and couldn't keep from smiling, too. He glanced at her small hand, which was already growing a couple of calluses. "What would your friends back in Dallas say?"

"One more thing I don't have to worry about," she said.

"Why do you need to be the one to fix everything?"

"You're my accountant. You know why. Because I've got gobs of money, so I need to use it to make things better."

"But why you? Why not other people? For that matter, most people with gobs of money sure as hell don't give it away like you do."

"Maybe they feel like they deserve it," she said.

He looked into her eyes and saw something he hadn't glimpsed before. "You really don't feel like you deserve it?" he said.

"Why should I have things easy when other people have them so hard? What did I do to deserve to live like a princess? Nothing. So I got the sperm jackpot when it came to my father. How is that fair?"

"You feel guilty," he said, the realization hitting him. "This is all about your guilt. How much are you going to have to give away to appease the guilt monster?" He shook his head. "Lord, you're even willing to marry someone you don't love."

She pulled her hand away and glowered at him. "Well, thank you very much, Dr. Jackson, amateur shrink, for that lovely analysis. I came down to the barn to feel better, to maybe even be able to sleep when I went back to bed, but you've totally ruined that."

"Sorry," he said. "I just hadn't realized you were so motivated by guilt, and it's guilt for no reason."

"Again, thanks for nothing," she said as she turned away.

Feeling a slice of his own guilt, he followed after her. "Wait a minute. I can turn this around."

"You already did," she said.

He reached for her shoulder. "Come on. Give me a chance."

She stopped, although he could tell she didn't want to, and shot him a dark glance. "Why should I?"

"Because I promise I'll make you feel different," he said.

She paused, then let out a sigh. "Not the best sell I've ever heard," she said.

"And you know I don't promise what I can't deliver," he told her.

She moved her head in a circle. "Okay. I'll give you five minutes."

"Deal." He took her hand and led her back toward Rowdy's stall.

"Where are we going?" she asked. "Why are we—"

"Just do what I tell you, and I promise you'll feel different."

She slowed her steps. "I'm not sure I'm going to like this."

"You will," he said firmly, tugging her the last few steps to Rowdy's stall. The gelding immediately walked to greet them. "See how happy he is to see you?"

"Because I give him treats," she said.

"He's like most men. They all want your treats, one way or another," Jackson said, his own gaze straying to her curves. "You have a lot of treats."

She shot him a wary glance. "Careful, that was almost a compliment."

He pulled a lump of sugar from his pocket. "I want you to give this to him," he said.

"I did that last night. And tonight I gave him an apple."

"I know, but then I want you to do something else."

"What?"

"I want you to stroke him."

She bit her lip. "Why is this so important to you?"

"Because it's important to you," he said. "I can tell that it is, and I can help you if you let me."

"You sound pretty confident," she said.

"I told you before I don't promise what I can't deliver." He lifted her hand and put the sugar cube on her palm. "Give it to him, then pet him."

She bit her lip again but slid her hand toward the horse. Rowdy immediately took his treat. Then Jackson lifted her hand to the horse's neck, guiding her to rub him. Rowdy responded like a gentleman.

"Look. He's wiggling his nose," Jackson said, liking the way her hand felt within his. "He likes it."

She gave a soft half laugh and rubbed the horse on her own. "I think he does." She stroked Rowdy a couple times more, then slowly moved backward, which put the back of her body against his.

Jackson felt an overwhelming urge to slide his hands around her belly and bury his face in her hair. It wasn't rational. In fact, if he went through with it, it would be as stupid as hell. He burned with curiosity about how she would respond. Depending on her mood, she could slap him or give in to whatever it was that shimmered between them.

She turned around and looked into his eyes. "Thanks," she said and lifted on tiptoe to skim her lips over his cheek.

The breezy kiss made his gut knot. The little caress was her way of saying, *Thanks, but don't count on getting too close*. It got under his skin enough that he gave in to an impulse. He reached for her hand and pulled her back.

Her eyes widened in surprise. "What—"

"I promised I would make you feel different," he said, pulling her closer.

"You did," she conceded.

"That was step one," he said and lowered his head. "This is step two." He pressed his mouth against her soft, puffy lips and immediately felt himself grow hard.

She opened her mouth as if she couldn't decide to quit or continue, and he made the choice for her when he slid his tongue past her lips. He felt her body stiffen in an instant of surprise, but then she slid her hands around his shoulders, pressed her breasts into his chest, and lured his tongue deeper into her mouth.

She rubbed her curvy female body against his, and it was all he could do not to rip off her clothes and nail her against the wall of the barn. The force of the primitive urge took his breath.

Sliding his hands low on her back, he pulled her against his aching crotch and slid his tongue over hers. He felt her tug his shirt loose and rub her hands over his bare abdomen, and the temperature in the barn rose exponentially.

Jackson sucked in a quick draft of air and pulled his mouth from hers, swearing under his breath. He stared into her eyes, dark with arousal, and swore again.

She licked her lips as she gasped for her own breath, and she might as well have stroked him intimately with her pink tongue. "If that was step two, what is step three?"

"There is no step three," he said, more for himself than for her. "You are a client. There shouldn't have been step two."

She narrowed her eyes. "I'm not just a client to you."

"That's right. You're the key to a promotion and a bonus, and you're a pain in the ass."

She glanced away, but not before he glimpsed a flash of hurt in her eyes. Then she lifted her chin, and her gaze trailed down the front of him, lingering on his crotch before she met his gaze. "Your ass isn't what's going to be hurting tonight. Enjoy your cold shower," she said and walked out of the barn.

Jackson was left with the tempting, taunting image

of her round ass and a hard-on that showed no signs of quitting.

Geoffrey dutifully helped Lori clean the cabins the next morning. When she went to clean the stalls, he wandered to the corral and watched Maria finishing up the morning session with horse therapy. She was firm with the horses, yet gentle and encouraging with the children.

One young girl kept reaching to touch Maria's long wavy hair. Maria picked her up and set her on her hip, allowing the girl to play with her hair. She was so beautiful she took Geoffrey's breath away.

There was something wild and wounded about her that stirred him. He wondered what her story was, why she seemed to carry a chip on her shoulder, what kind of men she'd had in her past. There had to be dozens who'd tried to get her affection.

That body, that fire, could drive a man to do something reckless. As if she knew he was watching her, she glanced up at him. She met his gaze for a searing few seconds, then glanced away as if dismissing him.

She may as well have thrown down a gauntlet. Her dismissal was a challenge. He would love to take her up on it. Closing his eyes, he thought of his family obligation. No matter how tempting Maria was, he had to stick to the plan. Lori Granger was the woman who could save his family. Not Maria.

That afternoon, however, Geoffrey wasn't sure how it happened, but Virginia assigned him the task of helping Maria in the kitchen. Lori had left to go grocery shopping with Virginia.

Maria sighed and shook her head. She muttered in

Spanish for several moments as she chopped a whole chicken into pieces. Although he didn't understand the words, her tone was unmistakable.

"Pardon me, but if you're going to insult me, would you please do so in a language I can understand so I can at least defend myself?"

She chopped off a chicken leg and met his gaze. "I was talking to myself, but if you must know, I was saying it was stupid to pretend that you would actually help me in the kitchen."

"Why is that stupid?"

"You know how to cook?"

He knew how to use a microwave, a toaster, and a teapot. "I've spent some time in the kitchen. Why don't you give me a try?"

She gave him a considering glance. "Okay." She went to the cupboard, pulled out two large onions, and gave him a knife. "I need these diced."

Geoffrey shrugged. "Right-o. Where's the food processor?"

Maria smiled. "*You* are the food processor."

Geoffrey faced the task like a man—more importantly, an Englishman. Englishmen didn't cry, and he was bloody well determined not to cry.

After he finished the first onion, his nose started to run, so he began to breathe through his mouth. As he completed the last of his slicing and dicing, he triumphantly offered Maria the spoils of his victory. A pile of diced onion.

She lifted a dark eyebrow. "*Bueno,*" she said. "I'm surprised."

"No need to be," he said. "I told you I'm quite handy in the kitchen."

Maria pulled two more huge onions from the cupboard. "Then you won't mind dicing a couple more."

With the stiff upper lip bred into him, Geoffrey sliced and diced the second two onions. This time, however, he decided to take advantage of the opportunity to indulge his curiosity about Maria.

"You're not married, are you?" he asked.

"No," she said.

"Do you have a lover or a boyfriend?" he asked. "Or several?"

She frowned at him. "That's none of your business."

"That must mean you have a dozen lovers but you don't like to show off."

She glanced up at him, her eyes widened in surprise. "I do *not*—"

"Aha," he said, continuing to chop and dice. "But you could have."

"Not around here," she said. "There aren't a lot of men around." She shrugged as she placed chicken parts into a casserole dish. "It's probably for the best. Men aren't dependable."

He blinked. "That's a bit of a global generalization, wouldn't you say? Surely some men are dependable."

"Very few," she said.

"That you've met," he corrected. "Have you always lived in Texas?"

She nodded. "Yes."

"Do you like it here?"

She shrugged again. "I know nothing else. I know I like Virginia's ranch much better than my father's house."

Geoffrey studied her expression and felt an uneasiness about the way her voice lowered when she mentioned her father's house.

He paused for a long moment. "He was abusive to you," he said.

She didn't look up at him. "Yes. He gave me the scar."

He looked at the jagged scar that ran from her cheek nearly to her jaw. "This may sound crazy, but I don't notice the scar unless you mention it."

That must have gotten her attention, because she glanced up to meet his gaze. "How can you not notice it?"

His lips twitched. "You have so many other things to look at."

She gave him a hard look, then glanced away. "You lie."

"I do not," he said, unable to keep indignation from his voice.

She met his gaze again. "It's impossible not to notice my scar. It covers half my face."

"It depends what you're focusing on," he said, setting down his knife. "Take your hair, for example."

"What about my hair?"

"It's long and beautiful, wavy. I wonder how it would feel in my hands. I wonder how it smells."

She gave him a half glance of flashing eyes before looking away. "It smells like onions and chicken."

He chuckled. "Then there are your eyes, so dark, full of secrets. You have many other very watchable—" He cleared his throat as his gaze wandered to her breasts and hips. "Attributes."

She met his eyes, and her lips tilted in a reluctant

smile. "You are a strange man. Are you finished with the onions?"

"Two more minutes," he said and quickly finished the task. He offered her the pile. "Don't tell me you have more for me to do."

"No," she said. "Four is enough."

"That was a stinky job," he told her.

"Yes."

Something about this woman made him feel reckless. Just looking at her made his adrenaline hum. "I believe it made my lips go numb."

She wrinkled her eyebrow as she studied his mouth. "They went numb? Are you allergic to onion? *Ay caramba,* you should have told me," she said as she drew closer to him.

"Actually, you can fix them if you wouldn't mind."

"How?"

"I believe you just need to press your mouth against mine, and then they would be better."

She blinked in surprise, then shook her head at him. "You are either very brave or very stupid to ask me to kiss you when I have a knife in my hand."

"Agreed," he said, throwing a wary glance at the knife out of the corner of his eye. "I'm hoping such bravery and the dicing of four onions will be rewarded."

For three seconds, she considered it. He saw the temptation in her eyes and got a rush from it. One second later, she tossed her head and turned away. "You are *loco.*"

As his gaze refused to budge from her gorgeous backside, he couldn't agree more. He was definitely *loco.*

*"It's always best to let a man feel like he's chasing you.
When he finally gets you, he needs to have that same
feeling he has when he bags an elk."*
—SUNNY COLLINS

Chapter Thirteen

Jackson stayed away from the barn for the next two nights.
The situation with Lori was getting too screwy. Her fear
of horses was none of his business, but he wanted to help
her. She got under his skin and into his head way too easily. He didn't just want to help her. He wanted to help
himself to her. And she wasn't exactly kicking him away.

By the third night, though, he was restless and decided
he should check on her. She was, after all, the reason he
was here.

He went to the barn and saw that the duke hadn't joined
her. He found that curious. If Geoffrey were smart, he
would be spending every spare minute with Lori.

She stood at the far end of the barn, crooning to
Rowdy. Straining against the door, she stroked the horse's
neck. He felt a rush of pleasure that she had made such

progress. For a woman who pretended to be a blonde air-head, she possessed a lot of courage.

He watched, unable to breathe, as she pulled open the door and stepped inside Rowdy's stall. Swallowing an oath, he wondered if this was her first time. He hoped Rowdy wouldn't frighten her or, worse, hurt her.

That last thought twisted his stomach, and he rushed to the stall. Inside, she stood next to the large horse, petting him and talking to him. Rowdy nodded in approval. Jackson stood staring as if his shoes were nailed to the barn floor. The image before him snapped inside his brain like a photo of Lori, small, vulnerable, but determined, and the horse responding to her.

He finally exhaled and Rowdy pricked up his ears and looked at him. Lori's gaze followed. Surprise widened her eyes, and then she turned back to Rowdy, stroked him once more, and moved toward the stall door. Rowdy followed.

She opened the door and slid through the small opening. "I didn't expect you."

"I didn't mean to interrupt your rendezvous," he said, shoving his hands into his pockets to keep from touching her.

"It's okay. He let me in his stall with him last night," she said and smiled. "He's like a little kid. Really sweet."

He nodded, feeling his heart tugged by the expression on her face. "Are you ready for the next step?"

She shook her head. "I don't know when I'll be ready for that."

"You've come a long way."

"Baby steps," she said. "And he's a good guy. Maria has made sure of that."

"She isn't as generous in her comments about you," he said.

"She's in a different position, and she doesn't know me," Lori said, then laughed. "Not like those who love me know me."

"So, if I grabbed a bridle and invited you to go for a ride tonight, how would you respond?" he asked on a very rare impulse.

She shrugged. "I'm safe because it's all supposition."

He nodded and rubbed his chin. "Okay. Hold that thought." He walked to the tack room, grabbed a bridle, and returned. "Hey, Rowdy," he said in a low voice to the gelding. "Wanna go for a little ride?"

Rowdy immediately moved to his stall door and pricked up his ears. Jackson chuckled. He put the bridle on the horse, led him outside the stall, and mounted him bareback. He looked at Lori. "We're past supposition now. What are you going to do?"

Backing away, Lori inhaled and glanced at the horse. Nerves danced in her stomach.

Then she looked at Jackson. Strong and in control, he hugged Rowdy with his thighs and held the reins not too tight and not too slack. He could take care of her, she thought. In the next moment, with sickening clarity, she remembered that accidents could happen.

Her palms clammy with fear, and her throat tight with apprehension, she stood there frozen. She felt him study her and hoped she didn't look as terrified as she felt.

"Hey, if you're not ready," he began.

Despite her crippling fear, or perhaps because of it, Lori felt something inside her rip. She was tired of being afraid. Sick of it. She lifted her head. "I'm not, but it's time," she said and forced her feet to move toward him and Rowdy.

"You sure?"

"Not at all," she said, lifting her hands for him to help her. "But I don't want to overthink this. I just want to do it."

He bent over and wrapped his hand around hers. "Give me your best jump," he said.

She leapt, and a second later she sprawled onto Rowdy's back. She clung to Jackson, wrapping her hands around his taut torso. As if Rowdy sensed this was a momentous occasion, the horse danced and snorted.

"Hold tight," Jackson said and brushed one of his hands over hers. He swore under his breath. "Your hands are like ice. Are you sure—"

"Don't ask, just ride," she interrupted him.

"Okay," he said and nudged Rowdy slowly forward. They took a couple slow walks around the barn. Lori figured he wanted her to get used to being on a horse again. The rocking motion felt alternately foreign and familiar. By the fourth time around, Lori was ready for more.

"Step it up," she said.

"No need to rush."

"I'm already here," she said. "You may as well give me a real ride, Jackson."

The urgency in her words made every muscle in Jackson's body tighten in attention. He felt a surge of pride that he'd been the one to get her to ride again, that he'd tapped a little of the passion she'd shut down for years. He couldn't help being curious about all that banked passion and how many different ways she would release it. The strange intimacy between them wrapped around him like a spell of the night, making him aware of every breath she took, every exhale against the back of his neck, the sensation of her breasts crushed against his back, her thighs open and hugging him.

"Okay," he muttered and nudged Rowdy into a slow trot and away from the safe circle of the corral.

Lori's heart beat in her throat, making it difficult to breathe, and when she did, she caught a draft of Jackson's clean male scent. She felt the remnants of terror, but exhilaration was taking over. Holding tightly to Jackson, she relished the wind in her hair and even the bumpiness of Rowdy's trot. Her bottom might be a little sore tomorrow, but she didn't care. The night was clear, and the stars sparkled brightly against the black sky.

She sensed the horse's desire to go faster, to break free of his in-between pace. She felt the same itch. "Let him run," she said.

"Hold on," Jackson said, and seconds later, Rowdy began to run.

The speed gave her a thrill she hadn't experienced since the last time she'd ridden a horse. Another shot of exhilaration bolted through, and she laughed.

"You okay?" Jackson asked.

"No," she said, clinging to him. "I'm wonderful."

She didn't know how long the ride lasted, but she felt as excited as a kid when the barn came in sight and he slowed to a walk. Lori inhaled and blew out a long breath, dipping her head against Jackson's broad, strong back. "Oh, that was great."

A half beat of silence followed, and then he gave a low chuckle. "I'm glad it was good for you."

Giddy, she laughed with him. He led Rowdy on a cooldown walk and stopped just outside the barn. "Scoot back a little," he told her and swung his leg over to get off the horse. He lifted his hands to her. "Your turn."

She looked into his eyes for a moment, feeling something monumental shift inside her. He had taken care of her. She could trust him. She couldn't remember feeling that way about another man. Jackson wiggled his hands, prompting her to move. Stretching out her arms, she slid downward. Jackson caught her against him, her head above his.

Lori saw a flicker of powerful emotions shoot across his gaze—awareness, passion, and something else she couldn't name. He paused and allowed her to slide down his body, making her intimately aware of his strength and her own desire. It was all she could do not to kiss him. Blindsided by a blast of need, she could barely breathe. She felt a sudden snap of clarity.

"Let's get married," she said breathlessly.

He stared at her in disbelief. "What?"

She took another quick breath. "Let's get married."

Jackson blinked, then swore under his breath. "Have you lost all your marbles?"

"No," she said, trying not to feel disappointed by his response.

Staring at her as if she'd sprouted a third eye, he released her and backed away. He shook his head and opened his mouth.

"Hear me out," she interjected, talking before he could turn her down flat. "It actually makes a lot of sense. You're a very practical man. You know why I want to get married. I trust you. And you would get a very nice salary to put up with me. You're ambitious, and you like to be in control. The money you make from marrying me could give you the ability to do a lot of things on your own. You wouldn't be held back by the limitations at the accounting firm. In a way," she added, "it would provide you with more freedom than you've ever had."

He looked at her for a long moment, then scrubbed his face with his hand. "By tying myself to you," he added.

"For six years," she said. "And I haven't gotten the impression you've been spending your spare time looking for love or romance." Maybe sex, she thought, but not the former two she'd mentioned.

"I'm not like your British duke," he said. "I know too much about you."

"What do you mean by that?" she asked, offended.

"I know that when you walk through the door, trouble's coming right with you."

Emotionally smashed, she bit her lip. "I assume that means your answer is no. You have no interest in taking on the horrendous job of being my husband for a limited time even though you would earn a nice check from it. Because I'm obviously more frightening and dangerous than dancing in a rodeo clown suit in front of an angry bull. Heaven knows, I never dreamed I could scare the mighty Jackson—"

"Okay, okay," he interjected. "You've made your point." He rested one hand on his hip and studied her with a level gaze. "You took me by surprise," he said with a shrug. "I'll think about it."

I'll think about it. Insulted, she swallowed a dozen pithy retorts. She nearly bit her tongue in half not to say them aloud. Instead she took a deep breath and smiled. "You do that," she said and stepped closer to him. She lifted her head, moving her lips in a moue and making a soft kissing sound. "Thanks for the ride. It was the best."

Stepping back, she saw a flash of heat cross his eyes. "Sweet dreams," she said and walked away. Cursing his name with every other step she took.

Jackson stared after Lori, feeling as if he'd been hit with a tire iron. What made it worse was that he had a hard-on that felt like iron, too. He swore under his breath. What the hell was she thinking telling him they should get married? What had inspired that insane idea in her head?

Hearing a snort from Rowdy, Jackson glanced behind him and looked at the horse. The light dawned. It was the ride, he realized. The ride on the horse had done it. He twisted his lips. Who would have thought the way to Lori's pocketbook would have been through a ride on a horse?

His mind raced with possibilities as he led Rowdy to his stall and settled the horse down for the night. She was offering a lot of money in exchange for being her husband. He could use that money as his stake for the real-estate venture he wanted to start. That kind of money could change a man's life. He could move his mother and brother to a better place. His mom wouldn't have to work so hard.

But how would a sane man survive being married to Lori? She was a combination of crazy and irresistible. Would she ever learn to control her spending? Would he be able to stand by and watch her go through her daddy's money like toilet paper? Even for good causes?

What about sex? He would have to be committed to an asylum to agree to a marriage with no sex. Being around her every day, he would have to take her. And he suspected he would need to do so repeatedly. The strength of his sexual desire for her caught him off guard.

He swore under his breath again and shook his head.

He wasn't going to think about this anymore tonight. He still had her perfume on him from the way she'd clung to him during the ride. He still remembered how her breasts and inner thighs had felt against him. He remembered the thrill he'd felt that she'd not only been willing to go with him, but also how she'd urged him to go faster.

The scent of her alone was enough to mess up his head this late at night. No. He would put her and her crazy offer out of his mind until he could think straight. He just hoped that would happen in this century.

Bored out of his mind and unable to sleep, Geoffrey roamed the house and made his way to the only place he'd ever really felt at home, in front of a keyboard. Closing the door to the room at the end of a vacant hall, he sighed with relief. Since a tuner had come to repair the old piano, he'd been playing it every chance he got during the last couple of days.

His stepmother had called his cell phone approximately eleven times during the last twenty-four hours, but he hadn't picked up. She wanted a progress report, and Geoffrey knew, even though he'd proposed to Lori, that the situation was moving at glacial speed.

His stepmother would harp and pressure him, and he bloody well didn't want to hear it. He was supposed to be wooing Lori, but God help him, he was totally fascinated by Maria. She was female fire personified. It was as if her very presence caused an internal combustion inside him, and she barely gave him the time of day.

He slid his hands over the keys, listening for pitch problems. Nothing so far, he thought, concentrating. A melody tugged at him, slipping through that part of his mind that he'd never understood but found magically seductive. He played the first notes, added a chord, another measure.

He felt a flicker of excitement and tried to commit the notes to memory. More of the melody slipped through his mind, and he chased after it the same way a child would chase a butterfly. Struggling with a chord, he heard the rusty sound of the door opening. He immediately stopped. "Sorry if I woke you," he said to whoever had come into the room. "I thought I was far enough away not to interrupt anyone's sleep." He glanced over his shoulder and saw Maria in the doorway.

His breath stopped in his throat. She wore a T-shirt that hugged her ample breasts and pajama shorts that showed the graceful length of her curvy tanned legs. Her expression, for once, wasn't hostile.

"I couldn't sleep, so I decided to clean a closet down the hall," she said with a shrug. "I heard you."

Unable to tear his gaze from her, he nodded. "Oh."

A silence followed, filled with curiosity and that fire she emanated that always seemed to start a blaze in him. "Well, you don't have to stop."

He blinked. "You'd like to hear more?" His mind boggled by her nod, he turned back to the piano and played a Brahms intermezzo he'd memorized years ago. When he finished, he glanced up and found her standing beside the piano.

She sighed. "So beautiful. I always wanted to learn to play a musical instrument. Music is like magic, don't you think?"

He nodded. "Yes, I've always thought so."

"Can you play something else?"

He gave a half smile. "I can play a lot of things. What would you like to hear?"

"Something sweet, but passionate. What was the song you were playing when I walked in?" she said and sat down on the bench beside him.

"Oh, that was something I heard in my head," he said, too aware of her proximity. She smelled like a combination of roses and fresh spices.

Her eyes widened in surprise. "You mean you just made it up?"

"Well, I heard it. It was just a few chords, a few measures, really."

"Have you made up other things?"

He reluctantly nodded. "I've tried."

"Play one," she commanded. "Play one you've composed."

This was the nicest she'd been to him since she'd hauled him back to the ranch on the back of her horse. He bloody well wasn't going to refuse her. "Okay, but no rotten fruit or pies," he said.

He played one of his recent compositions and held the last note for a few beats, then turned to her.

"That was beautiful," she said. "Can you play another?"

He would play all night to see that soft look in her eyes. "Of course," he said and played another. That piece eased into another and another.

Maria sighed at the end. "It's late," she said but didn't move.

He nodded. "It is."

She met his gaze. "This was nice."

"Yes, it was." Her face was inches from his, and it was

all he could do not to lower his mouth to her exotic lips. He wanted to explore her texture, taste her, plunder her.

She glanced downward for a second, then met his gaze again, her dark eyes full of secrets he wanted to learn. "Thank you for the private concert, Geoffrey."

"My pleasure," he said, feeling his gut tighten in a dozen knots. "I'm quite inexpensive," he said. "If you should like another—" He cleared his throat. "Session."

Her lips tilted in a sensual smile and she stood. "Thank you. I look forward to it." She lifted her hand and brushed his hair from his forehead. "You should go to bed. Morning will come early."

"Yes," he said, but he had a strong feeling that he wouldn't sleep. Maria had infiltrated his senses, and it would take more than a shower to get his equilibrium back.

The following morning when Geoffrey saw Maria in the kitchen, his heart squeezed tight in his chest. "Good morning, Maria. How are you?"

"Busy," she said in a dismissive voice. "Everyone else has eaten and left. There are biscuits and eggs in the warming pan." She nodded her head toward the opposite counter.

"You waited for me," he said, feeling a rush of delight.

She looked at him as if he were crazy. "No." She lifted two large bags. "I was preparing lunches for the campers. Don't forget to clean up," she said and left the kitchen.

Geoffrey felt like a fool. Why did he care what this woman thought of him? The tender side of her he'd glimpsed last night must have been an aberration. Yes, she was full of fire, but she clearly wanted to use that fire only to keep him away. Yes, she fascinated him, but nothing would come of it.

Being pissed provided Lori with extra energy to clean the bathroom floors. She'd made a huge mistake by telling Jackson they should get married. In the light of day, she knew she'd been impulsive.

That didn't change how much the ride had meant to her, though. Even surrounded by the scent of ammonia and scrubbing a white porcelain sink, she could easily recall the sensation of wind on her face, the combined scents of horseflesh and Jackson, his taut abdomen beneath her hands.

The exhilaration and sense of freedom had been the most exciting, amazing thing she'd experienced in years. The ride had made her feel alive and she wanted more. With him. She scowled at the thought.

"Hullo," Geoffrey said from the doorway. "So sorry I'm late this morning. Can I help?"

She glanced up at him and saw a glum expression on his face. "Are you sure you want to? The floors in the main cabin are all that's left."

"The activity will do me good," he said. "Can't have you thinking I'm a bum."

"Of course not," she said. "Anything wrong?"

He shrugged. "My stepmother is stalking me."

She winced in sympathy. "Oh. Can you put her on ignore?"

"I did that. She filled up my entire voice mail with messages. I probably shouldn't tell you this, but she thinks I'm completely incompetent. She has no confidence in me or my judgment."

Lori thought of Jackson and felt a bitter twist. "I can identify with that. I got the same thing from my father and—" She broke off. "Others."

Geoffrey looked up in surprise from the mop he was pushing. "That's bloody ridiculous," he said. "Look at you. You're perfectly capable of doing whatever you want. You have a good head on your shoulders and you can even—" He waved his hand. "You've become an excellent cleaner."

Lori laughed. "Are you trying to flirt with me? Telling me I'm a great bathroom cleaner."

"No flirting. I'm completely sincere."

"Thank you." She rubbed a spot on the mirror above the sink. "I'm not sure Maria would give me her stamp of approval yet."

"Yes, well, she doesn't seem to approve of much," he said in a testy voice. "Looks down her nose at most everyone."

"Oh, no," Lori said. "I thought she was getting less hostile toward you."

"Oh, no," Geoffrey said, shaking his head. "She looks at me like I'm something off the bottom of her shoe."

Lori frowned. "I wonder if I should talk to Virginia about it. Maria is entitled to her opinion, but she shouldn't be permitted to act nasty."

"No, I think you shouldn't involve Virginia," Geoffrey rushed to say. "She appears to have enough on her mind."

"That's true," Lori said and turned to him. "So you and I have something in common. People think we're incompetent." She felt a trickle of irritation run down her back. "What gave these people the right to be so judgmental? For that matter, why should we care?"

Geoffrey met her gaze and nodded. "You're right. Bloody hell with them."

> *"There will always be more than one man.*
> *The trick is choosing the best one."*
> —SUNNY COLLINS

Chapter Fourteen

Bloody hell with him. Or them, Lori mentally corrected herself. Geoffrey's phrase became her mantra. The more she thought about Jackson's response to her quasi-proposal, the more pissed off she became.

Sure, she'd surprised him, but he hadn't said one positive word in response. Unless she counted his grudgingly muttered *I'll think about it.*

She hadn't met Jackson's gaze once during dinner. She would have felt more satisfied if she hadn't sensed that he was ignoring her out of complete disinterest.

She heaped a helping of mashed potatoes onto her plate, feeling another rush of pique. "Virginia, the meal is delicious."

"Thank you." Virginia beamed. "But Maria helped."

Lori felt resistant to offering any compliments to Virginia's capable assistant. Was there anything the young woman couldn't do? "Thank you both," she said and turned her attention to Geoffrey sitting beside her. "You're enjoying it, too, aren't you?"

Geoffrey patted his stomach. "Yes, I am. Thank you, both of you. With a meal this good, I should sing for my supper, but I don't want to hurt your ears."

Lori laughed. "Perhaps you could play something on that old piano upstairs. Didn't you say you could play?"

"I suppose I could," he said, and Lori thought she saw him shoot a quick glance toward Maria. She suspected he feared her unceasing criticism.

"That sounds grand," Virginia said. "Since the campers have left and we won't have any for another couple of days, we can all take the time to enjoy it."

"I need to do some evening chores with the horses," Maria quickly said.

"I already mucked out the stalls," Lori said cheerfully.

"Thank you, Lori." Virginia nodded in approval. "Then it's decided. We'll take our desserts upstairs for an after-dinner concert."

"That room is very dusty," Maria said.

Everyone glanced at her, and she gave a forced shrug. "I would think it would be dusty," she amended. "Since no one has used it in a while."

"I'll take care of it," Lori said, rising. "I've become a dusting rock star in the past week. So if you'll excuse me."

"I'll help," Jackson said, also standing.

She glanced at him in surprise. "It's not necessary. I can—"

"Two are better than one," he said, his focused gaze on her making her stomach dip. "We can get the job done more quickly."

"Okay," she said and took her plate to the sink.

"I can get that," Virginia said.

"It'll be one less for you to do," Lori said, sliding her arm around the older woman's slim shoulders and dropping a quick kiss on her forehead. "This way I get my dessert faster."

Virginia laughed and shook her head. "I'm so glad you came, Lori. You've brought a lot of joy with you."

"Thank you," she said, Virginia's words filling up a hollow place inside her. She took her dish to the kitchen, rinsed it and her flatware, and automatically reached for Jackson's when she sensed him behind her.

"Do my eyes deceive me? Are you turning into Suzy Homemaker?"

"Just trying to be helpful. Useful. I realize you may believe that's a huge stretch for me, but—"

"I didn't say that," he said.

"No, but you thought it," she said in her best couldn't-care-less voice. She rinsed his plate, and his hand caught her wrist like a handcuff, stopping her midmovement.

He pulled her toward him, searching her face. "What is going on in that head of yours now?"

"Nothing out of the ordinary," she said and forced a smile. "Just the regular stuff. Trying to be a better person. Exploring my options." She tried to pull her hand loose, but he wouldn't allow it.

"Options," he prompted.

She nodded. "I have you to thank for that. You've told me there's more than one way to solve problems, so I'm exploring all my options."

He narrowed his eyes. "If you're talking about the duke—"

"Lori, sweetheart," Virginia said as she entered the room, "you don't have to load the dishwasher."

Lori seized the opportunity to remove her wrist from Jackson's clutch and immediately put his plate into the dishwasher. "I'm done. I'm sure Jackson will help with the rest. I'll scoot upstairs and get the room ready for our little concert."

She dashed out of the room without looking back, but she could feel Jackson's eyes boring a hole into her as she left.

Five minutes later, she'd dusted the room and pulled out a vacuum cleaner to use on the scarred wooden floor partially covered with an area rug. Maria hadn't been exaggerating when she'd called the room dusty. Lori quickly took care of the floor, then used the vacuum attachments on the chairs.

A hand on her back startled her, and she whirled around to find Jackson looming over her. She put her hand to her chest, her heart racing. "A little warning would be nice. You scared me to death."

"Do you need some help?" he asked, surprising her with the offer.

She blinked, then glanced around the room. "I don't think so. It looks okay to me."

He looked up at the light fixtures and ran his finger over a sideboard. "I'll take care of the tall stuff."

"Thanks," she said, feeling something strange unfurl within her stomach. Maybe it was the mashed potatoes, she told herself and turned back to the chairs.

Stealing a glance at him and watching his broad shoulders stretch as he dusted the top of the sideboard, she felt an odd sense of expectancy, anticipation, as if something big was about to take place. It wasn't rational, which meant she should probably dismiss it. It wasn't as if Jackson had decided he was in love with her and couldn't live without her.

She rolled her eyes at herself. That couldn't be what she truly wanted. If it was, she was just pathetic. The truth was he probably expected to take her to bed. Lori's emotions veered again, this time to indignation. "Bloody hell with him," she murmured under her breath, determined to get her mind back on track.

"Excuse me?" he said, turning toward her, his eyebrows lifted in inquiry. "What did you say?"

Shrugging, she felt her cheeks heat. "Nothing," she said and turned again to her task.

Two minutes later, Virginia and Maria stood in the doorway carrying trays of slices of pie and cups of coffee. Geoffrey stood behind them. "I offered to help, but they wouldn't let me."

"You're providing the entertainment. That's good enough," Virginia said.

Geoffrey raked his hand through his hair. "*Entertainment* may be stretching it," he muttered.

His nerves were obvious as he sat down on the piano bench and cracked his fingers. Feeling sorry for him, Lori squeezed his shoulder and tried to reassure him. "Relax, this isn't an audition."

Lori heard the clash of a spoon against fine china and glanced over her shoulder at Maria, who may as well have been shooting lasers through her. Lori lifted her shoulders. What was that woman's problem?

Lori sat down in the only seat left, next to Jackson. All too aware of his closeness, she noticed the strength of his legs stretched out within sight of her, one of his large hands resting on his leg. During the ride they'd shared, she'd become intimately aware of Jackson's strength and the easy way he'd kept Rowdy under control.

She didn't want to think about that now. Closing her eyes, she tried to concentrate on the romantic show tune Geoffrey played. She was surprised at how well he played. He stroked the keys, producing and evoking heart-wrenching emotion. When he stopped, everyone in the room was silent.

"That was beautiful," Lori said. "You really do have a gift," she said to Geoffrey.

He ducked his hand in modesty. "Thank you. Another?"

"Yes, yes," Virginia said, clapping her hands. "More. More. You've already earned back every bite we've fed you."

"In that case," Geoffrey said and began another song. He played for thirty minutes, and although Lori knew the listeners could continue, she didn't want to take advantage of Geoffrey.

"We'd probably better stop now if we ever expect to talk Geoffrey into playing for us again," Lori said, rising. "I should get some pie for him."

"I already got his pie," Maria said, following Lori to her feet.

"Good," Lori said. "Do you want some tea with it?"

"I can get his tea," Maria retorted.

Taken aback by the woman's response, Lori shrugged. "Fine, thank you." She glanced at Geoffrey. "You want to go for a walk after you have your dessert?"

His gaze slid toward Maria, then back to Lori. He

paused an extra beat, and she wondered what was going on.

Jackson cleared his throat. "Lori, let's check on the horses."

She sighed. "Okay, but I'll be back soon," she said to Geoffrey, who still looked like a deer caught in headlights.

"I'll take the dishes downstairs," Virginia insisted, shooing Lori away. "And Geoffrey, thank you for the beautiful concert."

Lori followed Jackson downstairs and out the front door into the dark night. The way his wide shoulders narrowed to his hips in a perfect V shape drew her gaze. Nothing feminine about this man. Nothing even metrosexual. She wished he didn't capture her attention so easily. She wished she didn't care what he thought of her or how he felt about her.

Thoroughly distracted, she caught her foot on a tree root and went sprawling forward against his back. She automatically flung her arms around him.

"What the—" He covered her arms with his hands and whipped around, drawing her against him.

"Sorry," she said, breathless from the fall, not from her proximity to him, not from the intensity of his gaze on her, and not from the sensation of being in his arms. "I tripped."

His gaze wrapped around hers for a long moment, and her heart beat ten times before she remembered to pull away. Pushing against him, she stumbled backward.

"Okay," he said, glancing behind her. "I guess we're far enough away. What's your game with the duke?"

She blinked. "Game? There's no game. It's all out in

the open. His family needs money. I need a husband. He has asked me to marry him." She paused and added, "Again."

He narrowed his eyes. "When did that happen?"

"This morning," she said.

He gave a whistle and shook his head. "I knew you were fickle, but this takes the cake. You propose to me one night, and less than two days later—"

"I didn't propose," she interjected. "I said we should get married. It wasn't as if I got down on one knee and begged you." Every muscle in her body stiffened. "If you thought I would beg you, then you're wrong."

"But you couldn't give me fifteen minutes to consider it."

"You took more than fifteen minutes, and you haven't exactly been banging down my door to get to me since we had the discussion."

"Was I supposed to bang down your door? Was that what you wanted?"

She bit her lip at the raw sexuality in his gaze. "I didn't say that. What I'm saying is that you haven't overwhelmed me with your eagerness."

"I didn't know that was part of the job description," he said, moving toward her.

"It wasn't," she said, her nerves jumping. She shook her head, flustered. "I just got the impression you weren't interested."

"So you moved on to the next guy," he said. "Is this what our marriage will be like? If I don't give you the answer you like whenever you want it, however you want it, then you'll move on to the next man?"

Lori's heart stopped. *Is this what our marriage will be*

like? That sounded as if Jackson was actually considering marrying her. She stared at him, terrified, thrilled.

"Well?"

Lori opened her mouth and moved it, but no sound came out. She closed it for a moment to gather her thoughts. "No," she said and cleared her throat. "If you and I get married, I won't be moving on to the next man if I don't like what you say." She paused a half beat. "If that were the case, I wouldn't have mentioned the idea in the first place, because it's not as if I've liked every word that has come out of your mouth."

He stepped closer. "Then why me, Lori? Your duke would probably go along with everything you want. He would never argue with you. You know we will."

"Well, you wouldn't prevent my access to the money."

"No, but I would do my damnedest to persuade you not to donate your entire inheritance to Designer Duds for Dogs charity."

"I have to agree that there are more worthy causes."

"Why me?"

Lori's heart squeezed tight in her chest. Why him? Because she felt things for him. Things she'd never felt before. But she didn't want to tell him that. "I told you. I trust you."

He stood silently, towering over her for what felt like an eternity. "Okay. I'm in."

Lori felt light-headed. The bones in her knees seemed to melt. Her pulse pounded in her head. Oh. My. God. He'd said yes.

His eyes widening in alarm, he swore as he reached out to her. "You're white as a ghost. You look like you're going to faint."

She clung to him and took baby sips of air. "I'll be okay," she said in a voice that sounded wispy to her own ears.

"Did I scare you?"

She gulped over the lump in her throat. "No. I'm just surprised. Very surprised."

"You sure you're not having second thoughts?" he asked, studying her.

Try tenth or twelfth thoughts, she thought. "Oh, no," she said in a high-pitched voice. "I asked you. Remember."

"Yes, but—"

Her mind going a million miles a minute, she moved her head in a circle. "Vegas," she said. "Let's go to Vegas."

"Vegas," he repeated, blinking.

She nodded. "Vegas. Tomorrow night."

He swore again. "Tomorrow night? Why so soon?"

So she wouldn't chicken out, she thought. "If you're sure and I'm sure, there's no need to wait. Is there?"

He met her gaze, and she saw the second he decided to accept her challenge. "No. There isn't."

"A new pair of shoes can brighten any day."
—SUNNY COLLINS

Chapter Fifteen

Maria slammed the teapot down on the tray so hard Geoffrey was surprised it didn't break. She looked at him with eyes so fiery he briefly wondered if she had some kind of superpower that would make his internal organs explode if he looked at her too long. Ridiculous, he thought, but he still looked away.

"How much sugar do you want?" she asked.

He glanced at her and, rising, shook his head. "Thank you. I can do it myself."

"No," she said, the spoon poised above a tiny sugar bowl.

Geoffrey assessed the situation, thankful there were no knives within Maria's reach. "Two, thank you."

She stabbed the spoon into the sugar and dumped two heaping spoonfuls into the cup. "Cream?"

"Please," he said.

She dumped a generous amount of cream into the cup

and banged the spoon in a circular motion. "Here," she said, shoving the cup and saucer into his hands.

Geoffrey nearly spilled the liquid all over himself, but he managed to confine the splatter to the saucer. He cleared his throat. "Thank you."

She crossed her arms over her generous breasts and stared at him. "Well?" she said expectantly.

He paused a half beat. "Well, what?"

"The tea," she said, nodding toward the cup. "Did I make it right?"

He glanced down at the steaming cup. "I'm sure you did."

"Taste it."

It was still too hot, but heaven help him if he tried to tell her that. Gingerly lifting the cup to his lips, he took a small sip of the too-sweet, too-weak tea. "Perfect," he lied with a smile. "Perfect."

Her glare softened a smidgen, and she pushed a strand of her bangs behind her ear. "Good." She glanced away, dropped one of her hands to her hip, then lifted her arms again to cross her chest. "I don't suppose *Lori* has made tea for you."

He blinked at the odd question and chuckled. "Not at all. I'm not sure she knows how."

Maria lifted her chin, and her lips lifted the slightest bit into an almost smile. "She can't cook, either."

"I wouldn't be surprised if she couldn't," he agreed. "After all, she has staff for that."

Her face fell again. "I'm not wealthy," she said. "So I'm sure you wouldn't be interested in me."

When she turned to walk away, he felt an overwhelming sense of panic. "You would be wrong," he said, the words bubbling up from somewhere inside him. Somewhere that wouldn't be denied.

She stopped, her hand on the doorknob, and he watched her shoulders rise and fall as she took a breath and released it. "What do you mean?"

"I mean," he began, then broke off, utterly conflicted. "Please come back. Just for a few moments." Setting down his cup of tea, he returned to the piano and began to play the melody that had burned its way into his brain and heart over the last couple of days. He hadn't needed to write down the notes, because he couldn't escape the song. It followed him everywhere all the time, even when he slept. The music brimmed with passion and hints of sadness, strength, and vulnerability.

He stopped when the notes and chords in his mind stopped, although he knew it wasn't the end of the piece.

Silence clung to the air like humidity just before a summer rain. The only sound he could hear was his heart beating inside his head.

"Finish it," Maria finally whispered, walking toward him. "It's beautiful. Finish it. I want to hear the rest."

"That's all I know," he said, meeting her gaze. "I know it's not finished, but that's all I know."

"It's so beautiful. Why didn't you play it tonight for Virginia? And Lori." Her eyes narrowed slightly, more in pain than any other emotion he could read.

"It's not finished," he said, then added, "And it's a personal piece."

She lifted her eyebrows in surprise. "Then why did you play it for me?"

His heart hammered in his chest. This was so right.

Yet so wrong. But he couldn't seem to stop any of it. "The name of the piece is 'Maria.' "

She stared at him for a long moment, her gaze fixed on his, a dozen emotions flying through her dark eyes. Then she bit her lip and her eyes grew shiny. "You wrote it for me?"

"I wrote it because of you," he said. Because her being had taunted and tormented him from their first meeting. "I wrote it about you." He took a deep breath. "That was you in music. The reason it's not finished is because that's all I know."

She sat beside him on the piano bench. "No one has ever written a song about me." She lifted her hand to his face. "Why did you do it?" She shook her head. "Why didn't you write one for Lori?"

"Lori is a lovely person," he said, watching her gaze darken as he said the words. She started to pull her hand away from his face, but he caught it in his. "It's true. She is lovely. But she is not the woman who has captivated me like no other woman has. I never dreamed a woman could affect me this much. Never."

She lifted her chin, challenge and fire mixing in her gaze. "You are an odd man."

He blinked at her response. It wasn't exactly what he'd been hoping for, although if he got what he was hoping for, he'd be in a bloody vat of trouble. "I'm not sure what to—"

"Don't say anything right now," she told him. "You talk too much."

Affronted, he opened his mouth to correct her.

She covered his lips with her index finger and leaned against him. Her gorgeous, delicious breasts, about which he'd fantasized, brushed his chest, rendering him mute. "But your British accent makes up for it," she added with a smile. "So polite on the outside, but I can tell you're lusting after me in your heart."

His heart wasn't the only organ she was affecting at the moment. Holding his breath, he shifted slightly, praying she wouldn't move away from him.

She didn't. Instead, she leaned closer, mashing her splendid breasts against his chest. She lifted her lips to his. "You are very odd," she said against his lips. "But you are also cute. All those proper English manners. I wonder how bad you are underneath," she said, then took his mouth in a scorching kiss.

Geoffrey felt as if a fire blazed straight through him. His heart raced, his mind thundered. Music poured through him. A new sound, a new movement. He couldn't breathe, but he didn't care. He never wanted her to move away.

Her tongue taunted and tasted his, daring him to go deeper. He took the plunge, delving into her silken, sexy mouth. She was everything voluptuous, sexual, wild, and free. So amazing he couldn't have dreamed a woman like this.

Hungry, he devoured her mouth and slid his hands around her back, drawing her as close as he could. The soft catch of her breath and moan hit him like pure whiskey.

He lifted one of his hands to the side of her breast and she arched against him as if she wanted more. The movement made him hard as a rock. Pulling her onto his lap so that she straddled him, he slid his hand beneath her shirt and upward to cup her breast.

"Yes, yes," she said in a husky, sexy whisper, arching again, wiggling against his crotch.

He wanted to feel her flesh, her bare nipple. Struggling with her bra, he searched for the fastening in the back.

"It's in the front," she said and ran her tongue over his lower lip, still wiggling her lush bottom over his crotch.

Sweating with arousal, he slid his hand between them and unhooked her bra. Her breasts sprang free against her shirt, and he immediately took one in his hand. Her nipple was already turgid, and the knowledge that she was so aroused sent him spiraling.

She suckled his tongue, making passionate noises of approval while he fondled her breasts. She continued to undulate against his erection, and suddenly it was too much. A roaring orgasm swept through him, and he went over the top.

Moaning and swearing, he clung to her. Bloody hell, he hadn't done that since— Had he ever done that? He was amazed and embarrassed. What must she think?

"I don't know what to say. I apol—"

"Oh, don't you dare apologize," she said, her eyes flashing with anger. "Unless you are ashamed of your feelings for me."

"God, no," he said. "But—"

She stood, leaning over him, her legs separated by his between hers. "If you think that was hot, my odd Englishman, you should know I was just getting started."

He inhaled, drawing in her scent, feeling like a damn stallion scenting a mare in heat. She made him feel as if he was in rut. Permanently.

He slid his hand to her denim-covered thigh and then up to her rounded hip. "Is that an invitation to continue?"

She tossed her head back and laughed, brushing aside his hand as she stepped away. "Later," she said and added, "if you please me. Work on my song. Play more for me next time, and we'll see," she said and sauntered out of the room.

Geoffrey stared after her, feeling as if he'd been whacked with a slab of stone that weighed a ton.

The following afternoon after Lori finished her regular cleaning chores, she found Virginia at the kitchen table, clearly mulling over her bank accounts. Lori rubbed Kenny's soft fur and watched the older woman mutter as she scribbled, erased, then scribbled again. Virginia raked a hand through her gray hair and wrinkled her brows.

Lori's heart twisted at the sight of the woman struggling. It wasn't fair. Virginia was trying to do something good. She worked hard. She didn't deserve to have to worry so much, especially after the loss of her husband.

Lori would be able to take care of that very soon. If everything went as planned, she and Jackson would be married by tonight, tomorrow at the latest, and Lori would gain more control of her inheritance. The first thing she was going to do was write Virginia a check. It was all she could do not to tell the woman, but she and Jackson had agreed not to tell anyone until the deed was done.

"Virginia?" Lori said.

The woman looked up and immediately smiled, sliding the accounting book to the side. "Well, hello, girl. I didn't expect to see you here so early. Are you already finished cleaning the cabins and the stalls?"

"Already done," Lori said. "I'm getting a little faster, although I doubt I'll ever get Maria's approval."

Virginia reached over to pat Lori's hand. "You're a big help. Don't let Maria bother you. That chip on her shoulder is all self-defense. Her father always told her she wasn't good enough. It's a darn shame, but she'll probably be fighting those words the rest of her life."

"That is a shame," Lori agreed. "Is there anything I can do to help?"

Virginia shook her head. "Heavens, no. That would just make it worse. Let her work it out. She'll come around."

"Okay," Lori said, not sure she agreed but not willing to push the matter. She cleared her throat. "Something has come up, and Jackson and I need to leave for a couple of days. It's business," she said and swallowed an ironic laugh, because she was telling the truth. She and Jackson were getting married for business purposes. "We won't be gone long, but I was wondering if you would mind watching Kenny while I'm gone?"

"Of course I will," Virginia said, reaching for Kenny, who willingly curled into the older woman's arms and licked her chin. "Me and your little Pom are buddies. I won't sneak him too many treats, but he's so sweet it's hard not to spoil him."

"I know. It's hard to believe something that weighs under five pounds can offer so much comfort." It was silly, but Lori couldn't help wishing she could take Kenny with her. Her little dog had always had a calming effect on her, and she was about to take a giant leap of faith. She just hoped this leap wouldn't send her careening over a cliff.

"You should give the prenup agreement I asked my attorney to draw up to your own attorney before you sign it," Jackson said.

"I trust you," Lori said, her red-high-heel-clad foot vibrating in a staccato rhythm as she sat beside Jackson in the SUV. She wore designer jeans that molded to her every curve and some kind of red top with pink lace that showed just a hint of cleavage. Enough to keep him glancing at her every third second.

Jackson rolled his eyes at the same time his gut tightened. He was driving toward the nearest airport to catch the next flight to Vegas. Or to Insanityville. Or both. Once Jackson made up his mind, there was no going back. This time, however, even he'd had second, third, fourth, and fifth thoughts. Ultimately, he knew the agreement was more than fair, and some part of him was dead-ass certain he could help Lori. Unless he was just using that harebrained idea as some kind of crazy justification for marrying her.

"You shouldn't trust anyone," he told her. "Not with that amount of money."

"I can always sue you if you do something dishonorable, because you're still my accountant," she said, her foot still pumping.

He had to restrain the urge to put his hand on her thigh for her to stop, but Jackson knew touching her thigh wouldn't be enough. He knew he could get totally sidetracked thinking about her thighs and how good she would feel if he . . .

Focusing on the road, he shook his head and tried a softer approach, even though it went against the grain. "It will make me feel better if your attorney reviews this before. I already instructed my attorney to e-mail a copy to yours. You can call your attorney and tell him to review it during our flight."

She sighed. "Okay, okay. I'll call him."

Jackson listened as she took a moment to go through the contact list on her cell phone, placed the call, and talked with her attorney.

After she finished, she turned to Jackson. "Happy now?"

"I'll be happy when you're more responsible with your inheritance."

"Is that why you put that clause in there about consulting with you if I was planning to spend anything that hit six digits?"

Surprised she'd actually read the agreement, he shot a quick glance at her. "Partly," he said.

"I noticed the agreement didn't give you the power to veto my spending. I would have told you to take a flying leap if it had."

His lips twitched at the heat in her voice. "I don't want to stop you. I just want to help you . . . pause."

"If I'm really determined, discussing anything with you won't make a bit of a difference."

"I know that," he said. "And if you're not really determined?"

A long silence followed. "Okay. I may not follow all my impulses."

"Is that bad?"

Another silence followed. "I don't know. I guess I'll find out, won't I?"

He felt her gaze on him. "You may find out after your attorney looks at the agreement and you sign it and we both make it to the justice of the peace," he said. This was such a wild card that he still wasn't counting on anything.

"Is that why you're making us fly commercial?"

He nodded. "Until we're married, you're still broke."

She tossed her hair over her shoulder and shook her head. "That's an exaggeration. I'm not *broke*."

"Unless you want to slash your budget, you're broke," he said bluntly. "If you want to give up your job as philanthropist to every imaginable cause on God's green earth and get a real job, then you're not broke."

Her toe started to pump again, and she crossed her arms over her chest. "Just drive, please," she said.

Six hours later, Lori stood in front of the concierge at the Bellagio Hotel, feeling as if she were going to jump out of her skin. The flight had seemed interminable. As soon as the jet landed, she talked with her attorney, who began the conversation by telling her not to do anything rash. During the drive from the airport, she boiled down all his concerns about the premarital agreement to essentially none.

Luckily Tim, the concierge, was also a notary. He witnessed her and Jackson's signature on the agreement. "There you go," he said. "I'm happy to be of service."

"Can we get married now?" she asked him.

"I'll have to check availability," Tim said. "We're usually booked. If we can't accommodate you, I can help you find a chapel."

"For tonight," she said.

"I'll try to find something," he said and picked up the phone on his desk.

"You're tapping again," Jackson murmured into her ear.

She curled her toes inside her shoes. His closeness

only made her feel more jittery, but she didn't want him to know that. "I just want to get it done."

"If you're this nervous about doing it—"

"I'm not nervous about being married to you." She bit her lip, trying to compartmentalize her thoughts and feelings. "I know you'll keep your end of our agreement."

"Are you sure you don't want to get a dress or pick out some flowers? I thought women spent their whole lives dreaming of being dressed like a princess on their wedding day."

"The princess thing is way overrated. I've been doing that most of my life." Without invitation, a vision of what she had pictured for her wedding day slid through her mind. In her fantasy world, Harlan had walked her down a garden aisle, and her mother, visiting from the hereafter, sat in the first row of white chairs with her half brother. Lori's two sisters would be bridesmaids.

Lori had always been so infatuated with the idea of having all her loved ones alive, in the same place, and not screaming at each other, that she hadn't spent much time thinking about her Prince Charming.

This wasn't a real marriage, she told herself. She couldn't deny, however, that the notion of making life-long promises with no intention of keeping them seemed creepy.

She couldn't let sappy, emotional thoughts stop her. She needed to think like a man about this. Taking a deep breath, she forced herself to meet his gaze. "What we're about to do is business. I understand—"

Tim lifted a hand as he held the phone against his ear. "I can get you an Elvis wedding in thirty minutes. Will that work?"

> *"Your honeymoon night should always be a once-in-a-lifetime experience . . . no matter how many times you get married."*
> —SUNNY COLLINS

Chapter Sixteen

Elvis was just over five feet tall and appeared to be approximately three hundred years old. Lori hoped he'd make it through the ceremony. He wore a jet black toupee and a white suit that hung on his skinny body as he warbled "Love Me Tender." Lori quickly walked down the aisle, carrying a bouquet of artificial white roses. Based on Jackson's grim expression and her own sense of facing the gallows, Lori thought "Jailhouse Rock" would be more fitting, but she hadn't been given a choice. Apparently this Elvis had a very limited repertoire. The hired witnesses, an older woman and young man, sat on the front row of the chapel. The young man was texting on his cell phone.

Clutching the white rose bouquet in her hands, she tapped her foot as she waited for Elvis to finish the song. Jackson moved closer and put his arm at her back, startling her. He lowered his head. "You're tapping again."

She tried to stop. She really did. But tapping was better than wrapping her hands around the skinny throat of Elvis and asking him to get on with it.

Elvis finally finished. Adjusting his thick eyeglasses, he looked at Lori and stretched his mouth in a denture-filled smile. "You're a beautiful bride," he said, then turned to Jackson. "Isn't she a beautiful bride?"

Jackson met Lori's gaze, and she felt an odd dipping sensation. "Yes, she's beautiful."

"Every bride needs to hear that she's beautiful," Elvis said, pretty much negating the compliment. "We're gathered here to unite this couple in joyous matrimony. If anyone can show just cause why they may not be lawfully joined together, let them speak now or forever hold their peace."

"The credit card went through just fine," the older woman said.

Elvis nodded and pulled two sheets of paper from his inside breast pocket. He paused a moment as he appeared to study the paper. "Jackson," he said. "Is that right?"

Jackson nodded.

"Jackson, do you take . . ."

After that, everything was a blur. In a detached way, as if she were watching herself from the back of the room, Lori heard Elvis officiate and she responded appropriately, but the scene became more surreal than real. Was she really pledging her troth to Jackson? And what exactly was a troth? Some corner of her mind took in the slight snore of the older woman sitting on the front row and the nonstop pecking of the young man texting. Looking into Jackson's eyes, she wondered what he was really thinking. She wondered if he secretly wanted to run screaming from this place. Of all her fears, that one was the biggest. Lori wanted to get the wedding done before he reconsidered and backed out.

"I now pronounce you husband and wife," Elvis said, the words snapping Lori out of her fog. "You may kiss the bride."

She and Jackson stared at each other for a frozen moment of incredulity. Omigod, they'd done it.

"Go ahead," Elvis urged. "I have one more song for you."

Slowly and deliberately, Jackson slid his hand behind her back and pulled her toward him. He lowered his head, and she lifted her mouth. To the sound of Elvis butchering "Can't Help Falling in Love with You," they sealed the deal.

Twenty minutes later, she'd returned the faux bouquet and the faux rings they'd borrowed for the ceremony, and she and Jackson climbed into the limo that was part of the ceremony package.

Jackson exhaled and rubbed his face. "That's over," he said, then sat up and glanced at the bar. "There's a bottle of cheap champagne. Do you want any? I think I want a scotch."

"If it didn't taste so bad, I'd want some scotch, too," she said.

He glanced over his shoulder at her and chuckled. "Then what will it be, my beautiful bride?"

"Cheap champagne," she said, her stomach knotting at the word *bride*. "This is going to sound horrible, but it felt like a funeral."

Jackson poured a glass of scotch and tossed back a

gulp. "There were a few times I was worried Elvis might not survive the ceremony."

She watched him open the champagne and pour the bubbly liquid into a flute. "It's hard to believe that people deliberately choose that kind of ceremony."

"I think we got the second string."

"Or third," she said, accepting the glass as he handed it to her.

"Or fourth," he said and laughed again as he clinked his glass with hers. "It's done now, Lori. You can spend money."

She nodded, fighting a sudden hollow feeling. Glancing outside the window as she took a sip of champagne, she stared at the lights. "I've never been to Vegas without my father," she said.

"You're kidding," Jackson said.

"No." She glanced back at him. "He always thought this was the perfect place for me to get in trouble. And of course, he always saw it as his job to keep me out of trouble."

He nodded, silent for a moment as he took another drink from his glass. "What kind of trouble did you want to get into?"

Her stomach dipped again at the expression on his face. "I don't know," she said, shrugging. "The usual stuff, I guess. Shoot some craps, visit some clubs." She laughed. "Dance on a tabletop."

Pausing, he tilted his head to one side. "We might be able to cover some of that tonight."

"Tonight?" she echoed, surprised. She'd anticipated going back to separate rooms and separate beds and pretending nothing was different between them. With the exception of the legality, she supposed it wasn't.

"We're here. We may as well. Within reason, you can shoot craps while I play blackjack. The only problem is you'll finish a lot faster than I will."

"I could do the slots," she said, warming to the idea. "Or watch you play. Are you any good?"

"I do okay," he said in a humble voice.

"You must be very good," she said.

"I wouldn't say that," he returned.

"If it's the truth, why not?"

"When you're in Vegas, if you don't want to lose big, never brag about how good you are," he said. "Or how much money you have."

"Why?"

"Because there's always somebody ready to show you how to lose, and there's always somebody ready to relieve you of your money."

"Okay," she said, unable to keep a smile from her face. "I'm going to do Vegas."

Jackson kept an eye on Lori while he raked in the chips at the blackjack table he'd chosen after careful scrutiny. It was a hot table with a fun crowd and a flirtatious dealer intent on making sure everyone had a good time.

He'd watched Lori win, lose, and win again at craps. He was impressed when she'd walked away after winning. Now she was feeding the slots while she sipped her second margarita.

Thirty minutes later, he felt a foot on his ankle that slowly moved up his calf. Surprised, he glanced around the table and caught the vixen gleam in the eye of the dealer. "My shift's over soon," she informed the group, but her gaze lingered on Jackson.

The dealer was attractive and had a good sense of humor. He wondered if he would have taken her up on her offer in other circumstances. At the moment, he couldn't even consider it.

He was just about to fold and walk away when Lori appeared beside him. "How's it going?" she asked.

"Not bad," he said. "I was just getting ready to leave."

He felt the dealer's foot fall from his ankle. "Does the lady want in? Are you two together?"

"Yes," Jackson said.

"No," Lori said at the same time, then looked at him. "I don't want to play. I just came to watch."

"I was telling her that you and I are together," he said. "We just got married."

The group around the table crowed and oohed and ahhed.

The dealer smiled. "Just married and you're here on the floor. I would think you would have better things to do."

"Soon," he said, slipping his arm around Lori's waist, feeling her stiffen in surprise. With his other hand, he scooped up his chips. "Thanks. Have a nice evening," he said and led Lori away.

"What was that about?" she asked, staring up at him.

"The dealer was extra-friendly," he said.

She gave him a blank look. "How? Did she give you extra chips or something?"

He couldn't swallow a chuckle. "No, but she wanted to give me something else."

Her eyes widened. "She solicited you?"

"It was more of an invitation than a solicitation."

"Hmmph. That's—" She broke off, as if she couldn't come up with the right description. "Bold."

"Vegas isn't known for subtleties."

"True," she said, glancing over her shoulder at the dealer with a frown.

"Let's cash in my chips and I'll take you to a club," he said, wanting to get her in a better mood.

She met his gaze again and slowly smiled. "That could be fun. We can dance."

"Dance?" he said. "I thought you wanted to dance on a table. I'm not dancing on a table."

"I was joking about that. You don't have to dance on a table."

"I don't dance."

She sighed. "I guess that means I'll have to find someone else to dance with me."

Shit. He was going to have to dance.

Twenty minutes later, Jackson was wedged intimately between Lori and someone else he'd never met in his life. The dance floor was packed with writhing bodies, and he and Lori were positioned in a dark corner. The good news was that the moves he made were so limited, no one could see that he couldn't dance.

Lori spun around, wiggling her ass and jiving to the music while Jackson shifted from one foot to the other. She rocked her booty against him, clearly unaware of her effect. He would have to be inhuman not to grow hard from the way she brushed him.

She emanated exhilaration. Throwing her head back and laughing, she danced with abandon. Her sense of freedom written on her face, she turned and looped her arms around his neck and shimmied against him. Torn between pushing her away and pulling her against him, Jackson couldn't stop looking at the expression of sensual joy on her face.

"Do you like it?" she asked, raising her voice so he could hear her.

He hated it. Except for the way she was rubbing against him. "Do you?"

"I love it," she said, removing her arms from his and spinning around again. She rubbed her booty against him and he got so hard he felt as if he would explode. Even though their marriage was a business arrangement, he couldn't help thinking about the natural follow-up to the ceremony. The honeymoon night, which in Jackson's mind meant nonstop hot sex.

The fast song ended and a slow one began. Lori turned to face him and met his gaze for a long moment. Unspoken thoughts, desires, wishes, and fears flowed from her to him and back again. The next second, she moved against him and slid her arms behind his neck.

Jackson automatically wrapped his arms around her waist and drew her flush against him. He knew he was playing with fire, but she was making it all too easy. Breathing in the scent of her hair, he skimmed one of his hands up her back, under the curtain of her hair to the nape of her neck. He felt her shiver in response.

She lifted her head and nuzzled his neck. Her breasts were pressed against his chest, and when he slid his knee through her thighs, she opened for him.

Jackson felt his arousal roar through him like a fire out of control. He wanted to feel her naked breasts in his hands, against his skin, in his mouth. He wanted to feel her bare, silky thighs opening for him with no fabric or barriers between them. He wanted to slide inside her and appease the hard ache she caused. He wanted to fill her up so that the only thing she could think about was him.

In some last corner of his mind, his rational self reminded him that this could be just a dance for her. Just because she was rubbing herself against him like a sex kitten didn't mean she wanted to go all the way. Especially with him. Maybe this was more about the three margaritas she'd drunk than him.

That last thought should have taken the teeth out of the gnawing, growling need that seemed to consume him. Maybe it would have, if she hadn't stretched up on tiptoe and pressed her mouth against his.

Every muscle in Jackson's body tightened. How was he supposed to turn this down? She slid her tongue over his bottom lip and his heart stuttered in his chest. Mentally swearing, he felt like a dog pulling at chains. One seemed to rip free, and he devoured her mouth, plundering her, kissing her the way he wanted to take the rest of her.

Lori made him too aware of his sexual need. She'd done it from the very beginning, and at this moment with her so close to him, he felt as if he were on a steep cliff over the ocean. It wouldn't take much to push him straight over the edge.

Jackson couldn't deny or hide the rough, edgy want for her anymore. He needed her to see it and feel it so she would either back away or decide she wanted him. He pressed his hand against her lower back, so that she rubbed against his aching erection. He waited for her response, expecting her to pull back.

Instead, she undulated against him and slipped her

tongue inside his mouth. Jackson thought he might explode right there on the dance floor. He sucked in a mind-clearing breath but inhaled her sultry scent along with the oxygen.

He lowered his mouth to her ear. "Sweetheart, if you don't want to finish this in bed with me, then we'd better stop."

She stopped and looked up at him, her eyes full of the same arousal that raged through him. He counted the seconds until she said something. One. Two. Three.

"I don't want to stop," she said. "Maybe we should head back to the limo."

"I'm not going to ask again. Are you sure?"

"Yes," she said without a heartbeat of hesitation.

Jackson immediately took her hand and led her out of the club. The night air was cool, but not cool enough to slow him down. With the limo parked just steps away, the driver spotted them walking toward him and he opened the door.

"The Bellagio," he said to the driver and helped Lori into the back seat. He pushed the privacy panel closed, and before the driver pulled out of the parking lot, he pulled Lori onto his lap.

They kissed with feverish intensity. He slid his hands underneath her shirt, searching for her full breasts. She immediately followed his lead and tugged at the buttons of his shirt, skimming her hands over his chest. The sensation drove him crazy. It was all he could do not to rip off his jeans and hers and drive himself inside her. He had never felt this overwhelming need for a woman before. Never.

Swearing under his breath, he pulled back. "We'll be at the resort in a few minutes," he said for his benefit as much as hers. "Which room? Yours or mine?"

"I don't care," she said. "Just so it's soon."

*   *   *

Ten agonizing minutes later, Jackson guided Lori from the limo. She halfway noticed that he paid the driver in cash, but she was in such a sexual fog, she couldn't be sure. Her body felt as if it were sizzling from the inside out, and all her most sensitive places screamed for Jackson's touch.

The intensity of the empty, aching sensation between her thighs shocked her. How had this happened? She'd known Jackson affected her strongly, but this?

A heartbeat passed, and he escorted her to the elevator. He mashed a button and as soon as the door closed, pulled her into his arms and kissed her. Lori felt boneless in his embrace, dizzy from his passion. His strength was an aphrodisiac, and his desire for her made her breathless.

The elevator doors whisked open, and he pulled his mouth from hers. She swallowed a protest as he tugged her down the hallway. He slid a card into the lock and opened the door. Tugging her inside, he immediately pushed her against the closed door and took her mouth at the same time he lifted her buttocks in his large hands and urged her thighs around his waist.

Eager for all of him, his scent, the sensation of his skin on hers, his tongue taunting and seducing her, she felt his hardness against the part of her that ached most. She couldn't help wiggling, and his groan vibrated inside her mouth.

"You feel so good," he said. "So good."

She slid her hands under his jaw, cupping his face as he devoured her mouth. His rough shadow of a beard abraded her hand deliciously. So masculine. So male. She craved his roughness, his hardness.

"Hang on," he said, barely giving her time to wrap her arms around his neck before he spun around and carried her to the large bed. Lowering her to the mattress, he followed her down, pulling up her top and unfastening her bra.

The cool air of the room whispered over her bare skin before his mouth took hers and she felt his half-naked chest against hers. A shocking urgency raced through her. Half-naked wasn't enough. She tugged at his shirt, releasing the buttons and pushing the sleeves down his muscular arms.

He pulled back slightly to shove his shirt the rest of the way off, giving Lori a secret moment where she could drink in the sight of his broad shoulders, his sculpted pecs, and the dusting of masculine hair across his chest.

"Lori Jean Granger," he said, surprise and teasing mixed in his voice. "Are you lusting after my body?"

She met his gaze, feeling a sexy exhilaration rushing through her. "Yes, I am," she managed breathlessly. "What are you going to do about it?"

His eyes darkened even further with arousal. "Make you lust a whole lot more," he said and unfastened her jeans and slid down the zipper. "Ready?"

"Yes," she whispered and arched her hips so he could pull the denim from her more easily.

She felt her shoes fall from her feet and heard the quiet thump onto the lushly carpeted floor just before he tugged off her jeans. Jackson's gaze fell over her, from her throat, down her lace-encased breasts, to her belly, and her bikini panties.

Holding her breath, she wondered if he noticed the scars, the contrast of the white lines and slightly thickened tissue against her fair skin. For Lori, those scars represented months of pain, more than a year of physical therapy, and eons of fear.

He paused, tracing the fine lines with one of his callous-roughened fingers. "Is the pain all gone?"

She bit her lip, then smiled. "I can get a little achy just before it rains."

He met her gaze, his hand tracing her abdomen. "So maybe you could go into business predicting weather?"

Her lungs expanded at the combination of his sensual expression and touch, and she shook her head. "It only comes on a day before. The satellites have got me beat on long-term forecasts."

He slid his thumb under the edge of her panties and tugged. Her heart stopped. She worked her throat to swallow over the lump in it, and she reached for his hips. "Your turn to take something off," she said and put one of her hands on the button of his jeans. Watching his eyes darken, she pulled it loose and his erection strained at the denim. She slid her hand down over him.

He gave a sigh, followed by a muttered oath. "The problem with me taking off my jeans is that I need something to slow me down."

"What if I don't want you to slow down?"

Jackson swore again. "You're killing me, Lori. You've been killing me since the day I met you."

"I thought you were completely immune to me the first day you met me," she said as he shucked his jeans and briefs and quickly returned to her. The sight of his proud, huge, naked erection took her breath.

"I was determined not to fall under your spell. Like Tilly," he said, speaking of her former accountant.

A breathless laugh escaped her throat. "You are nothing like Tilly."

"That's good to hear," he said in a dry voice, sliding between her legs. She savored the differences between them. She was soft where he was rough, giving where he was hard. His face just inches from hers, she lifted her hands to cup his face again.

"I like that," he said in a low voice. "I like the way you touch my face when you kiss me."

Closing her eyes, she lifted her mouth and rubbed her lips over him, drowning in the sensation of him. She wanted to taste him; she wanted to smell him. She wanted to feel him inside her.

"I hope my scars don't bother you," she whispered.

He rubbed his erection against her deliberately. "Does it feel like they bother me?"

"I guess not," she said.

Again, he slid his thumb beneath the elastic of her bikini panties, but this time he pushed them down. Her heart raced as he lifted himself slightly and pushed them over her hips and thighs. She slid her legs between his and the panties descended farther, down her knees, to her ankles.

She tangled her feet with the fabric. "I—can't—"

Jackson reached down and snatched them off. She had a distant image of pink flying through the air, but then he took her mouth. Moments later, he slid lower and her bra seemed to dissolve. He took both her nipples into his mouth and slid his hand between her thighs, finding her wet and swollen.

"Oh, my God," she said, burning from the inside out. Lori could hardly breathe, but she felt she would die if he stopped.

He lowered his head and kissed his way down her abdomen, kissing her scars while his fingers taunted her stiff nipples. The sensations made her light-headed. Intensifying the anticipation, he lowered his head between her legs.

Lori gasped at his tongue on her most sensitive place. She instinctively laced her fingers through his hair as he took her with his mouth. The tension inside her tightened like an overtaut rubber band.

She didn't think she could form a word. Every pump of her heart sent her blood streaming to her secret places, but in some corner of her mind, she heard her voice calling, "Jackson, Jackson."

A shower of sensation coursed through her like fireworks on the Fourth of July, and she arched before him, moaning.

Jackson quickly rose up her body and thrust inside her. She gasped at the overstretched sensation.

Jackson searched her gaze, his eyes dark, his face taut with need. He swore. "Are you—"

Lori took a careful breath. "Wow, you're really big."

"And you're really tight," he said in a husky voice. "Why didn't you tell me you were—"

She wiggled experimentally. "You distracted me." She wiggled again.

Jackson winced and swore. "Damn it, be still."

Lori let out a long breath. "That's no fun."

Jackson gave a rough laugh. "Does this mean you're not on the pill?"

"It doesn't matter. When I broke my pelvis, the doctors said I would have a difficult time getting pregnant."

"So I don't need a condom?"

She wiggled again, and he shook his head. "You feel so good. I have to have you . . ."

He began to pump. She met his thrusts, and moments later, he stiffened and took her mouth as he spilled himself inside her.

> "Sisters know everything about you but love you anyway."
> —SUNNY COLLINS

Chapter Seventeen

Geoffrey woke up with another hard-on.

"Bloody hell," he muttered, rolling over and gingerly climbing out of the twin bed he'd slept in since he'd arrived at the ranch. He glanced down at his boxers and sighed. Lord help him, at this rate, he'd have a hard-on until he died. He scowled. Knowing his luck, his erection would last past his death. He could see it now. He'd be in his casket, cold and dead, with his penis still poking out, waiting, hoping for Maria to assuage his ache the way she did in his dreams.

He shouldn't be thinking about her, he told himself as he pulled on a pair of jeans and headed down the hall to the shower. He was supposed to marry Lori. Lori was loaded. Lori was perfectly lovely, and Geoffrey had a special affection for her. Similar to the affection he had for his sister.

Scowling again, he turned on the shower and stripped off his clothes. For the three hundred and third time, he wondered what he was doing on this ranch. Yes, he knew his family needed money and he was expected to provide it. Yes, he knew that Lori was his best bet for achieving that goal, but it was still only a possibility.

Despite the uncertainty, he would be cleaning toilets today. Lori and Jackson were still out of town on business. In a different situation, he would feel offended that she hadn't mentioned the trip to him. Instead, he felt relieved. If only he could find some relief from his obsession with Maria.

Hours later, after he'd completed cleaning duties and eaten lunch, Geoffrey wandered to the barn. He told himself he was just stretching his legs, but he wanted to catch a glimpse of Maria. He hadn't seen her at all today.

He didn't see any campers in the corral, so he suspected she might be in the barn or riding one of the horses. Walking into the dark, cool barn, he heard noise from the other end. The closer he walked, the more he made out her voice. Muttering in Spanish, she sounded displeased. He was relieved that for once her displeasure wasn't directed at him.

He felt another surge of hunger burn through him. Everything about the woman oozed sensuality and womanliness, even her temper, God help him.

Rounding the corner to the tack room, he found her perched precariously on two boxes, struggling for a saddle out of reach. He watched her stand on tiptoe and shift her feet, which made the boxes shift.

Horror rushed through him, and he dove toward her to catch her. Too late. She cried out as she fell to the ground.

Geoffrey rushed to her side and searched her face. Her

eyes were closed. His heart plummeted. "Oh, Maria. Darling, are you okay? Are you okay?"

She lay there on the floor as still as death. Terrified that she was seriously hurt, he gingerly touched her shoulder. "Maria. Maria, wake up." He touched her face and lowered his ear to her lips, praying she was still breathing.

She was, but the fact that she was unconscious alarmed him more with each passing millisecond. He was so panicked he felt as if *he* were going to pass out. Geoffrey began to talk to himself. "Get yourself together. You've got to help her. She needs help." He rose to his feet, reluctant to leave her. Should he pick her up? Should he—

Over his screaming loud panic, he heard a moan. He stared down at Maria. Had she made that sound, or had he? Biting his tongue, he listened and heard the sound again. Sinking beside her, he watched as her brow furrowed in pain.

His heart wrenched. Oh, no, she couldn't be in pain. He couldn't let that happen. "Maria, what hurts? Tell me what hurts."

She moaned again, and her eyes fluttered open. "My head." She winced. "Oh, my head."

"Anything else?" he asked, desperate to help her. "I need to carry you to the house so we can get you proper medical attention."

She frowned. "I don't need a doctor," she said and shook her head. She stopped suddenly, wincing. "I'll be okay if I keep my head still."

He could see she was downplaying her injury. "A visit to a doctor is imperative," he said and slid one of his arms underneath her back.

Her eyes flashed open. "You're not going to try to carry me, are you?"

Surprised at the note of fear in her voice, he paused a half beat. "Of course I'm going to carry you. You can't walk the entire way. Don't worry. I'll carry you back to the house and then take you to a doc—"

She shook her head and winced again. "You can't carry me." She made a sound of exasperation. "I'm too big for you."

Geoffrey sighed. She couldn't be concerned about her weight. "That's ridiculous. You have a perfectly luscious body." He tugged gently to pick her up.

"Geoffrey," she said, her eyes wide with alarm. "You're too small. You'll drop me."

Geoffrey stared at her in disbelief. He'd thought she was self-conscious about her size. Instead she was criticizing his. Male pride rushed through every pore. "I am not too small," he said, the words feeling as if they were shooting through his teeth like bullets from a machine gun. "I would be quite happy to show you just how small I'm not," he continued, fuming. "And I will not drop you."

Adrenaline and indignation roaring through him, he pulled her into his arms and stood. Stomping toward the house, he felt a feral growl shoot up his throat from somewhere deep in his belly.

"Geoffrey!" Maria's eyes rounded in surprise. She was clearly shocked, however, no more than he. If he wasn't wrong, he thought he spotted a glint of admiration in her dark eyes. If he wasn't imagining things, she was looking at him differently.

He cleared his throat to keep from growling again. "So

you see I'm perfectly capable of carrying you. You are not too large, and I am *not too small*."

Five hours later, Maria lay in bed, with Geoffrey bobbing up and down every three minutes checking to make sure she was okay. In other circumstances, it would have driven her crazy to be stuck in bed, with someone fussing over her. If there was one thing Maria detested, it was feeling helpless. She would do anything to avoid it.

"I'm still breathing," she said, feeling just a hint of Geoffrey's breath on her cheek. "I fell in the tack room. I climbed on some boxes—"

"Which you'll never do again," he prompted with an edge to his voice. "You've nearly scared the life out of everyone."

"*You* nearly scared the life out of everyone, carrying me to the house, yelling for help like I was bleeding to death." She met his gaze, and a wave of tenderness washed over her, leaving her in a momentary state of shock.

Geoffrey studied her. "You look odd," he said. "Are you in pain? You must tell me if you have any unusual symptoms."

Symptoms like crushing over a pretty Englishman whose social status was stratospheres above her own. Not that social status had ever meant anything to Maria. But Geoffrey was different. So polite, yet urgent. So very passionate. How could she not be a little interested in the man? He'd written music inspired by her. She could tell he wanted her, and she couldn't deny wondering what he was like as a lover.

"I'm fine," she said quietly and reached for the orange juice on her bed stand.

"I'll get that." Geoffrey beat her to the chase and lifted the glass toward her, adjusting the straw.

She took a sip and looked into his eyes. "This is really unnecessary. I'm not sick. I'm not really hurt. You're pampering me when I don't need it."

"That's a matter of opinion," he said in that snooty uppercrust voice he used on very rare occasions. "More?"

She shook her head.

"Besides, from my point of view, it looks like you could do with some pampering. I may not be all that good at it, but I'd like to give it a try."

Another rush of warmth coursed through her. The man was getting to her. She'd always made a point of enjoying men on her own terms but never, ever putting herself in a position of weakness. She'd been in that weak place when she'd lived with her father, and she had the scars to show for it.

"Are you sure you wouldn't like something else to eat? Or another pillow?" he asked. "How can I pamper the woman who works twenty-five hours a day?"

Her lips twitched. "There are only twenty-four hours in a day, and I sleep every night."

"Hmmph. Could have fooled me. What can I do for you?"

She fought a rush of self-consciousness and decided to splurge. After all, Geoffrey was a delicious splurge. She knew he was the kind of man who would come around only once in a woman's life, and soon enough, he would be gone. The knowledge cast a shadow over her enjoyment, so she pushed it aside. "I'd like you to read to me."

He blinked. "Read to you." He hesitated a moment. "Are you saying you can't re—"

She laughed. "I can read. I just enjoy the sound of your voice."

"Really?" he said, his voice breaking slightly. He cleared his throat. "Really," he repeated in a deeper voice.

"Really," she said. "It's so—"

"English," he said.

"Yes," she said, unable to prevent a smile. "And it's kinda sexy, too."

His gaze latched on to hers, and she saw the desire flame. "You make it bloody difficult for this poor Englishman to keep his equilibrium."

She looked at his hand balled into a fist of tension and lifted hers to cover his. "Are you complaining?"

"Is your goal to torture me? Do you enjoy making me sweat?"

She laughed and couldn't keep a dozen wicked thoughts from her mind. "That's for another night. Right now I just want you to read."

"I think we missed late checkout," Jackson said as he slid his fingers down Lori's bare arm. Her skin was so pale and so soft that the sight and texture fascinated him. Her hair was a tousled mass of blonde waves, her eyes closed, and her mouth deliciously swollen and tempting. At the moment she was wrapped in a sheet, but he knew what was underneath. They'd spent the night in a blur of mindblowing sex and catnaps that enabled them to rest long enough to go at each other again.

This amazing, effervescent, scorching-hot woman was his *wife*. The reality knocked him sideways again. The desire to take her again, to mark her as his, scared the hell out of him.

Even though they were lawfully wed, he shouldn't feel this way about her. After all, it was temporary and it was business.

He felt a twinge at that last thought. Their business relationship had been blown to smithereens. He paused in stroking her bare skin.

"Don't stop," she said, lifting her arm so he would continue.

He smiled at her artless response. "I almost thought you were asleep."

She shook her head.

"You know we're paying for two rooms at the Bellagio when we're only staying in one," he said.

Her lips curved in a secret smile, and her eyes opened to slits of blue. "I saw how much you won at that blackjack table. You can afford it."

Shaking his head, he slid his hand down to her bottom and lightly pinched her through the sheet.

"Hey!" Her eyes flew open. "What are you doing?"

"Pinching the princess," he said without an ounce of remorse.

She met his gaze and slid her hand over his arm and tugged him closer. "Are you in a big rush to leave?"

His chest squeezed tight at her touch. "I could stay another night," he said in a voice that sounded a little rough to his own ears.

"That's nice to hear," she said. "I hope it won't be too much of a chore."

"No chore," he said. "But I almost feel like I should have trained for this."

She gave a low laugh, and her eyes swept downward. "Did you ever think about what it would be like if you got married?"

"Maybe a few times," he said. "But I've been wrapped up tight with school and my job for a long time."

"No time for a wife," she said, meeting his gaze.

"That's right."

"But when you did think about it, what were your thoughts?"

"I don't know. That it would be nice to go to bed every night with the same woman. Nice to wake up with someone who wanted to be in my life and who I wanted to be with me. We could go places together, do things."

"Like what?"

He shrugged. "Camping. Football games."

She fell silent for several seconds, then blinked. "Camping?" she echoed, grimacing.

He chuckled. "Hey, that's the male fantasy. I also thought it would be nice to come home to a hot meal and a hotter wife."

"With a cook and housekeeper, anything is possible."

He lifted his hand to her sassy mouth. "Okay, princess, what about you? Did you ever think about getting married? If you did, then what did you imagine?"

"I imagined going on adventures," she said. "To Paris or Italy or New York City. Or a Caribbean island. I imagined spending holidays with my husband, with my sisters and brother." She sighed. "And I imagined hot sex," she said. "Lots of it."

Jackson nearly choked over his shock at her bluntness. He cleared his throat. "I guess I can understand that, since you didn't get a lot of opportunities to—" He didn't want to finish that thought. It didn't feel right.

"Get laid," she said for him.

The woman was full of surprises. He lifted his hand to push a strand of hair from her face. "When we first talked about you getting married, you said you didn't think you would want to have sex. Why did you change your mind?"

She slipped her hands over his shoulders and chest, then down his arms to his wrists. "Because I wanted to be with you," she said. "And it seemed extra stupid not to be with you if we were married."

"Why me?" he asked, craving her touch. "Why not some other guy?"

She bit her lip. "I don't know. I just—"

"Just what?" he asked, feeling desire ooze through him again.

"I wanted to be with you. What about you? Why me?"

"Besides the fact that you're beautiful and sexy?" he asked.

She beamed. "You really think so?"

"Every man really thinks so," he growled and tugged her against him. He hated the sheet, but he craved her mouth beneath his. He kissed her, savoring her lips, and she responded, cranking up his arousal another few notches.

"I wasn't asking about every man," she said. "I was asking about you. Does that mean you like me a little bit?"

"Yeah," he said, his heart turning an odd flip as he pushed down the sheet. "A little bit."

"Can I be on top this time?"

He hesitated, feeling himself grow harder. "Top?"

"Yeah. I've never done that—"

If Lori wanted to be adventurous, then he definitely wanted to accommodate her. He immediately rolled onto his back, pulling her on top of him. The view was divine. Her hair shimmered over her shoulders, and her breasts swayed inches from his mouth.

"I'm ready when you are," he said.

Leaning forward, she braced her hands on his shoulders and positioned herself over him, pausing a few beats. Jackson held his breath and reined in the urge to plunge her down over him.

Mounting him, she enveloped his shaft, millimeter by wet, silky millimeter. When she had finally taken all of him, she took a little breath and whispered, "Wow."

He gave a rough chuckle. "Yeah. Wow."

She leaned down and took his mouth in a French kiss at the same time she undulated with him inside her. "I think I could like this," she said, her breasts pressed against his chest.

He slid his hands over her derriere and groaned. "That makes two of us."

The following morning, Lori awakened to the sensation of Jackson's breath tickling the back of her neck. His chest curved protectively against her back. His arm rested over her waist, and she felt as if she were in a delicious, sexy cocoon. Inhaling deeply, she caught a hint of his masculine scent.

She swallowed a moan of satisfaction. This felt delicious. She could grow to like this. After marathon lovemaking, they'd fed each other a midnight snack of cheeseburgers and chocolate cake. Afterward, they'd taken a shower together and crashed.

She heard a muted humming sound from somewhere in the room and wondered what it was. She carefully moved her head to glance at the bedside table to see if anything on top of it was off balance, but she didn't see anything. The sound stopped for a few seconds and she relaxed.

It started again and she frowned. What was it? Slowly lifting Jackson's hand from her waist, she wiggled away, not wanting to awaken him.

"Are you always this squirmy in the morning?" he asked and pulled her back against him.

She couldn't help smiling at his question. "Good morning to you, too. No. I'm not usually this squirmy in the morning, but there's some kind of humming noise. I don't know where it is, and it's driving me crazy." She paused and was very quiet. "Do you hear it?"

"Cell phone," he said. "It must be yours. I turned mine off."

"Oh," she said, not wanting anything or anyone to intrude on the short time they had together.

"You want to check it?"

"Not really," she said, turning toward him and burying her face in his throat.

"What are you afraid of, Lori Jean?" he asked, sliding his hand down her back. "I can tell something's wrong. Your body is tense."

"I'm not really afraid," she said and closed her eyes. "I just don't want to answer any questions about—" She took a breath. "About us."

He tilted her chin upward. "Are you wishing you'd married the duke?"

"Oh, no," she said. "I just don't want to deal with other people and their opinions right now."

"Tell them to stuff it."

"My sisters wouldn't like that. And that's probably not the best approach with the press." She sighed against his throat. "The last two days have been so wonderful. Do we have to tell other people yet? Can we wait a little bit until we figure out how to announce it?"

"If that's what you want," he said, sliding his fingers through her hair. "If you don't want a lot of attention, you'll probably need to go back to the ranch."

"That's fine with me. Will you go, too?" she asked, searching his face.

"Yes, but I'll need to resign from the firm soon and get started on the real-estate development I'm putting together."

"That's what you want to do with your husband money?" she said.

One side of his lips lifted in a dry smile. "Husband money," he said and shrugged. "I guess that's as good a description as any. But yes, I'm going to use the husband money to launch a midrange neighborhood development outside of Dallas, with pools, a park, shopping facilities, hopefully a school, and whatever else will draw in buyers."

"Did I read somewhere that real estate is in bad shape now?" she asked.

He nodded. "Yes, you did. But this would be for entry-level or second-time buyers. That's the group who wants a chance at the American dream. I have contacts with mortgage companies and construction outfits. With this combination, I think I can give these people a chance at getting a shot at owning their own homes."

He was so fervent, so positive. She admired his confidence and decisiveness and wished she had a fraction of it. "You sound like you have it all planned out."

"A lot of it," he said. "I've been thinking about this for years. I bought the property, and I've just been waiting for the opportunity to move ahead." He met her gaze and gave a wry laugh. "I never dreamed I'd get the chance by marrying the hottest girl in Texas."

Her stomach twisted and tumbled. It gave her a thrill to think that she could help make Jackson's dream come true. He was so strong, so independent that she couldn't imagine him ever really needing her. "You would have found a different way to get your funding. I was just in the right place at the right time."

"You have a lot of confidence in me," he said, cupping her jaw with his hand.

"You've earned it," she said and wondered if or when he would ever have the same confidence in her. If or when she would have the same confidence in herself.

> "Almost every woman regrets getting married.
> Give it a little time. Hopefully you'll get over it."
> —SUNNY COLLINS

Chapter Eighteen

Geoffrey read half of *Huckleberry Finn;* then Maria kicked him out of her room so she could sleep. Since he couldn't sleep, he spent most of the night at the piano. The next morning, Maria woke up as her snappy kick-ass self and insisted on performing her regular duties despite Geoffrey's protests.

After dinner, Geoffrey sulked for a bit, but since Maria just ignored him, he gave up on that and returned to the piano. Feeling the keys beneath his fingers and the vibration of sound throughout his body usually calmed him. But not tonight. He was so incredibly torn.

He wanted Maria with every cell in his being. How could he possibly marry Lori? His stepmother had called again today and left several threatening messages. What a bloody mess.

Raking his hand through his hair, he sighed and began to play the piece Maria had inspired. He played everything he knew of it so far but felt as if there was another line. The sensation was like having a word on the tip of his tongue that he couldn't quite summon.

The door creaked open behind him, interrupting him. He knew before turning who it was. Maria. He began to play a different song, one someone else had written. One to which he knew the blasted ending, which was more than he could say for his own composition.

"Why did you stop playing my song?" she asked, sliding beside him on the piano bench.

"You were listening?" he asked, glancing at her, feeling his stomach dip, his chest tighten, and something else grow hard. "I thought you were ignoring me."

Tossing her hair over her shoulder, she shot him a sideways glance. "That was because you were pouting."

"Because you're doing too much today. You should have rested more."

"It's my body," she said. "I'm the best judge of that. So why did you stop playing my song?"

He decided not to look at her. The woman made him a mess. "I'm stuck. I don't know what the ending is."

"Ah," she said.

"I know there's something else, something more—" He frowned in concentration. "But I just can't hear it. Yet."

"Maybe I can help," she offered.

"I thought you said you didn't know much about music," he said.

"I don't play a musical instrument, but I know what I like."

He nodded. "True, but how can that help?"

"There are other ways I could help," she said.

"How?" he asked, still not wanting to look at her. She

was too distracting. He wanted her too much. It was bad enough that her thigh was against his and he could almost feel the brush of her breast against his arm. She was one gigantic tease. From his peripheral vision, he saw her stand and straddle the piano bench so that she was facing him.

"Maybe I could inspire you?" she said and slid one of her hands over his thigh.

Geoffrey immediately felt his mental and emotional circuits crackle. His erection grew and his heart stopped. She lifted her head and rubbed her wicked mouth over his cheek, a caress that somehow managed to combine affection and seduction.

He couldn't move a muscle, at least voluntarily.

"You're not saying anything. You don't like—"

Panic raced through him. *Please, don't stop.* "I do like very much," he managed through his tight throat.

She lifted her hand to his jaw and swiveled his head so that he was forced to look at her. Her lips were curved upward in a tempting smile, her eyes lit with promises he prayed she would keep. "Tell me what you like about me."

"Everything," he blurted out. "Every bloody thing."

Her smile grew, and she lifted her mouth to his, nuzzling his lips. "I want a list," she said. "Give me a list."

He squeezed in a breath of air. "I like your hair," he said. "It's long and wavy, but soft." He lifted his hand to touch, but she pushed his hand aside.

"Not until you finish the list," she said playfully.

He wondered what kind of game she was playing but would do anything to keep her hand on his thigh or anywhere else, so he went along with her. "I like your eyes. They're sexy."

She squeezed his thigh and moved closer, brushing her breasts against his arm. Geoffrey was immediately consumed with thoughts of her breasts, touching them, caressing and kissing her nipples.

"Go on," she said.

Fortitude, my man. Fortitude. "I like the way you wrinkle your nose when you're displeased about something."

She lifted her eyebrows in surprise. "I do?"

"Yes, you do, and you look down your nose at people when you get impatient with them."

"I do not," she said and wrinkled her nose. Realizing what she'd done, she wrinkled it again and removed her hand from Geoffrey's thigh. He almost died. "Okay, maybe once in a while. What else?"

He cleared his throat. "Could you put your hand back on me?"

She met his gaze for a moment, then a realization crossed her face and she gave a wicked smile. "Does it help with the list?"

He nodded. She returned her hand to his thigh, this time higher, and he sighed in a combination of agony and expectation.

"More," she said and rubbed her breasts against his arm.

He could say the same thing. More. Please. Now. He closed his eyes for a moment. "I love your mouth. It gives away your emotions. The way you talk, the way you smile. The way you laugh." He sighed. "The way you kiss, although I don't have nearly enough experience."

A beat of silence followed, and he felt her lips on his

jaw, moving down to his neck. Her tongue darted over his skin, scoring him with her heat, then he felt her open mouth on his neck and he shuddered with pleasure. She squeezed his thigh and he turned to take her mouth, but she backed away, shaking her head.

"The list," she whispered, but he saw a hint of arousal in her eyes that gave him hope.

"I don't like how you got your scar," he said. "But I like what it says about you. You're strong. You're a survivor."

Her gaze turned solemn. "For a stuffy, self-centered Englishman, you see a lot."

Affronted, he sputtered. "Stuffy? Self-centered? I am neither stuffy nor self—"

"I know. Just wanted to see your reaction," she said and smiled again. "Anything else you like about me?"

Dammit, she was pushing him to the edge. "Obviously I like your body. You could make every clock in England stop. I like everything I've seen, but I haven't seen everything. I want to see more," he said and decided to hell with it. "I want to feel more. Do more."

"Me first," she said and slid her hand between his legs to his erection.

It took several seconds for him to respond. "Okay," he said. "Ladies first."

"Lady," she said, squeezing him gently. "Lady."

"Lady," he agreed, and one second later, she took his mouth in hers in a searing French kiss.

Geoffrey nearly came right then, but she pulled back. "You're wearing too many clothes," she said.

"Yes," he managed in a gruff voice. His clothes felt tight, his skin even tighter. "You're wearing too many clothes, too."

She opened her mouth to protest.

He shook his head. "Fair is fair."

Meeting his gaze for a long moment, she sighed, then unbuttoned her blouse and stripped it off. Her bra barely concealed her full breasts, her nipples just barely peeking above the white lace.

"Oh, my—"

"If you're going to be that distracted, should I put my shirt back on?"

"No, no, no, no . . ."

"Okay," she said and kissed him again, this time stripping off his shirt and rubbing her palms over his naked skin. Somehow he'd ended up more bare than her. How had that happened?

Her hands flowed down to his waist, where she unfastened his slacks with little fumbling. He didn't want to think about what that meant regarding her experience. How many men before him? He cut off the thought. He didn't want to go there. What was important was this moment. This woman.

Seconds later, she plunged her hands into his crotch, touching his bare erection. He forced himself not to growl, not to . . .

"What are you doing?" he murmured. "What do you—"

"I'm going to kiss my way down your chest," she said, lowering her wicked, wonderful mouth more and more. She pushed his jeans down farther, exposing him to her gaze. And mouth.

Geoffrey stifled a dozen oaths as her breath brushed over him intimately. "Oh. God."

Meeting his gaze, she lowered her head and took him into her mouth.

"Oh. My—"

Geoffrey was in ecstasy. The sensation of her tongue on him, the visual of her hair on his crotch, her mouth devouring the most sensitive part of him.

"Do you like it?" she asked, then slid her tongue over him. "Does it feel good?"

He was one millisecond away from losing it, and she stopped. She smiled at him with a sultry gaze. "Your turn."

Geoffrey acted purely on instinct. He lifted Maria on top of the piano and pulled off her bra. Her breasts spilled free—her nipples were large, dusky, and taut. He cupped her breasts and took a nipple into his mouth. She moaned.

Geoffrey fumbled with her jeans but succeeded in unfastening them. She graciously lifted her gorgeous hips so he could lower the denim to her thighs, then her ankles.

He caught sight of her swollen femininity. Her obvious arousal nearly did him in. "You're so gorgeous," he said, sliding his fingers between her thighs to where she was wet and velvety.

"That feels good," she said, wriggling beneath his touch.

He had to have her every way. Every way. Lowering his head, he spread her legs with his hands and took her with his mouth. She gasped and sighed and gasped.

The sound was like music to his ears. The taste of her drove him crazy. She grew more swollen with each stroke of his tongue. Her reaction was beyond gratifying. "Take me," she whispered. "Take me."

Sitting down on the bench, he brought her onto his lap. She struggled with her jeans, kicking them off, then rose again and plunged downward on him.

"Oh. My," he said.

"God," she said, undulating on him.

"I can't last long," he said.

"Me, either," she said.

And Geoffrey felt as if he'd died and gone to heaven. Or hell. Or both. He didn't care which. He just wanted to go again.

After they made love again, this time on a blanket on the floor, Geoffrey held Maria in his arms. She was warm, sensual, and lush. "You are the most amazing woman in the world."

"That's your woodie talking," she said, but she smiled.

"It is not," he said. "I don't even have a *woodie* at the moment," he told her, then chuckled to himself. "You took very good care of that." He slid his finger over the dark tendril of hair hiding one of her eyes. "Are you sure you're not a secret goddess?"

She threw back her head and laughed. "If I were a goddess, would I shovel horse manure?"

"I don't know. Would you?"

Her smile faded, but joy glinted in her dark eyes. "Perhaps."

"If you were a goddess, what would your life be like?"

She closed her eyes and her black eyelashes curled against her eyelids. "I would have my own house and my own horses. I would have a dog or two. I would have beautiful flowers in every room, and music. All of the furniture would feel soft against my skin. I would eat fruit and fajitas and pie. I would have enough money to hire helpers and pay them well. I would give money to Virginia so she wouldn't struggle. It would be beautiful."

"Would you have a husband?"

Her face fell again, and he felt some of the joy slip from her. "I don't know," she said and opened her eyes. "He would have to be a very gentle man. I would have to be sure that he would never ever hurt me."

A sharp longing stabbed him deep inside. More than anything, Geoffrey wanted to be that man for Maria. He opened his mouth to tell her, but the sound of Lori's Pomeranian yapping downstairs interrupted him. He glanced up. "What the devil—" He frowned. "What time is it anyway?"

"Around eleven, I think. We should go to bed," she said and shifted away from him. It took everything he had not to pull her back into his arms as she dressed.

Hastily pulling on his briefs and jeans, he darted to the window and spotted Jackson's SUV in front of the house. His gut sank. "They're back," he muttered. "Lori and Jackson are back."

Maria joined him at the window. "Lori," she said, her voice dead.

His heart hammering, he turned to Maria. "I want to be with you more than anything," he said. "But my family's finances are in dire straits. They're counting on me to get us out of the bloody mess. It's not fair. It's not right. But it is my duty. I must marry her if she'll have me."

"Tough being a duke, isn't it?" she said, with a sad smile. "She's pretty and rich, no scars—"

"Stop." Geoffrey pulled her against him. "She's not you," he said. "And you are who I want. You are who I wanted before I even knew you existed."

He saw the flicker of emotion and passion in her eyes before she closed them for a second. "But I don't have what you need. You would suffer if you didn't take care of your family. You must marry Lori." She lifted on tiptoe to press her lips against his. "I won't forget you," she whispered. "I've never felt so treasured. You've been gentle with me."

"You deserve so much more," he said, feeling helpless. "You deserve—"

"Shhh," she said. "We have this to remember, and I will always have your song. Good night, Geoffrey," she said and left him staring after her. He felt as if his heart had been ripped from his chest.

Lori awakened the next morning in her bed at Virginia's ranch house with Kenny at her feet. It could have been three days ago or two weeks ago. She closed her eyes and opened them again. Had she really gotten married?

Her mind flashed back to the awful wedding ceremony and the two mind-blowing nights she'd shared with Jackson. She couldn't have dreamed all that. She sat up in bed and thought about how they'd parted last night. He'd parked her duffel bag inside her bedroom and she'd held her breath, wondering if he would stay, wondering if he would ask her to join him. Instead, he'd muttered, "Good night."

She'd fumed over his lack of passion for a good hour, then fell asleep. Kenny moved toward her and rolled over to offer his belly to be rubbed. Lori smiled and obliged him. She shouldn't overthink her marriage to Jackson. The only rational part of it was that she now had access to her inheritance, and the first check she planned to write was to Virginia.

Rising from bed, she showered and dressed in jeans for the day. She walked downstairs and found Jackson, Maria, and Geoffrey in the kitchen. "Good morning."

Maria looked down her nose at Lori. "Good morning. Did you enjoy your vacation?"

"I took care of some business, but yes, I did have some fun, too. I think it's best to try to find the fun in as many of life's moments as you can. Don't you agree?" Lori asked, pouring herself a cup of coffee.

"It isn't always easy to have fun. Some of us have to work," Maria retorted.

"Yes, but—"

"I must go down to the barn now," Maria interjected and left the room.

"Whew!" Lori said, looking after her. "Looks like someone woke up on the wrong side of the bed."

"You shouldn't criticize her," Geoffrey said. "She hasn't had it easy like you and I have."

Lori felt as if she were striking out all around. She turned nervously to Jackson. "How are you?"

"Fine," he said. "I'll be here today, but I'm going to Dallas tomorrow."

She nodded, feeling an odd uneasiness at the prospect of him leaving. "I'll write the ch—"

"We can talk about it tonight," he interjected and stood.

"Okay," she said, wondering where the man who had ravished her body yet held her tenderly had gone. All she saw in Jackson's eyes was thinly veiled impatience. Her stomach twisted at his lack of emotion. She felt like a fool. Why? she wondered. It wasn't as if she and Jackson had professed undying love. Oh, wait. They actually had done that during the wedding vows. But she was certain he hadn't meant it. And neither had she. Had she?

"Do either of you know where Virginia is?"

"I think she's with the campers this morning," Geoffrey said.

"Okay, I'll give her—" She corrected herself. "I'll talk to her later." She turned to Geoffrey. Her second task for the day was to tell him she couldn't marry him. "I'm ready to get back to cleaning chores. Will you be joining me?"

He gave a heavy sigh and nodded. "You're not going to eat?"

Lori's appetite disappeared as she watched Jackson leave. "I'll just grab a biscuit on my way out the door."

Ten minutes later, she and Geoffrey walked to the cabins and began working. "Anything important happen while I was gone?" she asked him as she grabbed a bucket and headed for the bathroom.

"Just the regular everyday earthquakes and tidal waves," Geoffrey said soberly.

Lori appreciated his deadpan levity. "All in one day, here in the middle of Texas. I'm surprised it didn't make the news."

"I am, too," he said, grabbing a mop. "Lori," he said and she glanced up at him.

"Yes?"

He locked his jaw and closed his eyes as if he were in pain, then dropped to his knee.

Oh, no, she thought. Not another proposal. "Geoffrey, before you—"

He lifted his hand and shook his head. "No. I must. It's my duty. It's the only way. I must. I—" He broke off and wailed. "I can't do it." He rose to his feet. "I just can't. My family may lose everything, but I can't marry you."

Moved by his distress, she took a step toward him. "That's okay, because I—"

"I just can't," he said, his voice breaking. "I'm in love with Maria, and it would be sacrilege to marry you."

Lori felt her jaw drop. Shock raced through her. "Maria?"

"Yes, I'm sorry I've been deceptive. I tried to resist her. I really did, but the woman is a goddess." He cleared his throat. "You're perfectly nice and lovely, but Maria is—"

Lori bit her lip in amusement at the slight ego slap. "No, it's okay. Something has happened, and I couldn't marry you anyway."

"Of course," he said but clearly didn't believe her.

"No, really," she said.

"I'm sorry that I've wasted your time." He sighed. "There will be hell to pay with my family. If I'm lucky, they'll simply disown me."

Lori felt a tug of sympathy for the kind British duke who'd followed her to the middle of nowhere and ended up falling for temperamental Maria. "Out of curiosity, how much money do you need to get things back on track?"

He named a sum that would force her to go to Jackson. Lori grimaced.

"I know. It's a bloody fortune. And for you Yanks, the pound makes it doubly worse."

She nodded. "Is there any way you could make the house income-producing on its own?"

"I can't imagine how."

"I don't know. Make it a prestige bed-and-breakfast kind of thing? Have visitors pay to stay in a duke's house. Let them be duke for a day or something."

"It sounds a bit like prostitution. My stepmother would hate it." He paused. "Knowing how much she would hate it makes me like the idea even more." He sighed. "I don't want to be in a financial pit the rest of my life. What I'd really like to do is write music for film."

Lori's mind began to turn with possibilities. "Then why don't you?"

"For one, I don't have any connections."

"I could help with that."

"Would you?"

She nodded. "Do you have anything you could give someone?"

"Yes, but I suppose I'd also need some sort of backing or partnership to start up a company. It's too much to ask of you. You're too kind. I should take care of this myself."

"Well, there could be some benefit to me. What if you're a huge hit? I can say I knew you from the beginning. I helped launch you."

"You're too kind," Geoffrey said. "Why couldn't we fancy each other?"

"I like the idea of having you as a friend," Lori said. "I'll need to clear this with my consultant, but it shouldn't be a problem," she added, certain Jackson would have no problem with this financial move. After all, she might even see a return on this investment.

"The male ego is a very tricky thing."
—SUNNY COLLINS

Chapter Nineteen

"You want to do what?" Jackson asked, staring at her in disbelief.

Lori winced at his tone, glancing around the barn. The horses were resting in their stalls. All except for Rowdy, of course. "Lower your voice. You'll disturb the horses."

"The horses are not what is disturbed," Jackson said, shaking his head. "Two days. You're married two days and you're already spending half your inheritance."

"That's an exaggeration. I'm not spending half of it. Besides, I'm not really spending it except for the check I gave Virginia. And you knew I was going to do that as soon as possible."

"Yes, but this crazy scheme with Geoffrey—"

"It's a loan and an investment," she said.

"And what will you do if he never pays you back?" Jackson demanded. "Take his house in England and sell it."

She shifted on her feet. "That wouldn't be very nice."

Jackson rolled his eyes and rested his hands on his hips as he walked toward her. "Lori, you can't keep spending your money this way. I know you see yourself as a professional philanthropist, but if you keep going like this, the time will come when *you* will be the one needing charity. You can't fix everything."

She knotted her fingers together. "I know, but poor Geoffrey came all this way to marry me, and even though he's in love with Maria, it's not—"

"Maria?" he interjected.

She nodded. "It's not fair for him to go away with nothing."

"Then cover his travel expenses," he said.

Lori silently met his gaze for a long moment.

"You're going to do it anyway, aren't you?"

She nodded.

Jackson frowned. "He's taking advantage of you."

"No, he's not. It was my idea." Miserable that Jackson clearly didn't approve of her, she bit her lip. "I don't want you to be mad at me," she whispered.

Jackson closed the distance between them and slid his hand behind her back, tugging her against him. "Your generosity is amazing. I just don't want you to be hurt by it."

She snuggled against him, loving the sensation of his body against hers. "Did you think about me at all last night?"

He paused a half beat. "Yeah. I did."

She looped her arms around the back of his neck and looked up at him. "I thought about you, too, but when I woke up this morning, it almost felt like Vegas had been a dream."

He paused again and lowered his mouth closer to, but not touching, her lips. "Are you saying you need a reminder that you're married to me?"

Lori felt an illicit thrill race through her. "I might," she said, meeting the challenge in his gaze.

"You're telling me that you can't remember what we did for two days straight in that hotel room," he said.

Her heart pounded in her chest. "I didn't say I didn't remem—"

"You said it felt like it was a dream," he said and slid his hands under her bottom and hiked her legs around his waist.

Clinging wildly to him, she glanced over his shoulder as he strode farther into the barn. "Where are we go—"

"To the office," he said. "So I can remind you that you're married."

Lori felt a heady anticipation at his determined stride. He walked into the small office and closed the door behind him. And locked it. "What if someone comes?"

"It's not likely, but I'll take that risk," he said and rubbed his lips against hers. "Will you?"

She swallowed over a lump in her throat. "Yes," she whispered.

He took her mouth in a possessive, mating, claiming kind of kiss that made her feel dizzy. With the exception of a high, narrow window, the room was dark, making her acutely aware of the sound of his mouth and hers, their breaths, and the sensation of his erection pressed against her, where she was already moist.

Allowing her to slide down his body until she stood, he unfastened her jeans and pulled up her shirt. He tugged it over her head and immediately reached for her breasts. "You feel so good," he muttered. "Look so good."

He shoved her jeans down with a barely restrained savageness that thrilled her. There was nothing wishy-washy about every move he made. Suddenly she was naked and vulnerable, but she felt incredibly powerful.

He slid his hand between her legs and found her sweet spot. "This is a reminder," he said against her lips, kissing between each word. "I am your husband. You are my wife," he said and slid his finger inside her.

Lori gasped at the primitive nature of his strokes, his words. With trembling hands, she loosened his jeans and pushed them and his underwear down over his large, hard shaft. She stroked the length of him until she felt a drop of his essence. His breath was harsh against her neck. "And you are my husband," she said, her knees weak from the power of her desire.

"Damn right," he said and picked her up, backing her against the wall. Lowering her onto him, he let out a hiss of a sigh when she completely enveloped him. She felt so voluptuously full, so . . . taken.

Thrusting upward, he slid his hand between their bodies to where she was aching and wanting and rubbed her. The combination of his delicious caress and fullness inside her took her to another place, and she cradled his hard jaw with one of her hands and kissed him deeply.

The sensation inside her built with each stroke, each pump.

"Think you'll remember this?" he asked in a thick, gruff voice.

"Oh." She felt herself spiral over the edge. "Yesss."

Heartbeats later, she felt him stiffen and plunge one last soul-searing time.

"Will you remember?" she asked, slipping her arms around him, cradling him against her.

He swore. "I couldn't forget if I tried. You killed my knees, so I'm going to take us down now." He slid to the floor, pulling her onto his lap.

She was still breathless, her heart felt like a ping-pong ball, and now he was holding her in his arms. "Is sex always like this?" she couldn't help asking.

He gave a rough chuckle. "Depends on who your partner is."

"Why is it like this with us?"

He shook his head. "You're asking me to explain something as old as time."

She inhaled and felt her pulse calm just a little. "I want you to like me," she said.

He met her gaze. "What?"

"I like it that you want me, but I want you to like me, too."

He paused, then lifted his hand to stroke her hair. "I do. I just feel like I need to watch out for you. You need a reality check sometimes."

She rubbed her hand over his rough jaw and smiled. "I like the reality check you just gave me."

"You're making it hard to keep our marriage a secret," he warned her.

"Just a little longer," she said, lifting her mouth to his, enjoying the sensation of his lips and tongue. "I want it between you and me just a little longer."

*   *   *

Early the next morning, Jackson left for Dallas. Even though he'd always known money made a huge difference in how people treated a man, he was surprised at how quickly he found two highly reputable developers eager to work with him. He chose two construction companies known for producing quality work for a reasonable cost.

Since he owned the land and had already sketched out some plans, it would take little time to begin work. He'd originally planned this as a brief scouting trip, but since everything fell into place so smoothly, he stayed longer to iron out contractual details, choose a selection of layouts, and set tentative timelines.

Several times throughout each day, he felt the urge to call Lori, but he never did. He suspected she was busy with ranch work, and he prayed she wasn't sinking more money into a losing project. He was determined to make sure his own project would be a winner, and if he had his way, he would pay back every penny of the husband money she'd given him. The notion that he was finally succeeding because he'd married a rich woman stuck in his craw, no matter how much he tried to push the thought aside.

Eight days after he'd left, he returned to the ranch. Daylight was just turning to dusk. As he pulled up in front of the house, he saw Lori and Virginia talking to a tall man wearing a cowboy hat and jeans. The three of them appeared to be laughing. His gut twisted with something that felt like the color green.

Lori glanced up and began to wave as soon as she recognized his SUV. The delight on her face gave him a warm feeling. Cutting the engine, he got out of the car and watched in horror as she pitched forward on the steps.

"Lori," he called, rushing toward her.

The guy on the porch was closer, though, and grabbed her before she tumbled down the steps. "Where you going, nowhere fast?" the man demanded, his hand around her waist.

"Thanks for catching me, Cash. I guess my feet got ahead of me."

"Landsakes, you nearly gave me a heart attack," Virginia said, putting her hand to her throat. "Thank goodness Cash caught you."

Jackson felt another twist in his gut. "Good save," he managed to Cash and extended his hand. "I'm Jackson James."

"Cash Farley," he said, finally releasing Lori's waist and taking Jackson's hand in a strong grip. "Both Virginia and Lori have told me good things about you."

"Thanks. And you are?" Jackson ventured, glancing at Lori.

"He's our new hire," Lori said proudly. "Since Maria and Geoffrey will be going to England, Virginia needs someone to help with the horses and anything else that comes up. I'm trying to talk her into going on a cruise in the fall."

Jackson blinked, trying to take it all in. Damn, a man left town for a week and everything turned upside down. "Maria and Geoffrey are going to England?"

"After they get married here at the ranch," Lori said.

"Geoffrey decided he'd better take her as his wife so the rest of his family won't be able to argue too much," Virginia added. "Of course they won't want to tangle with Maria anyway."

"And don't worry. I haven't gone crazy with the wedding. Maria and I are looking at dresses on eBay," Lori said.

Cash looked at Jackson and laughed. "You look like you just got kicked by a mule. This girl knows how to make things happen, doesn't she?"

Jackson shot Lori a considering glance. "Yes, she does. So, do you live close by?"

Cash nodded. "My father's ranch is in the next county. He's had a knee replacement, but he's having a tough time handing over the reins. This way, I can help him out but give him the space to figure out what he wants to do next."

Jackson nodded. "No other family?"

Cash shrugged. "A brother, but he isn't interested in the ranch. No wife or kids, so this works out fine." He tipped his hat. "I'll see you ladies soon. Call me if you need anything."

As the man swaggered down the steps, Jackson fought the urge to put his arm around Lori and tell Cash she was taken. But was she really? He ground his teeth together.

"I can't tell you how grateful I am to Lori and to you," Virginia said to Jackson.

"Me?" Jackson echoed, shooting a quick glance at Lori.

"Lori told me you had to help her get access to her inheritance so she could donate money to the ranch. The money has already made a difference," she said, tears welling in her eyes. "Things have been hard since Skip got sick, and then after he died—" She choked up and shook her head.

Lori put her arm around Virginia's shoulder. "But in his own way, Skip is still here. He never really left. You've said thank you enough. I just want you to relax a little now. That cruise is not a bad idea."

Virginia laughed through her tears. "You are something, aren't you, Lori Jean? An angel," she said. "You're an angel. Don't you agree, Jackson?"

Jackson hesitated a half beat. Angel was *not* the description that came to mind when he thought of Lori. "I'm with you," he said. "Words aren't enough to describe Lori."

Virginia smiled. "We've already had dinner, but there's some leftover chicken. Let me pull it out for you."

"No," Lori said. "Let me do it. Jackson probably wants to bring me up to speed on my inheritance. We may as well get it done while he eats."

"Okay," Virginia said. "If you're sure. I think I'll pay a visit to the campers. I'll see you two later." She walked down the steps and took the path toward the cabins.

Lori looked up at Jackson. "Hungry?"

"Not for chicken," he said and lifted his fingers to her hair. "What about you?"

He watched her part her lips in an almost inaudible gasp. "I didn't know you would be gone so long," she said.

"Miss me?"

She glanced away and shrugged. "Since you didn't call . . ."

"Did you want me to?" he asked, studying her.

She bit her lip and crossed her arms over her chest. "Not if you didn't want to."

He slid his hand down her arm and laced his fingers through hers. "The phone works both ways," he said.

"Well, it's better if the guy calls," Lori said, not pulling away from him, but not moving closer, either.

"Who said that? Besides, we're married," he said.

"But it's not a normal marriage," she quickly pointed out. "And my mother said that in one of her letters to me."

"That makes it gospel?" he said, unable to keep the skepticism from his voice.

"No, but it makes sense," she said. "That way there's no confusion on the part of the woman."

"What about confusion on the part of the man?" he asked.

Lori paused and made a sheepish face. "Actually, my mother said it's best for men to remain in a state of confusion."

He chuckled. "If I didn't know how much those letters from your mother meant to you, I could be tempted to lock them away again."

She turned very serious. "But you would never do that, would you?"

"No," he said. "Even though I'll suffer from whatever wisdom she imparts from the hereafter."

Lori's lips lifted in a mischievous smile. "Don't worry. You'll benefit from some of it, too."

"You want to explain that?"

"Not really."

"I didn't think so. Anyone in the house?" he asked, looking around.

"Not that I know—"

He picked her up in his arms, and she let out a little shriek. He began to walk up the stairs.

"What are you doing?"

"Taking you to my room so I can remind you that you're married," he said.

"What if I haven't forgotten?" she countered.

"Then I'll let you remind me," he told her. Three minutes later, they were in his room, kissing and caressing. Three minutes after that, their clothes were on the floor. He was making her moan, and she was making him sweat.

He kept her in bed for nearly four hours straight.

"I should go to my room," Lori said. "But I don't think I can move."

"Then stay here," he said, lifting her hand and letting it plop to the mattress.

She rolled onto her side, her breasts exposed to his view. "You're tempting me," she said, wagging her finger at him.

"Nice to know it works both ways," he muttered, unable to resist fondling her breasts.

She closed her eyes in an expression of pleasure. "That's very distracting. Talk to me," she said.

Distracted himself, he forced his hands away from her nipples to her shoulders. "Talk about what?"

"I don't care. I just want to hear your voice. Talk about the housing development. Who you're working with. How it's going. What the drive was like. How many times you thought about me," she said with a smile, her eyes still closed. "You can even fuss at me for my mismanagement of my inheritance. I don't care. Just talk."

He felt an odd tug in his gut at her request. "The development is going better than I expected. I guess it's the old 'money talks and BS walks.' Long & Sons want in."

She opened her eyes. "That's great. They're very reputable."

"How do you know?"

"Daddy dabbled in lots of things, including real estate, and I remember him mentioning them."

Jackson moved his hands upward to toy with her hair. "I just wish I'd been able to find another backer."

She frowned. "Why? What's wrong with my money?"

The problem with her money was that it not only was hers, but it also came with the condition of marriage, and Jackson was learning that his agreement with Lori chafed at him more than he'd thought it would.

"There are lots of ways of getting financing, but you gotta admit this is one helluva strange one."

Pulling up the sheet, she sat up. "Are you going to renege on our deal already? What have I done to upset you?"

"Nothing," he said. "I'm not reneging."

"If you give back the money, you may as well," she said. "Don't you realize that you are one of the few truly fiscally smart investments I've made?"

"How is that? Marrying me just gave you access to more of your inheritance. You could technically spend all of it tomorrow and be poor the rest of your life."

"For one thing, under the terms of our agreement, I have to pause and discuss any major donations with you. For another thing, what you're doing will actually turn a profit and I'll see a return on my investment. My donation to the ranch is just that—a donation. I'll get a tax break, but that's it. My deal with Geoffrey is a financial crap-shoot. But you will go to hell and back to make sure your project is a success in every way."

Her faith in him did things to him, inside him, things he couldn't explain. The woman baffled him. "How can you be sure I'll make this deal work? I've never done this kind of thing before."

"Because of who you are. Defeat is not acceptable to you. If you're ultimately responsible, then you'll do whatever it takes to make it work." She sighed. "It must be nice to have that kind of confidence, that kind of will."

"You have some of it in your own way," he said. "You just go about it differently."

Her eyes widened. "Me? When I see a problem, all I do is throw money at it."

"The fact that you have the money and the desire to help people is huge. There are plenty of people who have the desire but not the money, and the reverse of that, too. As your financial advisor, I would just like to see you find a way to make at least as much as you donate. That way, you're set and your ability to donate the way you want is protected."

"You mean like a business," she said.

"Or investments in legitimate ventures," he said. "But you would need to be very selective. You would need to take a consumer's attitude."

She was quiet for a moment. "Do you really think I'm capable of something like that?"

He chuckled. "Lori Jean Granger, you're capable of whatever you want to do. You're the woman who was terrified of horses a few weeks ago. You're facing up to that. You're the woman who was told you couldn't have any more of your inheritance. Now you've gotten access to it again." He lifted his hand to chuck her cheek. "You're a lady who makes things happen."

She looked at him thoughtfully. "But none of that would have happened without you."

He shook his head. "You would have found a way."

She wrinkled her eyebrow and bit her lip. "I wondered if you would ever be able to think of me as more than the flighty blonde with more money than sense."

"I realized there was more to you soon after I met you. I just can't help wondering what kind of ball of fire you're going to be when you really realize it yourself."

She met his gaze for a moment, her blue eyes full of vulnerability, then she closed her eyes and took a slow breath. "If you keep saying things like that to me, I'll do something really scary."

He couldn't not pull her into his arms. He felt her take another slow breath. "Like what?"

"Cry," she said and opened eyes shiny with unshed tears.

He shook his head. "Don't want you to do that."

She offered her lips to his. "Then give me something else to think about."

> *"We are stronger than we look. We are stronger than we think we are. Don't ever forget that, sunbeam."*
> —SUNNY COLLINS

Chapter Twenty

Lori awakened to the sensation of Jackson's body against hers. She loved his masculine scent. She loved his broad shoulders and the way his strength permeated his body and his mind. She loved being close to him.

She loved . . . him.

The realization slipped into her consciousness. Her usual arsenal of denial and self-defense must have still been asleep. Lori looked at Jackson's face and knew she was in love with him.

How? When? Her lungs squeezed tight, taking her breath away. She'd known she could trust him. She'd known she was attracted to him. She'd known he would watch out for her. She'd also known he would never fall for her.

Crap. So now she'd fallen for her so-called husband, was stuck with him until she was thirty, when they would amicably divorce.

Panic raced through her. How was she going to manage

this? How was she going to keep it from him? Because heaven forbid, Jackson would probably just feel sorry for her, and she couldn't bear that.

Desperate for a moment alone, she rolled over to get up. A large, warm hand snaked around her waist and she closed her eyes. "Where you going?" he asked in a sexy, deep voice.

"I need to take Kenny outside. His bladder won't wait."

"Are you coming back?"

"I need to get my shower," she said, scooting the rest of the way out of bed and pulling on her clothes. "I'll see you at breakfast. Okay?" she said, more than asked, then raced out the door.

By the time Lori took care of Kenny, tried to wash away her feeling of panic during her morning shower, and arrived in the kitchen, Jackson was drinking his coffee at the breakfast table. Alone.

Darn, she'd hoped for a buffer from someone else this morning. "You beat me down. Have you already eaten?" she asked, picking up an egg biscuit from the warming pan on top of the stove. "Do you want a biscuit?"

"Already had mine," he said.

Pouring herself a cup of coffee, she sat across from him at the table. Feeling his gaze on her, she took a bite of the biscuit but found it hard to swallow. She wondered if he could sense a change in her. For such a practical man, Jackson could be incredibly intuitive. Her stomach felt like a jumble of nerves. She wondered if she could hide her feelings. Or would it be useless to try? Would he be able to read the fact that she loved him, as if she were wearing a billboard?

"What's going on?" he asked.

"Nothing," she quickly replied but nearly knocked over her coffee cup. "Oops."

"I repeat. What's going on? You seem jumpy," he said.

She forced herself to smile. "I guess I don't have the morning-after routine down yet."

He took a sip of his coffee and leaned back in his chair. "We're married. You don't have to do anything special," he said. "Unless you want to go back to bed."

She felt a wicked thrill at his suggestion but shook her head. "Someone would notice. There would be questions I'm not ready to answer."

"Why not?" he asked with a shrug. "Can't keep it a secret forever."

She bit her lip. "I know, but I haven't figured out what to say. How to explain."

"You just say you're married," he said.

"People will ask questions, like when did we decide to do it? And when did we realize we have feelings for each other?"

"Keep it general. We've had feelings for each other for a while and decided getting married was the right thing to do."

"Easy for you to say. Women are expected to give more details."

"How long do you want to keep this on the down-low?"

"I don't know," she said.

"Lori," Jackson said. "Are you embarrassed that you're married to me?"

"No," she said immediately. "No. I just don't know how—" She broke off, flustered. "I don't know—"

"I'm curious how you plan to handle come-ons from other men."

Another wave of confusion rolled over her. "Other men? There aren't a lot of other men around the ranch, except for summer-camp leaders, and they're gone within a week, since they arrive and leave with their specific groups. Geoffrey's gaga over Maria, so that takes care of him."

"What about Cash?" he asked.

"I didn't even think about him. If he approaches me, I'll just tell him I'm not available."

"So what are the rules, Lori? Do you expect us to be exclusive? Or are you and I just business partners with benefits?"

His question caught her off guard. "I thought we would be exclusive. We are married, even though—" She felt a heaviness in her chest. "I guess I can't require it, but—" She cleared her throat, feeling a rising tide of panic. "I did say there should be discretion. What is this about? Have you met someone? Is there someone else?"

He lifted his hands. "I'm not the one who wants to keep it secret."

She sighed. "It's my sisters."

"Your what?" he asked, raising his eyebrows.

Oh, no, his eyebrows were talking to her again. Unable to sit another second, she stood. "My sisters are madly in love with their husbands, and their husbands are madly in love with them. How in the world can I explain you and me to them? What do I say? I married you so I could get my inheritance, and I'm paying you to be my husband. Oh, and the rest of the deal is that we get divorced when I turn thirty."

Jackson shook his head and stood. He looked fed up. "Let me know when you figure out what you want. In the meantime, I'll head back to Dallas."

Her heart sank. "So soon?"

He nodded. "Yeah. Call me if you need anything," he said and left the room. Staring after Jackson, Lori heard steps behind her and turned to see Maria, who must have entered from the back door. Lori searched the other woman's face to see if she could read how much Maria had heard of her conversation with Jackson.

"Hi," Lori said after a long moment of silence.

"Hi," Maria said and wrapped up the remaining biscuits and put them in the refrigerator.

Lori chewed her lip. "I don't know what you may have heard—"

"It's none of my business," Maria said.

Lori cringed. Her statement said it all.

"But," Maria added, "I don't know a woman who would not be proud to call Jackson her man."

Lori sighed. "It's not that I'm not proud of him."

"It didn't sound that way," Maria said, lifting one of her dark eyebrows. "You sounded very wishy-washy."

Lori heard the front door close and knew it was Jackson leaving. She closed her eyes for a second at the searing pain that stabbed her. "He doesn't love me," she finally said, the words feeling as if they were torn from her.

"How do you know?"

Lori popped open her eyes. "I had to talk him into marrying me. I had to give him money."

"Did he ask for money?"

"No, but I know he expected it. As soon as we were married, he invested the money in a construction deal."

Maria frowned. "I still don't understand why you did this. You're skinny and a little spoiled, but you're pretty enough. Many men would take you."

"Thanks for the compliment," Lori said dryly. "I didn't want to marry just anyone. I wanted to marry someone I trust."

Maria's mouth formed a perfect O. "You are in love with Jackson."

"I didn't say that," she quickly said, not ready for the words to be said aloud.

"You are," Maria said. "You are in love with him."

"But he's not in love with me."

She shrugged. "You're married to him. Make him fall in love with you."

"Like it's so easy," Lori said. "Excuse me, but I'm fresh out of fairy dust and I've lost my magic wand."

Maria gave a careless shrug. "It's not so hard. Men are easy. You show them love, you tease them and please them, and they will beg. It happens all the time."

"Maybe for you," Lori said, envious of Maria's confidence. "Jackson is a very strong man. I'm not sure any woman could *make* him fall in love."

"Then maybe you're not the right woman for him. Maybe you're not strong enough for him," Maria said lightly. "Maybe you should let another woman have him."

A sizzling possessiveness raced through her with the power of a freight train. "Absolutely not. Why would I let another woman have him? He may not love me, but he's married to me."

Maria put her hands on her hips and cocked her head to one side. "You'll have to decide if you are strong enough for him."

Maria's words haunted Lori during the next days. The woman seemed to boil it all down very nicely, but Lori knew that seducing Jackson didn't mean he would give her his heart. If she were a different person, she would go after him and tell him she loved him, but she was terrified he would feel awkward because he couldn't return the affection. Her quandary drove her crazy.

After she didn't hear from him for two days, she decided to buck up and initiate the call. She dialed his number, and the rings continued so long that she almost hung up, unwilling to leave a message. Just before she decided to hit the disconnect button, his voice came on the line. "Jackson James."

Her heart raced at the sound of his voice.

"Hello? Jackson James," he repeated, impatient.

"Hello?" she blurted.

A half second of silence followed. "Lori?"

She nodded even though he couldn't see her. "Yes, it's me." She cleared her throat. "How are you?"

"Okay," he said. "Busy as hell, but okay. Is there a problem?"

Yes, I miss you. "Not really. I just wanted to check in with you."

"Hmm. Do you need more money? Did you want to make another donation?" he asked.

"No," she said, feeling more awkward with each passing second. Maybe this wasn't such a good idea, after all. "Well, I'm glad everything's okay with you. I guess I'll talk to you some other—"

"Wait," he cut in. "Why did you call?"

"I told you," she said. "I just wanted to check in with you." She took a deep breath and closed her eyes, mustering courage. "I wanted to hear your voice."

Silence followed. "Okay. Everything keeps moving

very quickly on the construction deal. I never imagined it would move this fast."

She heard the excitement in his voice and smiled. "That's great. Did you decide if you're going to have a pet park?"

"Yes. Good idea. The construction people love it. What about you?"

"I've been helping Maria with classes with the campers," she said proudly.

"Really? You've been riding?"

"So far just leading, no riding, but it's been a lot of fun. Those kids are amazing. They have all kinds of problems, but their disabilities don't keep them from trying."

"Yeah, it's fun to watch. Wait. Excuse me a minute," he said, and she heard him say something to someone else. "Listen, I'm meeting for drinks with some of my new business contacts. I'll give you a call tomorrow or the next day."

"That would be great," she said, the longing inside her stretching like the Grand Canyon. "Good to hear your voice," she said.

"Yeah," he said. "Good to hear yours, too. Bye."

Pushing the disconnect button, she replayed his last words five times in her head. Then another five. And another. Then she stopped, because she knew she was being goofy.

They talked every other day for the next week. Short calls that made her wish for his closeness. Every time they talked, she hoped she meant something special to him, but she couldn't be sure. She hated her sense of uncertainty.

Thursday dragged by. Rain started in the morning and didn't let up all day. Outdoor classes were cancelled, and

Maria and Lori played games with the children. One of the children, Reese, was especially challenging. Although mentally handicapped, red-haired Reese was physically strong and active, full of energy that Lori tried to help defuse by running races with him around the cabin.

In early afternoon, Maria announced that she and Geoffrey were going to town.

"Is it a date?" Lori asked, feeling a pinch of envy at the open affection Maria and Geoffrey shared.

Maria's cheeks bloomed. "Geoffrey wants to take me to dinner." She paused a half beat and lowered her voice. "We're also going to apply for the marriage license."

Lori couldn't help feeling a rush of joy. She was glad *someone* would get the marriage thing right. "Then you really need to decide on a dress."

Maria nodded. "I never thought I would be marrying an English duke. I never really thought I would be getting married at all. I still can't believe that Geoffrey thinks I'm the most beautiful woman in the world. Even with my scar," she said, lifting her hand to the jagged mark on her cheek. She sighed, then shook her head. "But yes, I want to get a dress. Did you wear a dress for your wedding to Jackson?"

Lori shook her head. "No. It was all done so quickly there wasn't time."

"Didn't you miss that? Didn't you want that romantic experience?"

Lori felt a knot form in her throat. "It wasn't supposed to be romantic. We don't have that kind of relationship," she said.

"Maybe you could if you would stop hiding your marriage," Maria said.

"That will happen eventually," she said. "But we weren't discussing my wedding. We were discussing your wedding."

Maria shot her a look of disapproval, but she couldn't hold it long. Her lips curved into a big smile of joy. "He is the sweetest man in the world. Thank you for not agreeing to marry him."

Lori laughed. "He wouldn't have been able to go through with it with me. He fell for you the first time he met you."

"True," Maria said. "Now, if you have any problems at all, just call my cell. Hopefully we wore out the little kiddies enough that they will settle down easily tonight. That cutie Reese was a little terror, wasn't he? I couldn't believe how many times you raced him around the cabin."

"And in the rain," Lori added. "There shouldn't be any problems here. Enjoy your afternoon and evening. You deserve it."

"Thanks," Maria said, then impulsively hugged Lori. "You're not as much of a stuck-up, clueless rich girl as I originally thought."

"Thanks," Lori said. "I think."

After Geoffrey and Maria left, Lori stayed indoors until dinner, when she delivered the evening meal to the campers. She and Virginia organized simple relays to entertain the children, then followed up by reading books to help the campers calm down.

Since Reese was still wound up with energy, Lori opened a big umbrella and took him for a walk to the barn. He enjoyed visiting the horses and protested when she took him back to the cabin.

Worn out from the day, Lori climbed into her bed and stared at her cell phone, willing it to ring. It remained silent, and she felt the distance between her and Jackson more than ever. She couldn't help wondering what the future for the two of them held. She fell asleep, cradling the phone in her hand.

A knock on her door woke her in the middle of the night. "Lori, Lori," Virginia said from the other side of the door. "We have an emergency."

Lori immediately sprang out of bed and flung open the door. Dressed in her robe, with an expression of fear tightening her face, Virginia shook her head. "One of the children is missing. He must have left after the camp counselors fell asleep. They've looked all around the cabin and the barn and can't find him anywhere."

Him. Lori had a sinking sensation. "Reese?"

Virginia nodded. "We have to find him. It's still raining out there. The streams are overflowing and the road is rained out. Maria and Geoffrey are stuck in town, and Cash can't get through, either."

"Oh, no," Lori said, feeling helpless. "Let me get dressed so I can start looking, too."

"I would take out one of the horses myself, but my arthritis has been giving me a fit," Virginia said. "Lori, I know the conditions are terrible, but our best bet is if someone takes Lady to do the search. She's sure-footed, gentle, and can always find her way back to the barn."

Lori's stomach clenched. Virginia needed her to step up. Virginia didn't know what she was asking, and Lori was terrified she couldn't deliver. "You think Lady can do this?" Lori asked at the same time she was asking herself if *she* could do it.

"I do," Virginia said.

Lori knew what she had to do.

> "The great thing about life is just when you think
> you're headed straight for the dump, you hit a curve
> that takes you to paradise."
> —SUNNY COLLINS

Chapter Twenty-one

Underneath her jeans, T-shirt, rain cloak, and hat, Lori broke into a cold sweat as she approached the barn. Rain pelted relentlessly against her vinyl raincoat. Armed with a lantern, flashlight, first-aid kit, and cell phone that would be intermittently useless due to lack of coverage, she wished she could just have a one-minute conversation with Jackson.

Just one minute and her heart rate would settle down, her breathing would slow, and she would believe that she could do what she needed to do. She hadn't ridden a horse alone in years.

Lanterns flickered nearby as two of the camp counselors searched for the little boy. Standing outside the barn, Lori closed her eyes and imagined Jackson's voice. "You can do anything you want. Anything."

Taking a deep breath, Lori stepped inside the barn.

Virginia and another camp counselor, Mrs. Aliff, greeted her. "Try the north pasture first," Virginia said.

Lori nodded and walked toward Lady's stall. "Hey, Lady, I'm counting on you." she whispered.

Mrs. Aliff came to stand beside her. "We hope you can find him. He's a pistol, but he means so much to everyone. His parents, the other children." The woman sniffed back tears. "He loves running games, races, tag, and hide and seek."

Pushing her own anxiety aside for a moment, Lori covered the counselor's hand with hers. "I know he likes to run. He ran circles around me this afternoon," she said and mustered a smile. "I think he's tough enough that he'll still be running circles tomorrow."

"I hope so."

"Lady and I will do our best," Lori said, feeling her nerves rise inside her again. Hauling the saddle from the tack room, she strapped it on, followed by the bridle, murmuring to the horse all along. All too aware of the horse's size and strength, she led Lady out of the barn and prepared to mount.

Swallowing over the ball of nerves in her throat that refused to go away, she fought the urge to run. Her body still wrapped in cold sweat, she fought the urge to panic, to splinter into a million tiny, useless pieces.

"Are you okay?" Virginia asked from behind her.

"I'm good," she lied, determined to make it the truth. Placing her left foot in the stirrup, she swung herself into the saddle and slid her other foot into a stirrup. For a second, the ground began to waver and swim. Light-headed, she gulped in deep breaths of air. She couldn't pass out. She couldn't. She had to do this.

No time to waste, she told herself and nudged the horse into a walk. Clinging for her life, she took it slow and moved north or, for her, right. The rain continued without abating, with the wind slapping moisture on her face every few moments. It was messy and miserable, and Lori could only imagine how frightened Reese must be.

The unpleasantness distracted her from her fear, and she urged Lady into a trot. "Not too fast," she said in a soothing tone. "I don't want you to slip, but let's not poke." Then she began to yell. "Reese! Reese!"

Two hours later, riding Lady was the least of her discomfort. Her throat hurt from yelling, and she was certain not one inch of her was dry. Worse yet, she didn't know where she was, and there was no sign of Reese.

"Okay, let's turn around and try a different direction," she said to the well-mannered mare. "If you were an eight-year-old boy, where would you go in the middle of a torrential downpour?"

Lady gave a nod and snort as if she knew better than to wander out in this kind of weather.

"You are definitely due some serious apples after this," Lori said and began to call for Reese.

An hour and a half later, she didn't know whether to keep looking or head back to the barn. Out of sheer frustration, she called out, "Hide and seek, Reese. You're it. Can you find me?" She repeated it for over twenty minutes. Her voice grew husky, breaking on every other word, and she paused and swallowed a sip from her water bottle.

She began to yell again but heard a faint sound. Rain splattered loudly on her drooping hat and vinyl raincoat. "Reese?" she croaked. "Reese?"

She heard another sound, high-pitched but indecipherable. Her pulse picked up. "Reese?"

"One, two, three on you," a voice called. "You are it!"

Lori's heart nearly exploded in her chest as she turned Lady toward the sound of his voice. "Reese, where are you? Come here."

"You are it," he called, his voice closer.

Swinging the lantern around, she spotted a tiny figure huddled under a large tree. "Come here, sweetie," she called. "Come here and let me take you home."

Reese began to cry, and the sound wrenched at her. Lori slid off the horse and raced toward the child, pulling Lady behind her. Reese cowered under the tree, sobbing. "One, two, three. You are it."

"Come here, sweetie. Let me take you home."

Reese continued to wail.

At a loss, Lori put her arms around him and held him. "You're okay. Wet, but okay. Don't you want a ride with Lady? She's very nice. She likes little boys. She wants to take us home."

"Ride?" he echoed, sniffing as he stared at the horse.

Lori nodded. "You bet. Let's go home."

After she got both of them on the horse, Lori tucked Reese's squirmy, wet little body under her raincoat and let Lady lead the way.

Jackson had been awakened by the phone call two hours ago. He'd been dead asleep, but it had taken only a moment for his heart to stop in his chest when Maria explained why she was calling so early.

Jackson had been in his car within two minutes. Driving through the constant downpour, he took his SUV off-road when the lanes were flooded. Rain shimmered down his windshield faster than the wipers could push it aside. Despite the vehicles he saw abandoned and the signs warning of flash floods, he drove on. He almost stalled out once but maneuvered out of the deepest waters. Sheer luck.

All he could think about was Lori. Although Maria and Geoffrey had been barricaded from returning to the ranch by flooded roads, Maria had learned that Lori had been looking for one of the campers for hours. Now Virginia feared that Lori was lost, too.

Jackson's stomach churned with remorse. He should have been there with her instead of focusing on this real-estate development deal. His pride had been mortally wounded when she'd insisted she didn't want her family to know she'd married him. Determined to make her proud of him, he'd worked night and day to pull this deal together.

She'd been the biggest headache of his life, and now she was the biggest heartache. His hands clammy as he clenched the steering wheel, he held on to a scrap of hope that her training had come back to her.

Lord help him, though, the woman was vulnerable. Her father had kept her wrapped in a cocoon, unprepared for life, let alone riding around on a horse in the middle of the night looking for a lost child.

Turning on the road to the ranch, he stepped on the gas. He would be there soon. The ranch was just three miles away. Just three miles. He saw the shiny puddle, or was it a lake stretching across the road? Swearing, he slowed. He didn't have time for this. Damn this rain. Damn the flooded roads. Damn it all.

Jackson swerved, but the engine gulped too much water and stalled. He tried to restart the SUV. It coughed and sputtered and died. Thumping his fist against the steering wheel, he swore again. Getting out of the car, he pushed it to the side of the road and started running. Two and a half miles to go. He had to get to Lori.

Twenty-five minutes later, he jogged toward the barn. He'd spent the last mile alternately praying and swearing. The chorus of voices and whistles he heard gave him hope. Brushing the rain from his face, he sped up his pace and ran to the far side of the barn that led into the paddock.

He stopped dead in his tracks. A small figure, covered in a hooded raincoat, rode Lady, the large, gentle mare, and held a small child peeking out from the raincoat. "One, two, three, I see you," the child called. "You are it."

The small group of people let out yells of praise. A volunteer stepped forward, reached up to the child, a boy, and carried him down off the horse.

"Lori, you're drenched," Virginia said.

The small woman on the horse was Lori. His heart racing, he ran to the horse's side and held out his arms.

"I tried to call you," she said in a croaky voice.

Lifting her foot from one stirrup, she slid down into his arms. "Sorry I'm so wet," she whispered, shivering.

Jackson held her close, so relieved that she was safe.

"She's been out in that rain for hours," Virginia said. "We should get her inside."

Jackson picked Lori up and headed for the house. "I'm so wet," Lori said.

"We'll get you dry," he said.

She lifted her hands to his face. "You're wet, too. What happened?"

"Another story," he said, still worried about her.

She coughed. "My throat hurts. I yelled and yelled and yelled," she whispered.

"You did good," he said. "You rescued that little boy. You're a hero."

She met his gaze from beneath the hood of her raincoat and smiled. "Me? A hero?"

His heart turned inside out. "Yeah, baby. You."

"Don't tell Virginia, but I was afraid I was going to throw up right before I mounted Lady."

"But you did it anyway."

"Yeah, I kept pretending that you were there talking to me. You kept saying, you can do anything you want."

"I would have given anything to do this for you," he said.

"I rode a horse again," she whispered as if she still couldn't quite believe it. "All by myself." She cleared her throat and winced. "My throat hurts."

"Be quiet," he said and carried her up the stairs into the house. He took her directly into the bathroom and turned on the hot water. He helped her strip off her clothes and dried her wet, shivering body with a towel before he ushered her into the tub.

She sighed as she relaxed in the warm water. "I could go to sleep right this minute."

"Not yet," he said. "I just want to get you warmed up."

Lori felt as if she were having an out-of-body experience. So weary she could barely stay awake, she felt herself drowning in Jackson's tenderness.

"Am I dreaming this?" she asked him, the warm water surrounding her, his concerned gaze latched on to her. "Are you really being this nice to me?"

He chuckled. "I guess."

She sighed. "Do you know how much I've missed you?" she asked. "I want you around even if you're fussing at me."

"Is that so?" he asked, his lips lifting in a half smile. He pushed a wet strand of hair from her cheek. "Why is that?"

Dizzy from stress, she shook her head. "I don't know. I just know I want to be with you all the time," she confessed. "Twenty-four seven. I'm crazy, aren't I?" She paused, wondering if she should have said all that. "I'm so tired. I must be half-dreaming."

"You've earned it, sweetheart," he said. "Time for bed." He coaxed her from the tub and dried her again, wrapping her in a big fluffy towel. He carried her to her room, and Maria appeared with a nightgown.

Everything blurred together after that.

"I'm sorry for every bad thing I've said to you," Maria said, her eyes wide with regret.

" 's okay," Lori said as she snuggled under the covers.

"Go to sleep," Jackson said, and she felt his lips on her forehead.

Drifting off, she whispered, "Love you . . ."

Or did she?

When she woke up the following afternoon, she immediately looked for Jackson. "Jackson?"

Maria gently squeezed her arm. "He had to go back to

Dallas, but he promised he'll be back soon. How are you feeling, sweetie?"

Disappointed that Jackson had left, she closed her eyes. "My throat hurts," she said in a husky voice.

"Virginia has some medicine that will make you feel better," Maria said. "I'll go get her."

Lori shook her head. "No, not now."

"Why not?"

Lori just shook her head. It required too much energy to do more at the moment. She drifted off again.

Sometime later, she awakened again. Her room was dark and Maria was curled up on a chair beside her bed. "Is Reese okay?" she asked.

"Reese is fine," Maria said. "Here, drink some water."

Lori lifted her head and sipped the cool water through a straw. "Why is it dark?" she asked in her croaky voice.

Maria laughed. "Because it's midnight."

Lori shook her head. "So late. Where's Jackson?"

"He's gone to Dallas, but he'll be back soon. He's called several times to check on you."

Lori sighed and closed her eyes.

"Drink some more before you go back to sleep," Maria coaxed.

Lori lifted her head and took several sips. "Did I dream that you apologized for being mean to me?"

A long silence passed. "No," Maria said. "You didn't dream it. I was very worried about you. You spent too much time in the rain. When I heard Virginia had sent you out to look for Reese, I was afraid you wouldn't survive."

"I'm stronger than I look," Lori said.

Maria laughed softly. "Yes, you are. Now you should take some of the medicine Virginia has for your throat."

Lori shook her head.

"You must take it. It will make you better," Maria said in a stern voice.

Woozy, but mostly cognizant, Lori recounted the days since her last period. She was late. "I need you to get something from the drugstore for me."

"No problem," Maria said. "I will stay with you, and Geoffrey will get it."

Lori shook her head again. "No. You. I need a pregnancy test."

"Dios," Maria said.

"Yeah. I could use His help, too," Lori said and closed her eyes.

When Lori awakened the next morning, a plastic bag waited in the chair where Maria had previously sat. She reached for the bottle of water on the nightstand beside her and drank half of it in no time.

She glanced at the plastic bag again, knowing what it held. She wasn't that late, and her body hadn't always operated like a Swiss watch when it came to her period. Her lateness could be due to stress. Getting married, falling in love, being apart from her husband, staying out all night in the rain . . .

Okay, enough of the procrastination. She rose from bed and felt reasonably stable. Amazing what more than twenty-four hours of sleep could do for a person. Grabbing the bag and a robe, she padded down the hall to the bathroom.

She read and followed the instructions for the test, pacing the small bathroom as she waited. When she saw the results, she took another test and waited. Same result.

"Dios," she whispered.

*   *   *

It took several moments to collect herself, but she finally managed it and took a shower. Wrapping herself in the cozy terry-cloth robe, she returned to her bedroom and found Jackson waiting for her.

"Well, hello," she said, her stomach jumping at the sight of him. Her voice still held a tinge of huskiness, but she no longer needed to whisper.

Jackson looked bone weary but gorgeous to her. Dressed in a dark business suit, he was leaning forward with his elbows resting on his knees.

"Are you okay? Maria said you had to go back to Dallas. It sounded urgent."

"I had to take care of the SUV first. I left it on the side of the road because I couldn't get through the temporary river in the middle of the road."

She patted her hair dry with a towel. "Is it okay?"

He nodded. "How are you?"

"Much better."

"You sound better. You had me worried."

"Sorry for the scare," she said, sitting opposite him on the bed.

"I have something to tell you," he said.

"I have something to tell you, too," she said.

"If you don't mind, I'd like to go first."

She felt a twisting nervousness at his ominous tone. Was he going to tell her he didn't want to be married to her anymore? Was he going to tell her he wanted out?

He squeezed the bridge of his nose. "I think I got in over my head."

Relief rushed through her. "You need more money? That's no prob—"

He lifted his hand and shook his head. "No. I meant I didn't know how being married to you would affect me and how much the money part would bother me."

The twisting nervousness returned. "You know my financial situation, so you know that in the scheme of things, it's not a burden."

"Maybe not to you, but it is to me," he said.

Lori bit her lip, bracing herself. Here it came. The big dump.

"I didn't expect to have such strong feelings for you. And I don't want the money thing hanging over my head, so I found someone else to back the project. I'm returning your money to you."

Lori gasped. "So fast? Does this mean you want out? Does this mean—"

"Out," he echoed. "Hell, no. I love you. I refuse to have the money issue between us."

Shocked at his declaration, she gaped at him, her mouth moving, but no sound came out. "Did you—did you say you love me?"

"Yeah. Joke's on me." He gave a dry chuckle. "It scared the life out of me when Maria called to tell me you were out riding Lady looking for that kid." He met her gaze. "The problem is I don't want to stick to the original bargain. I want to be a real husband to you. I want you to be my real wife. You may not be up for that."

Her heart pounded so hard she could hear it. She took his hands in hers and held on for dear life. "What if I am? What if I love you?"

He shifted their hands so that he enclosed hers in his. "Then we need to rewrite the rules," he said. "We go public."

"Yes," she said.

"You sleep with me every night," he said.

She smiled. "Yes." She closed her eyes for a moment, then opened them. "When did it happen? When did you start loving me?"

"The day I met you. I've been fighting it from the beginning. I wanted to believe you were a self-centered airhead heiress, but you're nothing like that." He lifted one of his hands to her cheek. "Look at you pulling off a rescue operation during a flood."

"Yeah, well, hopefully I won't be doing that again for a long time," she said.

"You rode Lady all by yourself. How was it?"

"It was okay after the first few minutes. I just pretended you were coaching me."

"That's what you told me when I carried you back to the house," he said.

"I don't remember much of what I said."

"I do," he said. "I remember you told me you loved me."

She felt a rush of warmth. "I guess I let that cat out of the bag."

"I'm glad you did," he said and lifted her hands to his mouth.

Lori could hardly believe this was happening, that Jackson really loved her. "Could you tell me again, please?"

"Tell you what?" he asked, leaning back and tugging her onto his lap.

"That you love me," she said.

"Yeah. I love you. You've brought magic and hope into my life. You once told me that your mom called you sunbeam, and I understand why your father was so protective.

I've never met anyone like you." He guided her mouth to his and kissed her.

Lori sighed. She'd never felt so complete in her entire life. She could almost feel her mother and father looking down at her, smiling in approval.

A knock sounded on her door. "Lori, what are the results?" Maria asked as she burst inside. The woman's eyes rounded. "Oops. Sorry. I didn't know you were here." She lifted her eyebrow in silent question to Lori. "I'll talk to you later," she said and left the room as quickly as she'd entered it.

Jackson shot her a look of inquiry. "Results? What was she talking about?"

"Oh." Lori bit her lip, fumbling for a way to tell him. "You remember how I had something I needed to tell you, but you said you wanted to go first."

"Yes," he said, drawing out the word expectantly.

"I'm pregnant."

He blinked. "But you said the doctor told you that you would have difficulty getting pregnant."

"Looks like he called that one wrong," she said and fought a sinking, anxious sensation. "Are you okay with it? We've never discussed having children, but—"

"You're sure about this?" he asked.

She nodded. "I took two tests."

His face lit up like the Fourth of July. "I thought you couldn't make me happier than when you told me you loved me. But you just did."

Seventeen days later, Maude, Cash, Lori, and Jackson witnessed the marriage between Geoffrey and Maria. Decked out in a tux, Geoffrey stood in front of the female minister. He shifted from foot to foot as he waited for Maria to appear.

Virginia smiled at him, and he managed a strained smile in return. He didn't doubt what he was doing. He just bloody well wanted to get on with it. He gave a nod to Cash and Jackson. Every millisecond that passed felt like an eternity. He had the sinking feeling that perhaps Maria had changed her mind.

The possibility made him sweat even more profusely. Although the sun was beginning to set, it was still hot as blazes. Folding his hands together in front of him, he told himself to settle down. Maria had declared her love to him. Despite the fact that he was broke, and likely to remain that way, and his family would detest her, she still loved him.

At least that was what she'd told him yesterday. What if she'd reconsidered? What if she was going to leave him sweating here at the altar waiting for her? Worse, what if she showed up and told him in front of everyone that she'd decided she didn't want to marry him?

Geoffrey swiped his hand across his damp forehead. He couldn't stand it. He turned to the minister. "If you'll excuse me just a moment, I will—"

A collective gasp from Lori and Virginia distracted him. Looking over his shoulder, he gasped, too. Maria rode toward him on Rowdy, just as she had the first time he'd laid eyes on her. His heart swelled at the memory.

This time she wore a strapless ivory gown of beaded lace and a lace veil on her head. Her hair shimmered over her tanned shoulders, and her beautiful skin contrasted dramatically with the ivory gown. She was everything lovely and beautiful he could have ever dreamed.

She pulled the horse to a stop in front of him, and he rushed to help her slide off. "You are a goddess," he told her.

"Just keep telling me that," she said and glanced over her shoulder at Cash, who led Rowdy several steps away. The minister began the ceremony, and Geoffrey treasured this moment in time, when he felt himself become more complete, stronger, and so grateful his wicked stepmother had sent him to Maria.

After they said their vows, all he could do was stare at her.

"You're supposed to kiss me," Maria said.

"Oh," he said, giving himself a shake. "Sorry. You're just so beautiful. And I'm so bloody lucky."

She smiled and pulled him to her, pressing her mouth against his. He wrapped his arm around her, savoring every sensation. He heard a new melody playing in his head.

She broke away far too soon and motioned to Cash, who brought Rowdy toward them. "We're riding the horse?" Geoffrey asked.

Maria gave a luscious, naughty giggle. "It will get you started on the honeymoon faster."

Geoffrey would have vaulted a skyscraper for the look in her eyes. "Then by all means," he said and helped her onto the horse.

"It's never too late to live your very own happily-ever-after."
—SUNNY COLLINS

Epilogue

NINE MONTHS LATER

Lori completely wrecked Jackson's nerves when she gave birth to a baby girl via cesarean section. White with fear, he squeezed Lori's hand as the doctor lifted their baby for them to see. The nurse cleaned up the baby and handed her to Jackson while the doctor stitched up Lori.

Exhausted but euphoric, Lori stared up at both of them. "Is she beautiful?"

"She's amazing," he said. "So pink. So perfect." He bent down so she could see and touch her baby, fresh into the world.

Lori's eyes filled with tears as she touched the head of her child and studied the face she'd waited nine months to see. "Oh, Jackson, she's beautiful. Look, I think she has your chin."

"I hope not. She'll be stubborn as hell," he muttered and shook his head. "Look what you did."

"What we did. Welcome to the world, Jacqueline Sunny James."

A nurse entered the room. "The group outside is getting a little rowdy. Would you like me to give them the news?"

Lori looked up at Jackson and smiled. "Take her out there and show them."

"But you—" He gestured toward the doctor.

"I'm not going anywhere," she said. "Go on. If you don't, then Delilah, Katie, and Maria will beat down the door. And your mother and brother will be right behind them."

"Okay. I'll be right back," he said and dropped a kiss on her forehead.

Lori closed her eyes and thought about everything that had happened since she and Jackson had gotten married. His mother and brother had come to live with them in Dallas, and his mother had become Lori's assistant. Lori had learned so much about discerning whom she could really help. Jackson's development was selling like gangbusters, and surprise, surprise, Geoffrey had been hired to write the music for two movies.

She couldn't help thinking about her mother and father. Both of them would love Jackson. Her mother would have loved Jackson's devotion to her and the way he challenged her to grow. Her father would have loved Jackson's levelheaded approach and his determination to protect her. She could almost feel them smiling down at her.

The door opened and Jackson returned with Jacqueline. "They all think she's perfect."

Lori beamed and lifted her hand to the baby, then to his face. "She came from good stock. But mostly good love."

Don't miss these other titles by
Leanne Banks!

Some Girls Do
(0-446-61172-7)

When She's Bad
(0-446-61173-5)

THE DISH

Where authors give you the inside scoop!

♥ ♥ ♥ ♥ ♥ ♥ ♥ ♥ ♥ ♥ ♥ ♥ ♥ ♥ ♥ ♥

From the desk of Sue Ellen Welfonder

Dear Reader,

My editor absolutely thrilled me when she told me this book's title: SEDUCING A SCOTTISH BRIDE (on sale now). After all, seduction plays a strong role in romance, and Scotland is the heartbeat in every book I write.

SEDUCING A SCOTTISH BRIDE conveys the grand passion shared by the hero, Ronan MacRuari, also known as the Raven, and his heroine, Gelis MacKenzie, youngest daughter of Duncan MacKenzie, the hero of DEVIL IN A KILT. The title also alerts readers that the book is Scottish-set. Of course, with Scotland being my own grand passion, readers familiar with my work already know that they'll be going to the Highlands when they slip into the pages of my books.

Passion and a vivid setting are only two of the magic ingredients that bring a book to life. I enjoy weaving in threads of redemption and forgiveness, a goodly dose of honor, and always a touch of Highland enchantment. Another crucial element is hope.

Heroines, especially, should have hopes and dreams. Lady Gelis bursts with them. Vibrant and lively, she's a young woman full of smiles, light, and laughter. Her greatest wish is to find love and happiness with her Raven, and even when terrible odds are against her, she uses her wits and wiles to make her dreams come true.

Lady Gelis also believes in Highland magic and takes pleasure in helping her Raven solve the legend of his clan's mysterious Raven Stone. And, of course, along the way, she seduces Ronan MacRuari. Or does he seduce her? I hope you'll enjoy discovering the answer.

Readers curious about my inspiration for the Raven Stone (*hint: a fossilized holly tree in the vault of a certain Scottish castle*), or who might enjoy a glimpse into the story world, can visit my Web site, www. welfonder.com, to see photos of the special Highland places they'll encounter in SEDUCING A SCOTTISH BRIDE.

With all good wishes,

Sue-Ellen Welfonder

♥ ♥ ♥ ♥ ♥ ♥ ♥ ♥ ♥ ♥ ♥ ♥ ♥ ♥ ♥ ♥

From the desk of Larissa Ione

Dear Reader,

In PLEASURE UNBOUND, the first book in the Demonica series, you met the three demon brothers who run an underworld hospital. There's Eidolon, the handsome, dangerous doctor. Wraith, the cocky half-vampire treasure hunter. And Shade, the darkly confident, insatiable paramedic.

Shade was a favorite of mine from the beginning, so naturally, I had to torture him a little.

Okay, a lot.

See, before I became an author, I was a reader, and as a reader, many of my favorite romances were those in which the hero and heroine are forced together by some external force. So when I started thinking about DESIRE UNCHAINED (on sale now), the second book in the Demonica series, I saw the perfect opportunity to employ a favorite plot element.

Shade was less excited by my decision . . . but then, his life was on the line, and the only way out of the mess would be death. Either his, or Runa's.

Yes, fun was had by all in the writing of Shade's book!

Oh, but it gets better—or would that be . . . *worse?*

Because not only do Shade and Runa have to deal with being forced together, they also have to

go toe-to-toe with a madman bent on revenge . . .
which is another of my favorite plot elements.

In real life, the need for revenge comes from powerful emotion that drives people to unbelievable
acts. We watch the news and wonder how someone
can snap like that. And if humans can lose it so im-
pressively, imagine what an insane demon can do!

Speaking of demons, I've put together a down-
loadable compendium of all species in the Demonica
world, available on my Web site, www.LarissaIone.
com. The guide, available to all Aegis Guardians,
aids in the identification of demons and includes de-
scriptions, habitats, and pronunciations.

Get yours now, and happy reading!

Larissa Ione

www.larissaione.com

From the desk of Leanne Banks

Dear Reader,

There are some personalities so powerful that they
refuse to die. Sunny Collins, late mother of Lori
Jean Granger, is the mother who keeps on giving.

Advice, that is. But it's not the typical, stand-up-straight, brush-your-teeth, study-hard-in-school kind of advice. Sunny wasn't exactly the typical mother, either. Here's a taste of her advice so you'll understand why she's unforgettable . . .

"High heels weaken men's knees."

"Dogs are generally more devoted than men are."

"When you're a teenage girl, think of dating as a visit to the candy store. Remember you can visit more than once, and make sure to try everything that looks interesting."

"The true test of a man's ardor is if he will go shoe shopping with you on Black Friday."

"If you must do a nasty chore, listening to rock and roll will help the time pass more quickly."

"Sanity is overrated."

"You will always be my little sunbeam."

You'll find more advice from Sunny in SOME GIRLS DO and WHEN SHE'S BAD. Enjoy!

Best Wishes,

Leanne

www.leannebanks.com

Want to know more about romances at Grand Central Publishing and Forever? Get the scoop online!

GRAND CENTRAL PUBLISHING'S ROMANCE HOME PAGE

Visit us at www.hachettebookgroup.com/romance for all the latest news, reviews, and chapter excerpts!

NEW AND UPCOMING TITLES

Each month we feature our new titles and reader favorites.

CONTESTS AND GIVEAWAYS

We give away galleys, autographed copies, and all kinds of fun stuff.

AUTHOR INFO

You'll find bios, articles, and links to personal Web sites for all your favorite authors—and so much more!

THE BUZZ

Sign up for our monthly romance newsletter, and be the first to read all about it!